What Readers Are Saying Ab

"God, greed, sex, con games, cas[ ] incredible gambling system that [ ] house! What more can you ask for? Great characters, fast moving pace and surprising plot twists that will keep you turning the pages. Armstrong has written a novel that takes on big issues and is simultaneously fun to read and interesting to ponder."
—Frank Scoblete, bestselling author, *Golden Touch Dice Control Revolution* and *Golden Touch Blackjack Revolution*

"Cutting-edge gambling fiction, written—with humor, insight and style—by the only author who can actually know whether God does or does not shoot craps!"
—Deke Castleman, senior editor, *Las Vegas Advisor,* author, *Whale Hunt in the Desert*

"Certainly the funniest, most suspenseful and thought-provoking novel to emerge from America's growing love affair with Las Vegas and gambling."
—Jane Cavolina, *New York Times* bestselling coauthor, *Growing Up Catholic*

"With *God Doesn't Shoot Craps*, world class copywriter Richard Armstrong has produced a highly literate nail-biter that takes you deep inside the steamier, seamier emporia of Atlantic City and Las Vegas—the casinos, the 'tanning' salons and the Italian restaurants that are frequented by some of the most deliciously disreputable characters you will ever meet."
—Denny Hatch, *Cedarhurst Alley* and *The Stork*

"I loved *God Doesn't Shoot Craps*. It's a fascinating blend of two subjects I know nothing about—gambling and flying—and two subjects I know quite a bit about—science and mail-order marketing. It's unique: a fast read and a riveting story combined with some rather deep philosophical thinking on the meaning of the universe, deftly plotted with lots of surprises along the way."
—Robert W. Bly, *The Science in Science Fiction*

"Bright, literate, pointed and oh-so-readable because of a sly and merry sense of humor. A talent too few writers possess is the ability to inject themselves inside the hides of others. Richard

Armstrong is rich in that talent, and the result is a story that seizes and involves the reader."
—Herschell Gordon Lewis, columnist, *Direct* magazine

"What can advertising scams, dice systems and topless dancers teach us about the nature of the universe? Read *God Doesn't Shoot Craps* and find out. Richard Armstrong deftly weaves these seemingly unrelated topics (and many more) into a wildly entertaining yarn that will have you laughing out loud and pondering the eternal mysteries at the same time."
—Brian Rouff, *Dice Angel* and *Money Shot*

"I don't read many novels, but this one grabbed me, held me, hypnotized me and even awakened me. A fun, easy, riveting book."
—Joe Vitale, *The Attractor Factor*

"A wonderful and at times hypnotic yarn for anyone whose fate has depended on a roll of the dice, and wished there were a way to improve the odds."
—Tom Collins, columnist *Direct* magazine, cofounder Rapp & Collins, author of *MaxiMarketing*

"A hilarious romp through the dark side of direct marketing!"
—David Garfinkel, author, *Customers on Demand*

"A great book to read while sitting in first class on your flight to Vegas to find unimagined wealth, then to *reread* while hitchhiking back home wondering how to make next month's mortgage. There may be no perfect system to beat the casinos, but this is one perfect book on how to try. Thought-provoking and highly entertaining."
—John H. Corcoran Jr., author, *A Few Marbles Left* and *True Grits*

"*God Doesn't Shoot Craps* has everything the great American novel should have: con men and cops, lap dancers and mechanical dogs, an airplane crash and a miracle, casinos and the Dalai Lama of dice. If you like Elmore Leonard and Carl Hiaasen, you'll love Richard Armstrong."
—Steve "Heavy" Haltom, gaming author and casino coach, www.crapsfest.com

God Doesn't Shoot Craps
A DIVINE COMEDY

Richard Armstrong

SOURCEBOOKS LANDMARK™
AN IMPRINT OF SOURCEBOOKS, INC.®
NAPERVILLE, ILLINOIS

Published by Sourcebooks Landmark, an imprint of Sourcebooks, Inc.
P.O. Box 4410, Naperville, Illinois 60567-4410
(630) 961-3900
Fax: (630) 961-2168
www.sourcebooks.com

Library of Congress Cataloging-in-Publication Data

Armstrong, Richard
  God doesn't shoot craps : a divine comedy / Richard Armstrong.
    p. cm.
  ISBN-13: 978-1-4022-0656-6 (alk. paper)
  ISBN-10: 1-4022-0656-9 (alk. paper)
  1. Craps (Game)--Fiction. 2. Gambling systems--Fiction. 3. Swindlers
and swindling--Fiction. I. Title.

PS3601.R577G63 2006
813'.6--dc22

2005033346

Printed and bound in the United States of America.
VP 10 9 8 7 6 5 4 3 2 1

To the memory of my father, Richard Athearn Armstrong Sr., who has found a good seat in heaven, I hope—directly across from the sixteenth pole.

ALSO BY RICHARD ARMSTRONG

The Next Hurrah
Leaving the Nest

Contents

Book One
INFERNO

---

*In which our hero finds himself enmeshed
in a world of sin*

Chapter 1

THE MAGICAL MIRACLE
WATER OF LOURDES

OR A MAN ON the verge of discovering the Holy Grail of casino gambling, Danny Pellegrino was in a rotten mood.

But it would be at least another hour before Danny realized he was in possession of the secret to beating the game of craps. At the moment, he was simply trying to make a tricky landing at Bader Field in Atlantic City.

"There's no good way to land at this freaking airport," he muttered under his breath, unaware or unconcerned that the voice-activated mike on the $2,000 Bose headset he recently purchased was sensitive enough to pick up the barest whisper and send it thundering out on the airwaves for all the world to hear.

"Bonanza Three-Four-Five-Juliet, do you want to repeat that transmission?" said the young lady manning the UNI-COM microphone at Atlantic City's Bader Field, in a tone of studied professionalism.

"Yeah, we'd love to hear that one again," chuckled another voice on the radio. The pilot behind Danny in the traffic pattern just couldn't resist making a comment.

Danny was not amused. "I said, 'Say your active runway

again, please' . . . could you do that for me, dear?"

"Bader Field is recommending runway two-niner, left traffic," the UNICOM operator replied curtly.

"Thank you ever so much," said Danny with exaggerated politeness.

Runway 29 or runway 11, what difference does it make? They both stink, Danny thought. One of them sends you directly into a headwind coming off the ocean that's so strong you can have an airspeed of three hundred miles an hour and a groundspeed of three. So you just sit there hovering like a helicopter, glancing at your watch, thinking to yourself you should be landing any day now. The opposite runway, runway two-niner, makes you do a kamikaze-like approach over the top of the Villagio Hotel & Casino. The pattern calls for you to fly much too high as you make your final turn—unless you want to scrape the penthouse with your landing gear—then swoop down at the last second to hit the end of the runway like a falcon diving for prey.

So, according to the UNICOM lady, today was going to be a kamikaze day, not a helicopter day. That suited Danny's mood just fine, since he was on his way to the aforementioned Villagio Casino to try out a new craps system that he knew was going to cost him some money—money he could ill afford to part with at the moment.

At forty-nine years old, with graying hair and a growing potbelly, the ability to fly an airplane in all kinds of weather and under all sorts of conditions was one of the few things left in Danny's life of which he was genuinely proud. When it came to flying an airplane, Danny left nothing to chance. This was in marked contrast to the rest of his life, where he left almost everything to chance.

It was mostly by chance, for example, that ten years earlier he had left an honest job as a copywriter for a mail-order encyclopedia publisher called Wonderworld Press to become a con man selling bogus gambling systems through the mail. It all started, as did so many of the pivotal moments in Danny's life, over a stiff martini.

He was having a long Friday afternoon lunch with an old friend at Spark's Steak House in Manhattan when the conversation turned to, of all things, religious relics.

"Every church in Italy has one of these freakin' things," said Danny, as he sipped his martini. "And it doesn't seem to matter how gross this stuff is. I mean, it could be a piece of St. Peter's toenail."

"Jesus, Danny, I'm trying to eat here," said his friend, taking a forkful of porterhouse away from his mouth and setting it back on the plate until the topic changed.

"Yeah," Danny said, warming to his subject, "it'll make you puke if you think about it too much. One church has a splinter from the cross. And another has a piece of Saint So-and-So's eyebrow. And another has a teardrop of the Virgin Mary. But what gets me is how does anyone know this stuff is for real? I mean, really, the Virgin Mary's teardrop? It could be a drop of Tanqueray for all we know. You've got millions of Italians coming to pray over this thing, and it could be nothing more than 7-Up."

"Well, it's like you've always said, Danny. It doesn't matter whether it's real or not, because people *want* to believe. They want to believe that the detergent is new and improved, because they're sick and tired of detergents that don't work. They want to believe the bonus gift is really free, even if they know deep down inside that nothing in life is free."

"You are correct, sir!" said Danny, imitating Ed McMahon, a figure of no small importance in the junk-mail industry. "And what is the copywriter's job?" asked Danny socratically.

"The copywriter's job is to LET people believe what they want to believe!" replied his friend, who had recited this catechism with Danny many times before.

Danny made a very Italian gesture, a little shrug of the shoulder and flip of his wrists as if to say, "Precisely so."

When the check arrived, Danny picked it up immediately and said, "Hey, you're a sport. Why don't we—"

"Oh no, not the coin flip thing again," his friend interrupted. "I've had lunch with you a hundred times and I've never won. I've picked up every single check."

Danny looked hurt. "Are you accusing me of cheating you? Would I cheat you? My oldest and dearest friend in the junk-mail business. I always let you call it in the air, don't I?"

"I guess so."

"Well, then call it!" Danny flipped the coin high in the air.

"Heads!"

Danny caught the coin with his right hand and slapped it onto his left wrist. Slowly he lifted his hand and peeked underneath. He made a face of infinite regret, like the Virgin Mary at the crucifixion.

"I'm sorry, Bill."

"Tails?

Danny showed him the coin.

"Jesus H. Christ! What are the odds? You'd think I'd win one freakin' time." He threw his American Express Platinum Card on the check like a losing poker player folding a bad hand.

It was a two-tailed coin, of course. Danny had purchased it at a magic shop in Las Vegas. The reason it seldom failed to work is because eight out of ten people who call a coin in the air will say "heads." Heaven knows why, but it's true. So Danny won at least 80 percent of the time. And on those rare occasions when some oddball yelled tails, Danny would snatch the coin out of the air and say, "I was just kidding ya, pal. Just wanted to see if you were a sport. Let's split the check."

Danny Pellegrino hadn't picked up the whole tab at a restaurant since 1977. But on this day, for some reason, he had a change of heart. He pushed aside his friend's card and put two $100 bills in its place.

"You're overdue for a win, old timer," he said.

Danny's first stop back at the office was, of course, the bathroom—where he urgently had to release the remnants of four double martinis currently stored, at great discomfort, in his bladder. It was an ironic twist of fate that if one of Danny's colleagues hadn't been suffering from a chronic bladder infection, and if that colleague hadn't accidentally left an empty urine sample cup sitting on top of the toilet tank, Danny Pellegrino probably never would've become a millionaire.

That's because after Danny relieved himself of the first gallon or so of urine, he couldn't resist picking up the sample cup and using it to catch the last squirt or two. He lifted the cup up to the evening sunlight streaming through the bathroom window, noted its rich, golden color, and said to himself . . .

The magical miracle water of Lourdes.

In a heartbeat, Danny was back at his desk, with a blank sheet of paper rolled into his typewriter and the urine sample cup perched at the end of his desk for reference, or possibly for inspiration.

Danny began typing feverishly. "Ever since a twelve-year-old girl named," . . . oh geez, he thought, what was her name? . . . BERNADETTE!

" . . . named Bernadette saw a vision of the Blessed Virgin Mary by a stream near her hometown of Lourdes . . ." Danny debated for a moment whether or not to add "France" after Lourdes. You'd have to be an idiot not to know Lourdes is in France, he thought. Wait a second, he changed his mind, these *are* idiots . . . "near her hometown of Lourdes, France, the waters of that stream have been thought to have miracle powers."

A few more paragraphs of this semi-historical nonsense and Danny was ready to start making some serious claims for the new product. But then he had a stroke of genius.

He decided not to make any claims at all. Instead, he would simply let his loyal customers speak for themselves. Of course, he didn't *have* any loyal customers at this point, or any customers at all for that matter, but that was a minor obstacle. He would rely on a technique he liked to call the "faux testimonial." Or, as he had explained it once to his staff, "If you can't get anyone to say anything nice about your product, you'll just have to say it yourself."

So Danny wrote a full-page advertisement for the Magical Miracle Water of Lourdes, more than two thousand words altogether, made up entirely of the enthusiastic comments of satisfied customers who didn't exist:

"I put it under my knee before I went to bed. In the morning, the pain and swelling of my arthritis was gone. It's a miracle!"—Mrs. Gwendolyn W., Pocatello, Idaho.

"Whenever I get a headache, I dab a few drops on my fore-head. It works better than Excedrin and it never upsets my stomach!"—Rev. Wilbur L., Amarillo, Texas. Danny loved using members of the clergy for his faux testimonials.

"My dog was dying of liver cancer. In desperation, I sprin-kled some of the water over his kibble. The vet said he'd never seen a cancer like that go into remission. That was six months ago, and Scooter still loves to play fetch!"—Miss Mary J., Winnemucca, Nevada.

So it went for paragraph after paragraph. Danny loved coming up with the names of the towns, most of which he pulled from memory of various trips he'd taken out West. Although he tended to rely on Nevada a little too heavily because he went there so often to gamble.

"I carried the bottle with me into the casino and sat down at one of those progressive slot machines. I couldn't believe it when those three sevens lined up and the change girl told me I'd won $45,000!"—Mr. Zachary B., Sparks, Nevada.

There's no reason we can't broaden the appeal of this stuff beyond good health, he thought. By the time he was done, Danny had broadened the appeal of the miracle water to include its use as a fertilizer for prize-winning plants and vegetables, a cologne or perfume to attract the opposite sex (Danny eventually settled on the words "toilet water," since it could apply to both men and women and since it was, after all, an unassailably accurate description of the prod-uct), a hair-styling tonic, a fabric softener (a police officer from Reno claimed that a shirt laundered with the miracle water actually stopped a bullet from penetrating his heart), a way to remove pet stains from carpets, a safe alternative to prescription drugs, a soothing way to shrink hemorrhoids, and a vitamin supplement for sprinkling on breakfast cereal.

He crossed the last one out. He would stop just short of encouraging people to actually drink the liquid—although there was certainly no harm if dogs like Scooter did.

Danny was so enthusiastic about the ad that he quit his job at Wonderworld the next day. He cashed in his profit-sharing plan and used the proceeds to buy a full page in the *National Enquirer.*

A few days after his advertisement hit the newsstands—the first day he could reasonably expect some orders—he went to the post office where he had rented a small mailbox. He peered into the little window of the box, hoping to find it jammed with envelopes, and was crestfallen by what he saw there.

Nothing.

Not a single envelope. Not a single postcard. Not a single coupon. Dejectedly he started to open the mailbox anyway, perhaps in the hope that a lone envelope might be stuck to the top or pressed against the sides. When he cracked open the little door of the mailbox, there was indeed something inside. Not an envelope. Not a reply card. Just a tiny slip of paper.

It read, *"Too much mail for box, see clerk at window."*

It was a few months afterward that Danny bought his first airplane. That was two airplanes ago. The one he was riding in now was new. It was a V-tail Bonanza, known around general-aviation airports as a "Forked-Tail Doctor Killer," because physicians could afford to buy these souped-up aircraft, but they rarely had the experience necessary to fly them.

When nosy people asked Danny how he got so rich, he liked to say, "I made my money in the water business," deliberately leaving the impression that he was heir to the

Pellegrino mineral water fortune—in fact, he was no relation. When pressed on the matter, he'd say, "I came up with a technique for turning wine into water."

After the Magical Miracle Water of Lourdes, Danny never looked back. He sold "Irish Lucky Charms" that had been chipped off the world-famous Blarney Stone in the Emerald Isle. (They were pellets of gravel from his driveway.) He sold rare and exotic diamonds from South Africa for just $49.95 each. (His supplier for these was a manufacturer of industrial diamonds, the kind used to make phonograph needles, who sold them to Danny for one dollar apiece.) He sold booklets about how to get rich playing bingo at church. (The secret, Danny said, was to ask the priest to bless your card.)

The enormous and unexpected success of the bingo books led Danny to venture into an area where he was destined to go anyway, given his passion in life: gambling systems. Finding the perfect marriage of his hobby and his work, Danny loved to invent gambling systems and write the junk-mail letters designed to sell them.

He wrote a book about blackjack that enabled people to "count cards" without relying on their memory. (Which isn't possible, but Danny didn't let that stand in the way.) He developed a slot-machine system that was so powerful, Danny claimed, it would guide people toward "loose" slots with the accuracy of a Geiger counter. He came up with a roulette system based on recognizing "biased" roulette wheels, the kind that came up with the same winning numbers over and over again. (Roulette wheels are engineered with the precision normally reserved for moving parts in the Space Shuttle, but what the heck?) He invented a craps system based on controlling the dice with your fingertips during the toss. (Another physical impossibility, but Danny was a big believer in reaching beyond the conventional boundaries of physics.)

Many booklets and many millions of dollars later, Danny found himself gradually running out of ideas. But this was not a problem because there were lots of aspiring gambling writers out there who could invent systems, but didn't know how to market them. Danny would scour the classified ads in supermarket tabloids looking for someone who was clever enough to have invented a new system, but dumb enough to try selling it through the classifieds. That was how he found *Win By Losing: Parrondo's Paradox and Brownian Ratchet Theory Applied to Casino Craps* by Virgil Kirk of Las Vegas, Nevada. And that was why he was on his way to Atlantic City today.

"Bader traffic, Bonanza Three-Four-Five-Juliet turning left base for runway two-niner at Atlantic City." I can't wait to get to the casino and start losing money, Danny thought.

It wasn't that he didn't like *Win By Losing;* he liked it a lot. It was one of the best craps systems he'd seen in a long time. He liked it because it took a spiritual, almost Zen-like approach to the game.

He also liked the fact that *Win By Losing* was based on the cutting-edge work of a real physicist and mathematician by the name of Juan M. R. Parrondo at the University of Madrid. Professor Parrondo, of course, had no idea that his ideas on "Brownian Ratchet Theory" were being applied to casino craps by some kook in Las Vegas. But his name and his theories lent a scientific imprimatur to the enterprise that would help the book sell. It didn't hurt that the author, Virgil Kirk, was something of a character, too. Danny had talked to him on the phone a few times to negotiate the royalties for the booklet and he came away from each call feeling like he'd just had a chat with the Dalai Lama.

But Danny had no illusions that the system would actually work in the casino. It was a gambling system, for chrissakes. The casinos *loved* players who had systems. They sent limousines and private jets to pick them up.

So Danny wasn't flying to Atlantic City because he wanted to *test* the system, he merely wanted to make sure he was thoroughly familiar with it. He had just launched a million-piece mailing earlier in the week and he knew he would start getting orders in a few days. Shortly after that, he would start getting phone calls and letters from customers asking questions about the system. "Am I doing it right?" "Why isn't it working?" "What did you mean by this?" "What did you mean by that?"

There would be a lot of questions about *Win By Losing* because it was a complicated system—which wasn't necessarily a bad thing. In fact, that was one more reason why Danny liked it. Complicated systems helped minimize returns, because people thought it was their *own* fault the system wasn't working. But complicated systems meant lots of questions, too, so Danny thought it only prudent to be prepared.

"Bader traffic, Bonanza Three-Four-Five-Juliet now turning final for runway two-niner at Atlantic City." Danny had managed to fly over the Villagio Hotel without scraping his landing gear. The wind was relatively calm today and everything was looking good at this point for a safe landing. But Danny had other problems on his mind.

They were mostly money problems. Producing, printing, and mailing a million-piece direct-mail campaign had stretched his cash reserves to the breaking point. Of course, the money would come back to him many times over when the orders started arriving. But that would take time. Meanwhile, he had just made a $300,000 cash down payment on the Bonanza and was continuing to make substantial monthly payments on the balance. So the prospect of donating several thousand dollars to the Villagio Hotel and Casino this weekend by testing this silly craps system—which normally wouldn't have fazed him at all—was very upsetting indeed.

"Bader traffic, Bonanza Three-Four-Five-Juliet is now on short final for runway two-niner at Atlantic City." As Danny throttled down almost to stall speed and aimed the nose of his new Bonanza at the big "29" printed on the runway, he could tell this was going to be a smooth landing. He calmly and confidently began his final descent when—THUD!—a seagull struck his windshield.

Or was it the other way around? Although it was just a glancing blow, it made quite an impact. It made Danny flinch so badly that the back of his head slapped sharply against the headrest, and it almost made him pull back on the yoke. On final approach, with the throttle at low power and the aircraft floating just barely above stall speed, pulling back on the yoke would've put Danny into a stall, a crash, a fire, a funeral.

But Danny did not pull back on the yoke. Instead, he yelled at the seagull, "Jonathan Livingston Sonofabitch, get out of my way!" He continued with his landing procedures as calmly as he could. And he landed safely.

"That was a surprise," said Danny in his best Chuck Yeager seen-it-all-before voice, as he cut the throttle and coasted toward the end of the runway.

But a much bigger surprise awaited him at the Villagio.

Chapter 2

THE HOLY GHOST
RIGGED DEM BONES

DANNY MADE A BRIEF pit stop in his hotel room before going down to the casino. It was the usual mid-level room in a mid-level casino hotel, about the same quality you'd expect from a Holiday Inn. The only difference was the price. On a weekend in July, this room could rent for as much $400 a night—roughly what you'd pay to stay at one of the best hotels in the country. On a weekday in February, the same room might go for as little as $50. But on this Friday night in December, Danny was getting it for free.

Not a high roller by any stretch, Danny was just enough of a gambler to qualify for a free room on a weekend night during a relatively slow season in Atlantic City. But Danny didn't care about the room. He would spend most of the weekend in the bars, the restaurants, and of course, the casino—which is where he was headed now. Danny liked to make a nice entrance into the casino, and he liked to dress the part.

Three very attractive women were guarding the entrance to the casino like MPs posted at a checkpoint. They were chatting aimlessly, smoking cigarettes, and judiciously evaluating every unattached man who entered. These women weren't prostitutes. Not exactly. Not yet. They were just extremely sexy young ladies who happened to enjoy the companionship of wealthy men. They liked the expensive dinners that such men bought them. They liked the little gifts that usually followed a winning session in the casino. And when one of these women asked for carfare home in the morning, she wouldn't mind if the man gave her three or four hundred dollars more than was strictly necessary to pay the cab. Women like this were commonly called "weekend warriors." In a few years, most of the ones who kept doing it would drop the pretenses and simply become whores.

One of them spotted Danny while he was still more than fifty feet away. With his Armani jacket over a black mock-turtleneck sweater, his Bruno Magli shoes, his gold Rolex, and his diamond pinkie ring, Danny was hard to miss.

"This one's mine, ladies," said the tall blonde in the middle, as she turned to face her friends. Then she expertly took one step backwards into Danny's path, perfectly timed to cause a collision.

"Oh, I'm terribly sorry," said Danny. "Are you okay? I didn't break any bones, did I?"

"No, I'm fine. Just a little startled, that's all. Where are you headed in such a big hurry?"

"I'm on my way to play craps."

"Craps! Oh, that game is so complicated. I don't even know the difference between the 'come' and the 'don't come.'" She winked at her friends, who giggled like school-girls. But with this remark, she revealed that she was very familiar with the game.

"Well, it has to do with whether or not you have prostate problems," said Danny. This drew a very big laugh from Petticoat Junction.

"I wish you'd explain the game to me," she said with a flutter of her false eyelashes. Danny assessed the situation.

"I doubt if I could explain anything to you that you don't already know, my dear."

"Oh, I bet you could," she replied suggestively, as she fingered the crucifix and teardrop heart hanging from Danny's gold necklace.

"Have you been doing this long?" Danny asked, as he put a fatherly hand on her shoulder.

She made a quizzical look on her face, as if to say, "Whatever could you mean?"

"Let me give you some advice. A real high roller never walks into the casino alone. He usually has one casino host on his left and another casino host on his right. Now, I'll grant you that this may make him a lot harder to bump into accidentally, but it's worth it. Because those guys have real money. A well-dressed, middle-aged guy like me is probably just a working stiff who is paying alimony to two ex-wives and can't afford to buy you much more than a cheeseburger."

"Well . . . er, uh, thanks, I guess," she said, somewhat dumbfounded by this unexpected homily.

"Don't mention it. Professional courtesy." He started to walk away, but she grabbed him by the sleeve.

"Hey, wait a minute. Aren't you Dennis Farina?"

"Oh no, not again," Danny muttered. With his olive skin, salt-and-pepper hair, and penetrating blue eyes, Danny was constantly being mistaken for a famous Italian American actor. The problem was, nobody could figure out which one. Pacino? No, he was taller than Pacino. DeNiro? No, he wasn't quite as handsome. People guessed Dennis Farina most often, but that wasn't quite right either.

"No, I'm not."

"Yes, you are!" the girl insisted.

"I assure you, my dear, I am not Dennis Farina."

"But you're somebody, right? You're *somebody*."

"No," he said with finality. "I am nobody."

That about sums it up, Danny thought, as he finally managed to extricate himself and continue walking toward the craps tables. At the core of Danny's being, there was an emptiness, an emptiness he tried to fill with sin. Danny was only as fulfilled as his next bet, his next drink, his next curse, his next whore, his next con game. He often felt a gnawing dissatisfaction—a sense that he could've been more, could've been better, could've done something meaningful with his life, but it was far too late to change now. There were no choices left in Danny's life, only consequences.

He married his first wife for love and had two beautiful children with her. Then he blew it by chasing anything that walked down the street wearing a skirt. The object of one of those adulterous flings became his second wife. But the ink was barely dry on their marriage license before it became abundantly clear that she was more interested in Danny's money than she was in him. After milking him for enough designer shoes to make Imelda Marcos blush, she, too, filed for divorce and asked for half of the community property. "Mental cruelty" was the official reason cited on the legal papers, but she privately told her friends that she didn't like Danny's "sleazy business." The rumors spread through their circle of friends, but Danny didn't put up a fight. He dealt with it the only way he knew how: he threw himself into his work and his flying.

At the age of forty-nine, Danny could not explain his behavior. He could only make allowances for it. So he deliberately withdrew from the lives of his two children, because he didn't want to hurt them anymore. He faithfully paid for their child support and expensive private colleges, but after they graduated, his contact with them diminished to an occasional telephone call and expensive birthday present. Better they should say, "I'm not in touch with my father," he thought, than say, "My father is a phony and a fraud and a skirt chaser who broke my mother's heart."

But tonight, as he walked past row after row of glittering, noisy slot machines, he looked like a man with the world at his feet. He did not give off a hint of insecurity or pain. Danny was good at taking the biggest regrets of his life and hiding them from public view like an oyster wrapping a cyst around an irritating grain of sand. All the outside world ever saw was the shiny pearl. He walked up to the first available craps table, where one of the pit managers recognized him and said, "Hey, Mr. P, how've ya been? Long time no see."

Pit managers or floormen (the public mistakenly called them all "pit bosses," but there was only one boss in a pit) routinely referred to their better customers as "Mr. First Initial." If a guy put $10,000 in action on a single night, as Danny frequently did, he was far too important to be addressed by his first name. But a floorman didn't want to use the last name either, because casinos were still sufficiently sinful that some people didn't want their last names broadcast too loudly.

"Hey, Jimmy," said Danny, "gimme five large." Danny threw a little plastic card down on the table. It was his

"Villagio VIP Card," and the floorman would use it to begin the process of securing a marker for Danny. A marker was like a counter check that would allow Danny to draw chips on his credit with the casino. If he had a winning session, the marker would be destroyed. If he didn't, it would be sent to his bank like a regular check. Or he could buy it back from the casino cashier later. At Villagio's sister hotel in Las Vegas, Danny would've received his money almost instantly upon showing his card. But here in Atlantic City, there would be lots of paperwork to fill out over the next few minutes. It was the difference between western laissez-faire and eastern bureaucracy in a nutshell.

Las Vegas was so loose about extending credit, in fact, that one time Danny dropped his health-insurance card down on the table by mistake instead of his VIP card. Strangely, the casino still gave him his money. Danny loved telling that story so, of course, he turned to the craps dealer next to him and proceeded to tell it again.

"You know, I was at the Villagio in Vegas once and I accidentally dropped my health-insurance card down instead of my VIP card. They were both little white cards. It was an honest mistake. But you know what happened?"

"What happened, sir?" the dealer asked with a smile.

"They gave me the freakin' money, that's what!"

The dealer laughed politely, as if on cue.

"I mean, it took them a little longer than usual. I could see them back in the pit looking at the card and whispering about it. I said to myself, 'What, am I back in Atlantic City where I gotta get my ass notarized before I can get my money?' But ten minutes later, they give me the chips. Then one of these goombahs says to me, 'Mr. P, this is your health-insurance card. But it's okay, your credit is always good here.'"

The dealer smiled again. With his slicked-back hair, rimless glasses, and handlebar mustache, this particular dealer looked like he could serve as the logotype proprietor of a chain restaurant in the suburbs, something called "Rickenbackers" or "Phineas T. Fuggwipers." A good-natured middle-aged man, he was Danny's favorite craps dealer at the Villagio and he'd heard this story many times before. But some of the other players at the table who hadn't heard it were chuckling out loud. Danny warmed to his little audience.

"But you wanna know the funny part?"

"What's the funny part?" The dealer waited expectantly for what he knew was coming.

"When I got back home, I didn't have any freakin' health insurance!"

Everyone laughed. Even the dealer. Danny was nothing if not charming. People tended to like him instantly and tonight he was at the top of his game. Friendly. Funny. Even more importantly, he had an amazing capacity to mirror the behavior, the attitudes, and the culture of the people around him. Now he was playing the part of the big gambler, because that's what the situation required. He was saying freakin' this and freakin' that and he fit in perfectly. But in a business setting he could talk like someone who'd received his MBA from Harvard. When he was at Giants Stadium for a football game, he chatted with the folks around him like a guy who worked in a steel mill. Had he ever found himself inside a church, there was little doubt he could whisper with the little blue-haired ladies about how he'd come to witness for Jesus.

Some of the people Danny knew in his day-to-day life—his barber, his dentist, his dry cleaner—would've been shocked to learn that he was just this side of being a criminal. He was so *nice*. So accommodating. So personable. You could say that they didn't know the "real" Danny. But why was the felonious side of him any more real than the charming side?

When all of the paperwork was done, the dealer standing opposite Danny at the table counted out $5,000 in chips of various denominations and pushed the pile toward Danny saying, "Good luck, Mr. P."

"Thanks, I'll need it," he replied.

Danny hadn't exactly memorized *Win By Losing*, but he'd read the booklet five or six times and he had a good sense of how the system worked. Basically, it called for him to play both the pass line and the don't-pass line on an alternating basis, while hedging his bets with certain exotic side bets on other parts of the table. The theory behind the system was that Danny could gradually "ratchet up" his winnings, even if he lost more often than he won. That was the theory anyway. Danny gave it about the same chance of working as the Ptolemaic theory. But what the heck? He put two green chips (or a total of $50) on the pass line and awaited the first roll of the dice.

The dealers were talking about football. Craps dealers only had two main topics of discussion: sports and cocktail waitresses. The sports discussions could be very intricate, detailed, and lengthy. The cocktail waitress conversations were sly, hit-or-miss affairs triggered by the sudden arrival, departure, or near-miss of a pretty waitress. During the football conversation, for example, Danny heard the dealers switch gears in mid-sentence:

"The Giants really stink this . . . *did you see that one?*"

"Yeah, her name is Michelle. She's new. I met her last night."

"You met her, yeah, right, like I met the freakin' Pope."

The boxman, a casino employee whose job was to sit at the craps table and keep an eye on the proceedings, shot the dealer a look. Saying "freakin'" was perfectly all right for players like Danny, but a definite no-no for dealers.

"No, she's a nice kid," continued the first dealer. "She's taking night classes at Atlantic County Junior College. She's really sweet, she . . . hey, get a load of *that* one!"

The only topic craps dealers refused to talk about at any length was craps. They were unspeakably bored with the game.

"Winner six, it came easy. Front-line winner. Pay the line, take the don'ts. The dice are coming out. Craps bets, yo bets, whirl bets, get your bets down, the dice are out," said the stickman.

It was the stickman's job to "call" the game by announcing the results of the previous roll and soliciting bets for the next one, particularly the worst bets on the table. Stickmen were supposed to keep up this patter with enthusiasm and panache. It was part of the show. But most of them were so bored, they recited the standard lines in the dry monotone of a priest handing out penance after confession.

Danny's $50 had magically turned into $100 and *Win By Losing* now called for him to move the $100 to the don't-pass line, where he would be betting against most of the other players at the table.

Don't-pass players were not well-liked in the world of craps. Some gambling writers referred to don't-pass betting—or wrong betting—as playing the "Dark Side of the Force." The reason for this bias is that while pass-line bettors (who make up the vast majority) play with a gathering sense of enthusiasm as the dice get hot, wrong bettors stand quietly at the table like vultures waiting for everyone else to lose.

Sometimes don't-pass bettors even *look* like vultures. Danny remembered one wrong bettor he'd seen at the El Cortez Hotel in downtown Las Vegas who was a classic example of the mold. Dressed in a long black trenchcoat, he was a tall, gaunt, ghostlike man with long gray hair arranged in a ratty ponytail. He carried a small spiral notebook and made notations after every roll. Other players at the table gave him a wide berth, not because he smelled bad, although he almost certainly did, but because wrong bettors were like lepers who were believed to infect a table with bad luck. As it happened that night in Las Vegas, the dice were hot. The vulture was losing. And Danny watched as he did what wrong bettors always do when they're losing badly. He melted away. He didn't walk away. He didn't slink away. He *melted* away before Danny's very eyes, like a slow dissolve in a movie. Danny had seen it happen a hundred times before, and each time he blinked his eyes and mumbled to the nearest dealer, "What the hell happened to the don't bettor?" It was weird.

As soon as Danny moved his $100 from the pass line to the don't-pass line, he felt the bad vibrations coming from other players at the table. The guys on either side of him decided they needed a little more breathing room and moved away from him. A player across from him gave him *il malocchio,* the evil eye. Even the dealers suddenly adopted the overly professional, slightly distanced attitude of a nurse who is forced to work with a patient who has a very infectious and somewhat distasteful disease.

"Seven out, line away. Take the line, pay the don'ts. There was no six. New shooter, new direction," said the stickman, indicating that the pass line had lost, the don't-pass line had won, and now the dice would be given to a new shooter at the other end of the table.

Danny's $100 had turned into $200. And he felt relieved as *Win By Losing* now called for him to move his money back to the pass line where he would rejoin the company of decent society.

"Seven, winner seven, front-line winner. Pay the line, take the don'ts," said the stickman. And Danny's $200 had now turned into $400.

"Craps bets, whirl bets, yo bets, place your bets, the dice are coming out," said the stickman.

And now, against his better judgment, Danny would start to play some of the exotic side bets the stickman was trying to promote. It was against his better judgment because these were some of the worst bets on the table. But Danny had to do it because *Win By Losing* told him to do so.

He placed a yo bet, which stood for eleven. No one knew for sure how an eleven came to be known as a yo. Perhaps it was because early craps dealers were urged to enunciate the word carefully so it wouldn't be mistaken for the seven, as in "Eeeeee-ooooo-leven." Later this mutated to "Yo-leven" and finally to yo. The eleven got a lot of action from players, despite the fact it was a bad bet, simply because they loved to say it.

Danny hated making such exotic bets, because they gave too much edge to the house. The chances of seeing an eleven on any one roll of the dice were 17-to-1, for example, but the casino only paid you 15-to-1 if it actually happened. That was a 16 percent advantage for the house, or roughly the same "vigorish" you'd expect to pay on a slot machine. But *Win By Losing* was adamant about making these bets under certain circumstances, so Danny tossed a $25 chip to the stickman and said, "Quarter yo."

"Eeeeeee-oooooo-leven!" said the stickman with more than the usual amount of enthusiasm as the six and five showed up on the dice. The stickman tapped his bamboo rod in front of Danny and told the other dealer to, "Pay Mr. P $375 on his yo."

"Parlay it," said Danny, which meant he wanted his winnings to go back up on the eleven.

That got the dealer's attention. The boxman, too. In fact, even the pit manager who had prepared Danny's marker wandered curiously over to the table to make sure he had heard what he thought he'd heard. If Danny won this bet, the payoff would be $6,400. To bet this much money on a so-called "proposition" bet was unusual to say the least, and in some casinos, even prohibited. But the pit manager nodded almost imperceptibly at the stickman to give his approval. Danny noticed their mild discomfort, so he tossed another $25 chip at the stickman and said, "Put the boys on the yo with me, too." This was the customary method of tipping the dealers. If an eleven showed on the dice, the dealers would get a nice $400 tip. If it didn't, they'd get nothing. So he had reawakened their interest in the game.

"EEEEEEEEEEE-OOOOOOOOOO-LEVEN!" shouted the dealer, with genuine enthusiasm now, as the six and five came to rest, face up, in a pile of chips at the end of the table.

"Thank you for the action, sir!" said the stickman as he tapped the stick in front of Danny again and said to the opposite dealer, "Please give this kind gentleman $6,000, and the dealers will go $400 and down." (Meaning the dealers were too smart to try for another yo.)

"Do me again," said Danny.

"Excuse me, sir?"

"Parlay the yo," said Danny softly.

But his quiet words caused a sudden flurry of activity in the pit. All four pit managers converged upon the table, including the actual pit boss, who, after ascertaining what was going on, picked up a telephone to call *his* boss, the casino shift manager.

What Danny was proposing to do now was technically against the rules. The table had a $2,000 limit on it. A little red sign in the corner said so in no uncertain terms. Players were not allowed to exceed that limit without securing permission from the management. Such permission was frequently granted to high rollers who wanted to exceed the limit on a pass-line bet, but it was extremely rare for someone to put several thousand dollars on a *proposition* bet like the yo. Not that the Villagio Hotel & Casino was going to go broke if it paid Danny $102,400. But if Danny eventually walked away from the table with more than $100,000 of the casino's money, it would be very noticeable on the daily profit-and-loss statement for that particular craps table, and someone somewhere would have some splainin' to do if they didn't get permission from upstairs.

Danny hated doing what he was about to do. Every cell and fiber in his body was screaming at him to take the bet down. He hated making proposition bets, even for a single dollar. He hated parlays. He was a firm believer in taking his bets down after a win. He even hated risking large amounts on a single roll, preferring to make his profits incrementally over the course of an evening. But he had promised himself he would follow Virgil Kirk's advice, no matter how stupid it was. In *Win By Losing*, Kirk had said something about yos coming in groups of three, particularly when there had been none at all for a long time. Danny remembered that Kirk had made some sort of bizarre allusion to the Holy Trinity to prove his point.

If the Holy Ghost can rig these bones to come up with a yo, thought Danny, I'm sending ten large to the archdiocese.

Although the archdiocese never did get its money, the two dice did indeed come to rest at the end of the table with a six showing on one and a five on the other.

Every player at the table screamed and cheered. The dealers cheered, too, because Danny had taken care to put an additional black chip on the yo for the crew. It was a $1,600 tip altogether. Only the pit managers seemed less than thrilled by the result. They stared at the table with the grim expression of a group of surgeons charged with informing the next-of-kin that the patient had died on the operating table due to their own dumb mistake.

So it went for the next seven hours. Danny simply could not lose. At one point he was nearly a half-million dollars ahead of the game. It couldn't possibly be because of this dopey system, Danny thought. He knew enough about the mathematics of craps to know that the system was seriously flawed. He knew as much after his very first reading of *Win By Losing*. The system called for making lots of idiotic hedge bets and proposition bets that couldn't possibly win in the long run.

The more he thought about it, the more frustrated he got. He actually found himself rooting against his own bets to prove to himself that the system was flawed, like every other craps system in the world. But no matter how much he rooted against himself, the money kept coming. And the more money he won, the more frustrated he got. Once, after raking in about $30,000, he actually started to break out in a cold sweat.

"Are you okay, Mr. P?" asked the stickman. "You look a little pale."

"I can't seem to stop making money," Danny replied.

To make the sweating stop and to restore his sense that the universe was still right side up, he forced himself to conclude that he was simply on the lucky streak of his life. That it had nothing to do with the system. That he was simply as hot as a firecracker tonight and could do no wrong. It was an unfortunate thought, because it caused him to do something very stupid:

He decided to try to lose.

"If I'm on the lucky streak of my life," Danny reasoned, "then the lucky streak should continue whether I stick with the advice in *Win By Losing* or not. But if all of my success tonight is really due to *Win By Losing*, then I should expect to start losing money as soon as I go off the system."

It made sense—at least to the extent that deliberately throwing away a windfall of $500,000 ever makes sense. So Danny went off the system and went back to his normally cautious, conservative, disciplined style of play. The only difference between the way he began playing tonight and the way he usually played was that he was betting with a basic unit of yellow chips ($1,000) instead of green ones ($25). But what the heck, he figured, he was playing with the house's money.

Which, of course, proceeded to disappear. Not all of it. Danny got down to a bankroll of about $50,000 before he realized that deliberately losing money at the craps table may not rank among the smartest things he'd ever done in life. And having taken a seven-hour roller coaster ride from

$5,000 all the way up to $500,000, then plummeting down in a heartbeat to $50,000, Danny decided it might be time to cash in his chips and get a drink at the bar. He needed to think.

Danny ordered a double martini on the rocks with an olive and began to chew over what had happened that night. Okay, so the system works, he thought. At least, it seems to work. He'd have to try it a few more times to be sure, but it certainly was working beautifully for seven straight hours tonight. *Why* does it work, though? It *shouldn't* work. Danny had twenty books in his gambling library that would gladly tell him the chances of parlaying a yo bet three times in a row were astronomically remote. The chances of doing it twice in one night, as Danny had done this evening, were not even in this universe. No, the system should not work.

But it did. Perhaps this Virgil Kirk was on to something, thought Danny. Perhaps the theories of this professor in Madrid—*what was his name? Pontouro? Bitondo?*—really could be applied to craps. Maybe there was indeed a way to take two bets that were supposed to lose in the long run, like the pass-line bet and the don't-pass bet, and combine them in such a way that they showed a net profit. Perhaps it was true, as Kirk and the Spanish professor proposed, that you could ratchet your winnings upwards by alternating randomly between two losing propositions.

What was the deal with Virgil Kirk anyway, Danny wondered. Didn't he realize how valuable this system was? In their few telephone conversations, it was clear that Kirk was some kind of scientist, or mathematician, or witch doctor. Perhaps he was only interested in it from a theoretical point of view. Perhaps he'd never even bothered to take it to a casino. God knows, Danny had sold a few systems in his day that he never tested in actual casino play. In fact, he was more likely to test a system he was retailing, like *Win By Losing*, than one he had invented himself. He knew how his own systems worked. Or didn't work. It was the retail systems you had to check out. Maybe Kirk had been reading about Brownian Ratchet Theory, applied it intellectually to casino craps, and sat down to write the booklet without worrying about whether it would really work in the casino or not.

"What a flim-flam man," Danny mumbled with admiration.

What exactly did "ratchet" mean anyway, wondered Danny in the kind of misty thought that would only occur after a shot-and-a-half of gin. He knew that elevators were built with ratchets. That's what kept them from falling. He remembered reading somewhere—was it *Win By Losing?*— that Otis used to demonstrate his new invention by standing on the platform of an open elevator and deliberately cutting the cable with an ax. The ratchets prevented him from plummeting to his death. A ratchet allowed upward movement, but prevented downward movement. Could that really happen in a casino? Could you really keep your bankroll moving steadily upward without ever worrying about it falling back down?

"Jesus H. Christ," Danny muttered to himself as the full implications of this thought dawned on him.

"You rang?" said the bartender.

"Another double martini," said Danny absently.

The more he thought about it, the more excited he got. He was getting tipsy now and it occurred to him that the alcohol might be causing him to be more excited than he should be. But another gulp of gin erased that reservation.

"I could make millions with this freaking thing," he said aloud. Fortunately, no one was there to hear him this time.

Then he had a scary thought. No sooner had he begun thinking about all the wonderful things he could buy with the money than suddenly he realized how quickly it might all disappear:

What if the casino changed its rules?

All they'd have to do was tell people that they had to choose between pass-line betting and don't betting. The casino would tell the players they had to make up their minds before they came to the table whether they were going to bet with the dice or against them. No alternating allowed. Heck, that's the way most people bet anyway. Danny could count on the fingers of one hand the number of times he'd seen players alternate between the front line and the back line. People were either right bettors or they were wrong bettors. It was a part of their self-image, a part of their personality, a part of who they were. If the casino told people they couldn't alternate back-and-forth during one playing session, there wouldn't be so much as a squeak of protest.

Danny realized that if he was going to make millions from this thing, he was going to have to do it fast and do it quietly. He would have to hit one casino after another, taking each one for at least the $500,000 he (almost) won tonight. Maybe he should shoot for an even million dollars per casino. It was no big deal for these casinos to lose a million bucks to a high roller, he thought. He did the arithmetic in his head. Finishing off his second double martini, it wasn't easy. But according to his best calculations, it meant he would make about $12 million in Atlantic City, about $40 million in Las Vegas, maybe another $40 million in the Mississippi casinos, riverboat casinos, and Indian casinos in the Midwest and Connecticut. Maybe as much as $100 million altogether.

You could live on that, he thought.

"One more double," said Danny to the bartender.

"Coming up."

"Extra olives, please."

Danny loved olives. Green ones, especially. In fact, the martini was his favorite drink, primarily because it was the only cocktail that came with olives. There must be a chromosome in the body of every Italian that makes them love olives, thought Danny. His thoughts were starting to get a little silly now.

The guy is drinking doubles and he likes olives, thought the bartender. So when Danny's third drink arrived, it looked like a cocktail glass growing in the middle of an olive grove.

Danny took a toothpick and started dipping olives in the glass like some alcoholic version of a Swiss fondue. He was feeling utterly on top of the world, on top of the entire universe, until a second truly mortifying thought popped into his head:

He had just put a million letters into the mail offering to sell the secret of *Win By Losing* to virtually every avid craps player in the United States.

Danny got up from the barstool and ran to the men's room.

"I wonder if it was the gin or the olives," muttered the bartender.

WIN BY LOSING!
Parrondo's Paradox and Brownian Ratchet Theory
Applied to Casino Craps
by Virgil Kirk

SECTION ONE:
THE BEGINNING OF WISDOM

"The test of a first-rate intelligence is the ability to hold two opposing ideas in mind at the same time and still retain the ability to function."
—F. Scott Fitzgerald

Craps is a lot like chess. I can teach you how to play it in two minutes, but you might spend the rest of your life learning how to play it well.

It is a game that is at once more simple and more complex than it first appears. Many people hesitate to play craps because it seems so intimidating. There are so many different bets on the table. So many players and dealers crowded around. People are usually screaming and yelling. They're using strange-sounding words and phrases to place their bets.

Once you've started to play the game, however, you'll discover how simple it really is. It is perhaps the easiest table game in the casino to learn how to play. After only a few hours, you will think that you have mastered it. But that's when the game of craps sets a trap for you. Because it's only when you believe you've mastered craps that it is gradually revealed what a subtle and complex game it really is.

For now, however, let's concentrate on the simplicity. The essential bet in craps is the pass-line bet. When you place your chip on the pass line, the next roll of the dice is called the "comeout" roll. If a seven or an eleven appear on the dice, you win. If a two, three, or twelve appear on the dice (these are known collectively as "craps" numbers), you lose. If any other number appears on the dice—a six, for example—then the object of the game will be to roll the six again before you roll a seven. The six, in this case, is called your "point." If you see the six again before you roll a seven, you win. If you see a seven first, you lose.

That's it! That's all there is to it. But just to make sure you understand, let's look at a few examples of how it might work in the casino.

Let's say you step up to the craps table and put a $5 chip on the pass line. The shooter rolls a seven. You win! It's an even-money bet, so the dealer puts another $5 chip next to your original one. You now have ten dollars. Suppose you "press" your bet by adding the two chips together and putting $10 on the pass line. The shooter rolls an eleven. You win again! Now you have twenty dollars. So you press your bet again and put $20 on the pass line. The shooter rolls a three.

Ooops, you lose! The dealer scoops up your twenty dollars. But that's okay. What's twenty dollars in the whole scheme of life? So you put another $5 chip on the pass line, but this time the shooter rolls a five. The number five is now your point. You want the shooter to roll the five again before he rolls a seven. So the shooter keeps rolling. He throws an eleven. No decision. He rolls a two. No decision. He rolls an eight. No decision. He rolls a five. You win!

But what if he had rolled a seven in the meantime? Then you would've lost. That's called "sevening out," and the shooter's roll would've come to an end.[1]

The other basic bet in craps is the "don't-pass" bet, which is simply the opposite of what I've just described. If you place a chip on the don't-pass line, you lose if the comeout roll is a seven or eleven. You'll win if the comeout roll is two or three. And if the comeout roll results in a point number—a four, for example—then you'll want to see a seven before you see the four again.[2]

There are many other bets on the craps table. But the pass line and the don't-pass line are the two most important. Not only are they the two most advantageous bets in craps, but they are also the two most critical bets for the *Win By Losing* system that I'm going to teach you later in this booklet.

The only other bet that we'll employ in the *Win By Losing* system is a seldom-used proposition bet called the "whirl" bet.[3] The whirl bet is actually a combination of five one-roll bets—the "yo," the "any seven," the "high," the "low," and the "ace-deuce." Again, it's not nearly as complicated as it sounds. When you make one of these bets, you are simply wagering that a certain number will appear on the very next roll of the dice.

When you bet the yo, for example, you're betting that an eleven will appear on the next roll. When you bet the any seven, you're betting that a seven will appear on the next roll. The high is a bet on the twelve. The low is a bet

---

1. That's why craps players sometimes refer to the seven as "The Devil" when it arises in this situation.

2. If you've been paying close attention, you may be wondering, "What about the twelve?" How come the twelve loses on the pass line, but it doesn't win on the don't-pass line? How very observant of you! You have a natural gift for this! If you're betting the don't-pass line and you see a twelve on the comeout roll, it's a "push," which means there's no decision. Your bet neither wins nor loses. It simply stays on the don't-pass line awaiting the next roll. This little anomaly is what enables the casino to bet against both sides and still make a profit.

3. Sometimes called "The World" bet.

on the two. And the ace-deuce is a bet on the three. When you make a whirl bet, you're simply combining all four of these bets at once.

All of these proposition bets have a very bad reputation in craps, because each of them carries a substantial edge for the house. But I want you to get comfortable with playing them anyway. Why?

Because you will never succeed at craps until you learn how to play the entire table.

Unfortunately, virtually every book ever written about craps seems eager to have you confine your betting instead of expanding it. I've read otherwise excellent books on craps that eventually come to the subject of proposition bets and say something to the effect of, "We're not going to talk about these bets because they're all bad, and you're much better off not knowing about them."

Isn't that astounding? Can you imagine a book about astronomy that gets to the chapter on Pluto and says, "Pluto is really far away, so it would be best if you didn't think about it."

In craps, the beginning of wisdom is when you realize that the casino doesn't make money when you lose. It makes money when you win. And it does so simply by paying you less than you deserve. Let me explain.

The real odds of getting an eleven on one roll of the dice, for example, are 17-to-1. But if you bet the yo, the casino only pays you 15-to-1. The casino, in effect, pockets the two additional dollars it *should have* paid you and uses them to buy a new volcano.

That's why the essence of good strategy in craps is to focus your betting on wagers where the house edge is the smallest. To their credit, the so-called experts who write books about craps have grasped this essential truth and shared it with their readers. The problem is, they can't seem to get beyond it.

There are similar strategies in other games. A basic principle of chess, for example, is to control the center of the board. In football, you want to control the line of scrimmage. In baseball, you should put your best fielders up the middle, from catcher to shortstop and second baseman to center fielder. But you can take this philosophy too far!

When I was a kid playing softball, we used to take our worst player and put him in left field. It seemed like a good plan until someone hit the ball into left field. Not only was this kid incapable of catching it, but he'd chase the ball around for a few minutes, fumble it once or twice as he tried to pick it up, and eventually make a weak throw to the exasperated cut off man. Meanwhile the batter was circling the bases, laughing hysterically at the slapstick in left field and scoring an easy inside-the-park home run. (What I didn't tell you is that the spastic kid in left field was me!)

The same thing applies to craps. Yes, you should concentrate on the so-called "good bets." Yes, you should avoid the so-called "bad bets" when the dice are cold. But when the dice are hot, you want to be playing the entire table. Failure to do so would be as silly as playing baseball without a left fielder.

Another reason proposition bets get such a bad rap is that the systems for playing them usually involve some form of the strategy known pejoratively as "the gambler's fallacy." Here is another issue that makes the so-called experts on gambling go ballistic.

"How could anyone be so willfully stupid as to believe in the gambler's fallacy?" they ask. "The dice have no memory!" they shout. "The dice are not intelligent. They don't know how long it's been since the last eleven!" To prove their point, these writers will often trot out the age-old example of tossing coins.

Let's say you toss a penny in the air a hundred times and in some bizarre twist of the normal rules of the universe, it comes up heads every time. The question is, what are the chances it will come up tails on the next toss?

Ask any hard-core gambler and he will tell you that the odds are overwhelmingly in favor of tails on the next roll. After all, tails is "due." It's *overdue. Way* overdue!

But the gambling experts, smug in their superior knowledge of probability theory, say no. They say the odds of tails showing up on the next toss are exactly the same as they've been on all of the previous tosses: fifty-fifty. The penny has no memory, they say. It has no idea what happened during the previous one hundred trials. The penny simply has one side that is heads and one side that is tails, and the odds of tails coming up on any given toss is exactly one out of two.

But F. Scott Fitzgerald once defined intelligence as the ability to hold two contradictory ideas in your mind at the same time. Which is why most gambling experts are not quite as intelligent as they think they are. Because my own feeling is that both the theory of probability and the gambler's fallacy are both correct in their own way.

It's certainly true that the odds of tails showing up on the 101st toss of the coin are exactly fifty-fifty. There's no reason to think that any one particular toss is any more likely to be tails than heads. But it seems to me that there's every reason in the world to expect tails to dominate over the next one hundred tosses to "make up," in effect, for the predominance of heads in the first hundred.

To make my point, let's keep tossing those coins—a thousand times, let's say. Over the course of a thousand tosses, you'd expect to see the theory of probability kick in pretty much the way it's supposed to. You may not have exactly five hundred tails and five hundred heads, but probably something very close to that. Maybe 497 heads and 503 tails.

But if for some reason the first five hundred tosses came up heads, you'd have every right to believe that the next five hundred would be *predominantly* tails. Maybe not all five hundred of them, but well over three hundred of them. In other words, a lot more than fifty-fifty.

In fact, there is a scientific name for this phenomenon. It's called "Regression toward the Mean." And while regression toward the mean has a much more scientific ring to it than the gambler's fallacy, it essentially means the same thing. In layman's terms, it means that over a period of time, weird fluctuations in probability gradually will even out to give you the results you'd normally expect.

The concept of something being due, in other words, is not as foolish as the gambling experts would have you believe. And that has very important implications for playing craps. If a little voice in your head says, "Hey, we haven't seen an eleven for quite a while," don't ignore it. By all means, throw the stickman a $25 chip and tell him to put it on the yo. In my experience, yos are like the Holy Trinity: they tend to disappear for a while and then come back in groups of threes.

It is not my intention to teach you everything you need to know about craps in the confines of this tiny booklet. I only want to teach you the three bets that you'll need to play my *Win By Losing* system effectively: 1) the pass line 2) the don't-pass line, and 3) the whirl. I urge you to continue your study of craps not only by playing as often as you can, but also by reading more books about it. I want you to view yourself as a pilgrim on the road to craps wisdom.

But as you continue your journey on this path, please do not become obsessed with the mathematics of the game, as so many "experts" on craps are. Mathematics may be the language of the universe, as Galileo said, but the poetry of the universe is something else again. It's wise to be fully informed about such matters as the house edge on various bets, the actual odds of bets, the casino's payoffs on bets, and so on. But don't miss the forest for the trees. If craps were only about numbers, you'd be silly to play it at all because the numbers are stacked against you.

Far more important than mastering the mathematics of craps is learning to how to master how you play the game. The emotional component of the game. The psychological component. The spiritual side. The side of self-discipline, self-awareness, and self-control. The biggest mistake most gamblers make is not the gambler's fallacy, but the fallacious belief that the "luck" resides in the dice, or in some mystical force outside of the dice. The luck, to the extent that it exists at all, resides in *you*.

To win at craps consistently, you must have the discipline to learn about the game, the desire to master it, and the wisdom to surrender to it. Those are the three secrets to winning at craps and they are the same as the secrets to winning at life. In the following sections of this booklet, we will take a look at each of those issues. Will you follow me on the road to craps wisdom, pilgrim?

Chapter 3

RECOVERY FROM UNUSUAL ATTITUDES

DANNY WOKE UP WITH the first light of dawn streaming through his hotel room windows, despite the fact that he had drawn the curtains shut as tight as possible the night before. Danny could never get hotel curtains closed enough to keep out the light in the morning. He was even in the habit of building barricade-like contraptions with the hotel's chairs and tables to hold the curtains closed. But somehow the light always slipped through them.

It didn't matter. He woke up at 5:30 a.m., even though he'd left a wake-up call with the operator for six. He wanted to get an early start. After he went to bed around three, he had stayed awake dreaming about all the money he could make with the new system and worrying about all the money he'd lose if the secret got out. He got about ninety minutes of sleep altogether, just long enough to wake up with a hangover instead of a high. Danny dressed quickly and took a cab to the airport.

It was extremely dangerous to fly on ninety minutes sleep and a hangover. In fact, it was illegal. But Danny was in a hurry to get home and this was the first time in his life that he would put personal expediency above aviation safety. He had a severe case of what pilots called "get-home-itis," which could be a deadly disease.

Danny wanted to get home before noon, which is when the Mailboxes, Etc. where he had rented a box for the returns on *Win By Losing* closed on Saturdays. It was less than a one hour flight from Bader Field in central New Jersey to Danny's "home drome" of Teterboro Airport in northern Jersey. But Danny had a peculiar habit that added several hours to almost every flight he took.

He was in the habit of practicing emergency landing procedures, stalls, stall recoveries, recoveries from unusual attitudes, engine-out procedures, and all the other aviation techniques related to those moments when bad stuff happens in the air.

Every pilot is supposed to keep an eye open for possible emergency landing sites, for example. The standard recommendation is to locate one every five minutes, a rule honored more in the breach than the observance. But Danny did that and more.

Every few minutes he would cut his throttle and begin to coast toward the landing field of his choice, run through his emergency checklist, mimic the various steps he was supposed to take, and prepare himself for a rough landing. Then at the last minute, he would slam the throttle forward, climb back to his cruising altitude, and resume his previous course.

Fifteen minutes later, he'd do it again.

But that wasn't all. He loved to practice stalls. Again, every pilot is supposed to practice stalls. But not as obsessively as Danny did. Stall recoveries have a serious application in aviation, as Danny's recent run-in with the seagull nearly proved. When an airplane is on final approach, with the throttle back, the flaps down, the landing gear extended, it is traveling just barely above stall speed. To stall an airplane when it's in this position will almost always lead to a fiery death unless the pilot does the exact right thing . . . and does it instantly and instinctively. So pilots are urged by the FAA to practice stalls and stall recoveries. But Danny always took a good thing too far.

What appealed to Danny about practicing stalls was that it was like taking a roller-coaster ride, except that the danger was real. In order to put an aircraft into a stall deliberately, the pilot is supposed to slow the aircraft down by cutting the throttle, lowering the flaps, and extending the landing gear. Then the pilot lifts the nose of the aircraft and starts aiming at the clouds above—gradually at first, more aggressively as the stall comes closer. Before long, the airplane loses its lift and the nose tips forward like the prow of a sinking ship poised for its final dive.

The danger of this maneuver is that every now and then something can go wrong. If the wings aren't perfectly level, for example, there's a chance that the aircraft could enter a spin.

Every pilot is taught how to recover from a spin, but the procedure is rarely practiced in the air. It's too dangerous. The FAA's official policy is that the best way to get out of a spin is to not get in one in the first place, because if a spin is allowed to develop too long, or develop in the wrong way, there's always a chance that it could become a *flat* spin. And even Chuck Yeager would find a flat spin very interesting.

Danny knew he was good at these emergency techniques and procedures. So what did he do? He practiced them more often. With all of his obsessive practicing, in fact, it wasn't unusual for a one-hour flight with Danny in the pilot's seat to take three hours or more. The habit was so ingrained that even when he was in a hurry, as he was today, he still went through these unnecessary motions. But there was a positive side to it, too, and not just that it made him a very safe pilot. It also helped him think.

Today he was thinking about all the spectacular failures he'd had over the years in the junk-mail business and devoutly wishing that *Win By Losing* would be another one. From the cheeseburger and milkshake diet to the stock-picking system based on the predictions of Nostradamus, Danny had dropped more than a few bombs in his day. But this was the first time he had ever *hoped* for one.

Danny landed safely at Teterboro, but he had only twenty minutes to get to the Mailboxes, Etc. near his home in Montblanc before it closed, and the trip usually took him thirty minutes. So he hopped in his Porsche Carrera and drove like a maniac.

The promotion for *Win By Losing* had dropped in the mail the previous Wednesday. The chance that there would be any reply cards in the box on Saturday morning was somewhat remote. Saturday was a slow mail day under the best of circumstances. Given how recent the mail date was, it was unlikely that even a spectacularly successful promotion could put more than three or four replies in the box so soon.

Every junk-mail expert is skilled at gauging the overall success of a mailing by counting the early returns, and Danny was no exception. Mathematical formulas printed in direct-marketing textbooks explain how to do it, but a veteran like Danny did it mostly by feel.

An empty box would be a bad . . . er, a good sign, according to Danny's mental calculations as he motored up Route 46 at 30 miles over the speed limit. A box with one or two envelopes would be marginal. That might mean that he'd only get several hundred orders altogether, and there was a chance, just a chance, that he could get away with not fulfilling those orders at all. He'd get some heat from his friends at the U.S. Postal Service, but even the postal inspectors knew how bad the U.S. Postal Service was, and he could talk his way out of trouble by saying he'd never received them.

But a mailbox with more than three or four envelopes in it on this Saturday morning would indicate that the mailing was a stunning success. In other words, a disaster.

He arrived at Mailboxes, Etc. just as the proprietor, a balding middle-aged man who found Danny quite amusing, was locking the door. Danny came up to him from behind and startled him.

"Oh, it's you, Mr. Pellegrino. I thought I was being mugged. You don't carry a gun, do you?"

Danny had neither the time nor the inclination for banter.

"Let me in, Bob, please, it's important. Five minutes, that's all I need."

"Sure, no problem. Hey, Mr. Pellegrino, I'm really glad you stopped by today, because . . ."

Danny brushed by the man so fast and so brusquely that the words literally froze in his mouth as he watched Danny rush to his mailbox and fall to his knees like a supplicant. As was his habit for nearly ten years, Danny peered into the window first.

There was nothing there. A sense of relief flushed through his body and came out of his mouth in the form of a satisfied sigh.

Oh, geez, he thought, this seems awfully familiar. He opened the box. Still nothing.

Except, of course, for a tiny slip of paper.

"That's what I wanted to tell ya, Mr. Pellegrino . . ."

The paper read, *"Too much mail for the box, see clerk at window."*

"Yeah, I wanted to tell ya, you got a boatload of mail this morning."

Chapter 4

A MATTRESS IN THE FEDERAL PENAL SYSTEM

ICHARD GOLDMAN, AN ATTORNEY in the Criminal Investigations Unit of the United States Postal Service, was sorting through his decoy mail on Monday morning when he came across Danny's letter. It was called "decoy" mail because postal inspectors like Goldman used phony names to get on the mailing lists of various scam artists, pornographers, and other disreputable characters who used the U.S. mail to further their criminal schemes.

These fake names and addresses, located all over the country, were like sitting ducks for every con game, Ponzi scheme, chain letter, or porn promotion that came down the pike. Only they weren't real ducks. These were venomous ducks, and they could bite. Each one could lash out with a $5,000 fine and five years in jail. If a con man like Danny Pellegrino got ten thousand orders for one of his bogus products, it was theoretically possible that he could spend fifty thousand years in jail and owe the government $50 million on the day he was released. Tax evasion and mail fraud were two things the federal government took very seriously.

And there were two things that caught Richard Goldman's eye about the letter he was turning over in his hands at this moment. First was the return address. A post office in Montblanc, New Jersey.

Ah, said Richard to himself, it's a Danny Pellegrino special. He couldn't help but chuckle fiendishly. He considered Danny a worthy adversary.

The second thing that caught Richard's eye was the teaser headline printed on the outer envelope in large block letters. It read, "WIN BY LOSING!"

Now there's a concept, thought Richard as he sliced open the envelope with the solid gold letter opener given to him by the Postmaster General himself for twenty-five years of faithful service to the USPS. He had started working there while his hair was still thick, black, and curly. It was still curly, but now it was thin and gray.

Win by losing, thought Richard. I could use something like that.

Not that Richard thought of himself as a loser. Not exactly. It's just that he hadn't quite lived up to the high expectations of his youth. He came from a good middle-class background. Both of his parents were also government employees in Washington, D.C. Jewish, but not particularly observant. They celebrated Passover and Hanukkah in their home each year, occasionally stopped by temple during Yom Kippur and Rosh Hashanah. That was about it. But they were good people and they cherished their son.

Since Richard was an excellent student, they gave some serious thought to sending him to one of the nearby private schools like Sidwell Friends or St. Albans (one was Quaker, the other Episcopalian, but plenty of Jewish kids went to both), which were prestigious and expensive. But being good liberals, they eventually decided they "owed it to the city" to send him to a public high school. It probably didn't hurt that this decision saved them $10,000 a year that could be applied to other worthy causes, like a Volvo. So Richard went to Western High School in upper northwest Washington, where he was one of comparatively few white students and extremely few Jewish students. He graduated as valedictorian.

After high school, Richard went to a small but prestigious liberal arts school in southern Minnesota called Carleton College. Born at the very peak of the baby boom generation, this was back in the days when it was difficult to gain admission to a college like Carleton. Even as valedictorian and with SAT scores well over 1400, Richard felt lucky to be accepted. His law degree came from an even more prestigious institution—Harvard University.

Nowadays, both of Richard's children, who, in his opinion, were indifferent, mediocre students, were going to colleges that were considered far more prestigious than Carleton. The girl, Leah, was attending Stanford. The boy, Seth, was at Dartmouth.

And they, too, made him feel like a loser sometimes. Problem was, he was paying approximately $60,000 a year, more than half of his annual income, to send these two sullen brats to college, and whenever he tried to engage them in some intellectual topic, like current events or the origin of the universe, they looked at him like he was the stupidest person in the world.

"What do you think of this new 'String Theory'?" he asked one night at the dinner table. "Have they talked about that at school?"

"Dad, I don't know if I've mentioned this to you, but I'm a sociology major," said Leah. "We don't discuss physics very often in sosh class."

Richard stared at her glumly over the wire-rimmed reading glasses perched at the tip of his nose. Then he forced a smile and turned to Seth. "What about you, Seth?"

"African American studies, Dad."

Richard and his family lived in a leafy section of Washington called Glover Park. It was home to what might be called the professional class of government workers, i.e., mostly lawyers. Sometimes it seemed to Richard as if *everyone* in Glover Park was a lawyer for the government. Even the children in this neighborhood wanted to be lawyers.

Once he was at a block party on 39th Street chatting with one of his neighbors, an attorney for the National Aeronautics and Space Administration named Jacob Friedman. A small child, scarcely more than ten years old, walked up and interrupted them.

The kid looked up at Friedman and said, "Mr. Friedman, you work for my *favorite* government agency!"

Friedman chuckled and said, "Is that so? Do you want to be an astronaut when you grow up?"

"Hell no," said the kid, "I want to be a lawyer!"

The only substantial group of non-lawyers in Glover Park was that of State Department employees, or "foreign-service officers," as they called themselves. Richard called them "Foggy Bottom Feeders," after the swampy section of Washington where State Department headquarters was located.

The Foggy Bottom Feeders looked down their noses at the ordinary government lawyers in the neighborhood because they led more interesting lives. Or at least they thought they did. But it was an illusion: the interesting part of their lives was always elsewhere. It was either in the past or in the future, never in the present. They were always talking about their last posting or their next posting. And the next posting—Richard found this very amusing—was always going to be Paris. They were constantly whispering to their neighbors over the back fence in the alley, "Don't say anything about this just yet because it's not confirmed. But it looks like we're going to be posted in Paris. Yes! Isn't that great? Gay Paree!"

But Paris almost always turned out to be located in a place like Uzbekistan. Which couldn't have pleased Richard more. He didn't like them very much.

He never really got the chance to like them, since they never stayed in Glover Park for very long. Their usual migration pattern was to spend two years in Uzbekistan, two years in Washington, two years in Pari . . . er, Kazakhstan, two years back in Washington, and so forth. They maintained ownership of their townhouses in Glover Park while they were away, usually renting them to a group of Georgetown University students. Five students to a townhouse was the norm. Graduate students, usually. In most cases, these students were themselves training to become lawyers or foreign-service officers.

Richard didn't like these kids very much either, but in fairness, he didn't know them very well. They never invited him to the parties (orgies?) they had almost every Friday and Saturday night. His only connection with them was a nodding relationship based on running into them when he hauled his garbage can out to the alley on Thursday nights.

"Good evening," Richard would always say to them on these occasions.

"Howyadoin'?" they'd always reply.

Richard found that "Howyadoin'" infinitely patronizing. To his ears it sounded like, "I can't believe you've settled for this in life, pal."

You see, these kids were still young enough to dream. The medical students all thought they were going to find the cure for cancer. The foreign-service students all thought they would become the United States ambassador to France. And the law students all harbored even bigger dreams. They thought they would spend a few years in Washington, move back to their ancestral home of Podunk, and run for the United States Senate as a stepping-stone to the presidency.

But Richard knew he'd have the last laugh on most of these kids. He knew that after ten years of pursuing their elusive dreams, the majority of them would move right back to Glover Park—not as renters this time but as homeowners. There they would settle into comfortable lives as lawyers for the government, physicians for Kaiser Permanente, or mid-level foreign-service officers. Their biggest dream at that point would be to own a flat-screen, high-definition television set.

High-definition televisions, DVD players, satellite dishes, and high-speed Internet connections were the drugs of choice in Richard's neighborhood. None of Richard's neighbors drank alcohol anymore; it wasn't healthy. (Expensive and exotic wine was the exception, but that wasn't really *drinking*, was it?) Most of Richard's neighbors had been heavy pot smokers in college, but they wouldn't touch the stuff now. It set a bad example for the kids, for one thing, and they had heard that marijuana now is much stronger than it used to be. In their minds, pot had metamorphosed into a dangerous drug. Most of Richard's neighbors had been heavy cigarette smokers at one time, too, but Richard couldn't remember the last time he'd seen anyone smoking a cigarette in Glover Park.

You need *something* to relieve the boredom, though, and many of Richard's neighbors found their opium in consumer electronics. Richard himself desperately wanted to own some of these gizmos, but whenever he announced that he was of a mind to buy one, his wife reminded him that they had two kids going to college at the same time. Dartmouth and Stanford, no less. So Richard limped along with a pitifully obsolete Macintosh computer (it was two years old), six color television sets, none of which had screens larger than nineteen inches, a temperamental VCR, and a PDA that he *absolutely needed* for work. He never used it.

The really good stuff belonged to the government lawyers in the neighborhood who did not have any children in college, and Richard would often stroll through the back alley on a summer's evening admiring the satellite dishes on his neighbors' houses like a botanist wandering through an Edwardian flower garden. You have to stop and smell the roses, Richard thought. That's the key to happiness in life.

Richard and Rachel were one of relatively few couples in Glover Park who were old enough to have college-age children. Most men Richard's age—particularly those with law degrees from Harvard—had long since moved out to the wealthier suburbs. But the tradition of civil service ran deep in Richard's blood, and he couldn't afford the multi-million dollar homes in places like Potomac, Maryland, or McLean, Virginia. Glover Park was considered a neighborhood of starter homes, although owning a $700,000 townhouse was an excellent way to start in life. As a result, most of the children in the neighborhood were grade-school age or younger.

Aside from consumer electronics, the two main topics of conversation in Glover Park were the teachers at the nearby Stoddert Elementary School and the appointment-level bosses at the government agencies where everyone worked. Neither was smart enough to satisfy the good people of Glover Park.

The Stoddert teachers simply didn't have the native intelligence to teach children who were as remarkably gifted as every child in Glover Park. It wasn't really the teachers' fault, everyone concluded, but an extremely gifted child like mine, like yours, needed special care. Many of Richard's neighbors yearned to send their kids to private school. Many of them could actually afford to do so, but it might mean doing without a Land Rover, so the matter took some careful consideration.

The other big topic of discussion was how hard it was to work for the idiots appointed to deputy-level positions by the current administration in Washington. Glover Park residents were 97 percent registered Democrats, so Democratic appointees were tolerable. Barely. But the current batch of Republican "Schedule Cs," as they were known, didn't have the sense to tie their shoes without making some sort of critical error that could put the nation in irreversible jeopardy.

The professional class of government workers in Glover Park could never figure out why *they* weren't allowed to run the country. They were the ones who had gotten 1400 (or more!) on their SATs. They were the ones who had gone to the good Ivy League colleges. Even more importantly, they were the ones who really knew how the government worked. How to get things done. How to make things happen. Chop, chop! Nothing pissed off a Glover Parker more than some Republican pol from Pocatello telling him how to do his job. And for Richard, this Monday morning at the office was a perfect case in point.

The word had come down from on high that the postal inspectors should spend less time focusing on petty fraud and con games and more time prosecuting pornography—especially child pornography.

But Richard had nothing against pornography. In fact, he enjoyed it. He and his pal Jake Friedman had recently spent a delightful afternoon checking out the porn on Jake's new satellite dish. Richard considered pornography a victimless crime, like prostitution.

So when his bosses at the postal service, and the patronage appointees at the Justice Department with whom he worked closely, told him to drop the petty fraud cases and concentrate on pornography, Richard did what any self-respecting civil servant would do. He did the exact opposite. He made a point of passing the porn cases on to his subordinates so that he could spend even more of his own time investigating the con artists.

He hated these scammers. Especially the ones who sold gambling systems. He hated them because he perceived their life to be so different from his own. He hated them because they could take a vacation in Las Vegas and write it off on their tax return, with a straight face, as a business expense. Heck, he thought, I bet these guys even write off whores as a "normal and reasonable" expense of doing business.

He pictured these guys walking into a casino, probably wearing an Armani jacket with a black mock-turtleneck shirt and a gold necklace, a blonde babe on one arm and a brunette on the other. He saw them drawing markers for $5,000, $10,000, enough to buy even the most expensive high-definition television set, and sign for it like they were signing a $10 check for breakfast at Denny's. These bastards didn't have any kids going to college, he thought. They didn't have to report every morning to a drab government office where the desks were made of steel and all the available light came from fluorescent tubes. God, how he'd love to put one of these jerk-offs in Leavenworth!

And there was no one, *no one,* that he would like more to find a jail cell for than Danny Pellegrino of Montblanc, New Jersey. He had been watching Pellegrino for years. Investigating him. Pestering him. Sending him cease-and-desist letters. Launching prosecutions that always seemed to peter out before they ever got started, in part because Danny had one of the best mail-order lawyers in the country on a monthly retainer. His name was Solomon Lefkowitz, and coincidentally he was at Harvard Law at the same time as Richard, although they didn't know each other there.

Thanks to the good offices of the honorable Mr. Solomon Lefkowitz, Esq.—but thanks mostly to his own genius— Danny Pellegrino's direct-mail copy was incredibly hard to prosecute. It was virtually bulletproof. In fact, as an attorney, Richard had a grudging admiration for it. He couldn't have written it better himself. Truth be told, he couldn't write it half as well, because Richard simply didn't have the larcenous turn of mind to make a fraudulent product seem both irresistible and perfectly legal at the same time. Try as he might, and he had tried on many occasions, Richard could never put Danny in jail based on the false and fraudulent claims in his copy. He had to attack him from a different direction.

Specifically, he had to hope that Danny would simply slip up someday and fail to fulfill his orders. That was as close as a mail-order con man got to original sin. That was the one thing that the government could *always* pin on you. When you accepted money for a product, then didn't send that product to the customer, Richard would always find a mattress for you somewhere in the federal penal system.

So Richard sipped his morning coffee and filled out the little yellow reply card that said, "Yes, Danny! Please send me my copy of *Win By Losing.*" He used his decoy name and gave the decoy address of a government-owned mailbox in Albuquerque, New Mexico, the contents of which were forwarded to Richard daily.

If, in a week or so, there was a booklet titled *Win By Losing* in that mailbox, Danny Pellegrino would probably slip away again. If there wasn't, Danny might find himself in a world of trouble. It was a slim chance, thought Richard, but heck, you've gotta take a shot.

Chapter 5

FROM A CATERPILLAR TO A BUTTERFLY

ANNY WORRIED ABOUT HIS predicament for the rest of the day on Saturday. Then he worried about it all day Sunday, occasionally stopping to daydream about what he would do with $100 million if he could figure out a solution. Then, on Monday, the dawn broke clear and bright, and his problem got worse.

He arrived at Mailboxes, Etc. at ten in the morning, shortly after the mail was delivered, and found five more giant mailbags waiting for him. About two thousand replies altogether, which Danny instantly calculated to mean about twenty thousand in total when the returns began to trickle off after a month.

"Congratulations," said the Mailboxes proprietor. "This looks like one of the most successful," he paused to consider the right word, "projects you've ever had."

Back home, Danny dumped the mailbags in a corner of his office and sat down heavily at his desk. This was very unusual. On previous occasions when he had received bags full of mail, he liked to empty them into the center of the room, sit down on the carpet in a lotus position, and play with all the envelopes. He'd let them trickle through his hands like spring water. Sometimes he'd pick up a handful and rub them on his face. He'd throw a few up in the air and watch them flutter to the ground. Of course, he'd always open at least twenty of the envelopes to make sure they were filled with checks, money orders, and cash. (It always amazed Danny how many Americans did not have checking accounts.) But today, Danny simply slumped in his big leather chair and stared out the window.

When the solution to his problem finally came to him, it came suddenly. It was more a sense of recognition than revelation. It was as if the answer had been staring him in the face for three days, as if it had been knocking on his head with a ball peen hammer saying, "Hey, stupid! Is anyone home?"

Why didn't I think of that before? Danny thought as he smiled and sat bolt upright in his chair.

He would execute what is known in the direct-mail business as a "dry test." Which meant that he would write back to all of his customers and tell them that he had decided not to publish the book after all. He would come up with some cock-and-bull story about changes in the economic climate and give them their money back. A dry test was a lot like the dry heaves: you still felt terrible, but at least you didn't make a mess.

"That sonofabitch in Washington won't like this much," mumbled Danny, who knew very well that he had a nemesis in the United States Postal Service who came to work every morning wondering how he could put Danny Pellegrino in jail. "But there isn't a hell of a lot he can do about it."

Danny figured that Goldman would probably send him a strongly worded letter, maybe even a cease-and-desist letter. But Danny would forward the letter to Lefkowitz, who would write an even more strongly worded letter back to Goldman saying, in effect, "If you don't have any evidence of wrongdoing on behalf of my client, then please get off his back."

So Danny fired up his computer and began typing his dry-test letter.

"Due to unforeseen circumstances and changes in the macro-economic climate," Danny began, "Pellegrino Enterprises has reluctantly decided to indefinitely postpone the publication of *Win By Losing*."

Danny had only written two other dry-test letters in his career—he hated to return money. And under most circumstances, he had no need to do so. The big mail-order publishing companies relied on dry tests, because it cost them a bundle to write, edit, design, proof, print, and distribute a lengthy hardback book. Danny's "books," on the other hand, were usually ten-page Xerox affairs that his assistant, Maria, ran off on his own photocopier and stapled by hand.

But dry tests weren't cheap. First of all, it meant returning all these checks and money orders and greenbacks sitting in the corner of his office. That would hurt. Second, it meant that the $300,000 or so he had spent on the mailing would go up in smoke, an investment he would never recover. Third, it was customary to throw the disappointed customer a bone of some kind when you did a dry test. The big publishing companies usually offered to send a similar book; they had large inventories of backlist books they could use for this purpose. But Danny only had one craps system in stock, and many of the people on his mailing list had already bought it.

Instead, he would try another common trick. He would send each customer a single dollar bill along with a nice postscript on the letter that said something like, "Hey, we know you're disappointed. And we know you spent some time and effort to mail us your order. So in addition to returning your own money, we're adding another dollar with our sincere gratitude and humble apologies for your trouble." This helped cut down on complaints. In fact, on the two other occasions when he'd done dry tests, he'd received dozens of notes from his customers saying, "Hey, Danny, thanks for the buck!"

The dollar bills would add another $20 thousand or so to his losses, not to mention the postage, paper, and labor costs. But what the heck, thought Danny, money is not a problem anymore. I've got myself a craps system that really works! All I've got to do is go back to Atlantic City and make a withdrawal.

Danny was putting the finishing touches on his dry-test letter when his assistant, Maria Falcone, walked into the office. She'd let herself in the front door with her own key.

"What's up, my *capo di tutti capi?*" Maria asked in her customary greeting.

"Look at those mailbags in the corner, *cara mia,*" said Danny, "and you'll see what's up."

"Holy moly," she said. "Are those the *Win By Losing* orders? On the first freaking day?"

"On the second freaking day, if you count Saturday, when we got another pile."

"You had a big mail day on a *Saturday?*" Maria knew enough about the business to know how rare that was. She worked for Danny four days a week in the afternoons and had been doing so for nearly five years now.

Maria was pretty in a New Jersey Italian sort of way, which meant she was pretty if you didn't mind a few minor facial flaws and far too much makeup to cover them. She also had a northern New Jersey accent that could make a dog stand up and leave the room. Born and raised in Bayonne with absolutely no intention of leaving, she had ventured into Manhattan only three times in her life. But she had a great butt, her face was cute, and she had a fun-loving personality that made the whole package more attractive than the sum of its parts.

At least three times a week Danny had to stop himself from asking her out for a drink. He told himself that "dating her now would be fun for a while, but it would mean losing a damn good secretary." He also told himself that Maria's current boyfriend—a rather disreputable-looking character by the name of Ricky Trepiccione—wouldn't take kindly to any expressions of interest on Danny's part. Both of these were excellent excuses, but they weren't the truth.

The truth was that Danny *did* love Maria. She was smart, good-looking, and incredibly loyal—both as an employee and as a friend. But there was something even more intriguing about her. Unlike his first wife, who had fallen in love with Danny while he still had a respectable job, and unlike his second wife, who considered Danny's business to be considerably less dignified than the image she wished to convey to the world, Maria always seemed slightly amused by the way Danny made a living. It was as if she understood he wasn't doing anyone any real harm—what's the big deal about selling bogus gambling systems anyway, she thought, even the most gullible people never really expected them to work—and she admired the creativity and ingenuity necessary to pull it off. Danny sensed that

Maria had a mischievous, if not fully larcenous, turn of mind like his own. The angel on her right shoulder was the dominant spirit of her personality, but it was the devil on the left that made him love her.

So he could easily see himself having a relationship with Maria—which is precisely why he refused to get involved. Every time he had felt that way in the past, he wound up hurting the object of his affection and hurting himself as well. So he made a deliberate decision to treat Maria like a younger sister—which, of course, drove Maria crazy because she, too, found him attractive.

Girls from Bayonne didn't run into guys like Danny Pellegrino very often. Not that good-looking Italian men were hard to find in northern New Jersey, but you rarely found them with Danny's intelligence, his education, his lively wit. Meeting a man like Danny in Bayonne would be like running into Pierce Brosnan on the PATH train. But it was more than that. For all the superficial trappings of his success, for all his raffishness and apparent disregard for the law, Maria sensed there was a decent human being in there somewhere.

"Yeah, but that's the good news," said Danny. "The bad news is that we're sending the money back."

"Get out of town!" Her favorite expression. "Why?"

"Because I flew to A.C. this weekend to try the system out and it sucked up a storm. I can't sell the damn thing, Maria. If I did, you'd be sitting here for the next year mailing out refund checks. That bastard in Washington would be on my back. I'd be sending money to Lefkowitz by the boatload. It would be a disaster."

Now this struck Maria as *very* strange. She had been working for Danny for five years and she had never once known him to back out of selling a gambling system just because it didn't work. Most of the time, he wasn't even mildly curious about whether it worked or not. But Maria wasn't the reason-why type. She would do whatever Danny asked her to do.

"So we're sending all this money back?"

"Yeah, 'fraid so. In fact, *cara mia Maria,* it wouldn't hurt if you could stay late tonight. Stay late for the next coupla weeks, actually. Because I'm writing a 'we've-changed-our-mind-about-publishing-it' letter. I need you to run off several thousand of these on the photocopier. Put them in our regular envelopes. Return the checks to these hard-working Americans. And put a dollar bill in each envelope. Can you do that for me?"

"Sure, I could use the overtime. But where are all the dollar bills coming from?"

"Come here," he said. She walked over to him. Danny opened his briefcase where he had stashed the $50,000 he won at the Villagio and took out four packets of hundred-dollar bills. Each packet contained fifty bills, or $5,000.

"Mama mia," said Maria softly. She'd never seen that much cash before. It was a year's salary for her.

"I want you to run these over to the bank and ask them to exchange them for 20,000 one-dollar bills. They'll have to put them in some kind of a money bag for you. There's a chance they could give you some static about it. They're so sensitive about money laundering these days. But money laundering usually goes the opposite way: Some *melanzane* walks in with lots of small bills and wants to exchange them for big ones. If they give you a hard time, ask to speak with Mr. Davis. He's my guy over there. Then if Davis gives you a hard time, tell him to call me."

"Okay," said Maria tentatively. The prospect of driving over to the bank in her beat-up old Camaro with $20,000 in cash was a little daunting. One of her windows had been broken by a petty thief who stole her radio, and it was patched up with a plastic trash bag and duct tape. She had an image in her mind of somebody punching out the bag and grabbing the money.

"Take the Carrera," he said.

Danny had read her mind.

"Really?"

"Sure," he said. "I've been meaning to let you take a spin in it for ages. You'll love it." He tossed her the keys. "But do it now, *cara mia,* because I'm flying back to A.C. for a meeting this afternoon. And if I have to talk to Davis, I'll have to do it soon. You know these freaking bankers. They leave work right after they get back from lunch."

When Maria left, Danny picked up the phone and dialed the number for the Villagio Hotel in Atlantic City. He called the VIP reservations number, the same number he always called. But when one of the low-level casino hostesses came on the line to take his reservation, there was an uncommonly friendly lilt in her voice.

"Oh, Mr. Pellegrino, so nice to hear from you!"

So nice to hear from me, thought Danny, what's that about? This broad doesn't even know me.

"David Invidia, your senior casino host, has asked that I immediately forward your calls to him."

"He has?" said Danny. Invidia had never paid much attention to him before. Sure, Danny got his free rooms, his free cheeseburgers, his free tickets to Villagio's own production show—a semi-nude extravaganza called *Flesh!*—but David Invidia had never bent over backwards for Danny.

Danny was a $10,000-per-visit player and he got no more in the way of comps than such a player would expect to get, which is to say, not much.

There was a click on the phone line, followed by the vaguely familiar sound of David Invidia's voice.

"*Mister* P! How are you today, my fine sir?"

"Pretty good, I guess," said Danny in the guarded tone of a schoolboy who had received an unexpectedly warm greeting from a nasty teacher.

"I heard you had a big score the other night."

"Well, it started big," said Danny, "but I gave most of it back."

Now it was beginning to dawn on Danny. He'd just gone from being a $10,000-a-night player to a $500,000-a-night player, which, to a casino host's eye, was like watching time-lapse photography of a caterpillar turning into a butterfly.

"Well, that's gambling, Danny, that's gambling," said Invidia, ever so chummy with the first name now. "But they told me you still walked away with a nice chunk of our change. Congratulations!"

"Thanks, David."

"So what can I do for you today?"

"Well, I'm coming back to A.C., actually. I was just calling to get the usual room."

This was precisely what Invidia had hoped to hear. "Let's put you up in one of our Tuscan Villa suites this time, Dan. I think you'll like it. Jacuzzi. Three color TVs, one in the bathroom. Telephone in the bathroom, too. They've all got great views of the ocean. How's that sound, Daniel?" Invidia seemed to be experimenting with every possible variation of Danny's name in order to come up with the one that implied the most intimacy.

Danny hated to be called "Daniel" for the simple reason that it wasn't his name. The name on his birth certificate was Dante Alighieri Pellegrino. He'd been named after the great Florentine poet, a distant ancestor on his mother's side. Almost from day one, his parents and friends called him "Danny." But hearing "Daniel" always grated on his ears.

"That sounds great, *Davey*," said Danny, returning the favor. "I'm going to fly down in my plane, and I should get there about seven this evening. I'll stay two or three days, depending on how it's going with the dice."

"I like a man who lives by the bones," said Invidia. "Let me make a blanket reservation for you in the steak house. I'll fix it up with the maitre d'. Just show up whenever you're hungry. Dinner's on Villagio. Tell Antoine I said so, and he'll take care of you."

"Thank you, David." He was starting to like this.

"And good luck at the tables tonight," said Invidia with what sounded like sincerity.

"Thanks again," said Danny. And he hung up thinking, I wonder what they'll give me if I put a million bucks in action tonight? First row tickets to Streisand followed by a candlelight dinner with Barbra afterwards?

Danny was feeling on top of the world again. Tonight he would make the management of the Villagio Hotel & Casino feel like they wished they'd never heard of him.

Chapter 6

SUSHI IN THE BATHTUB

C AN'T YOU *PLEASE* DO this for me, David?" asked the voice of an elderly lady with a New York accent on the other end of telephone line.

"Mrs. Abramson, you know I'd do anything for you, *anything* at all," said Invidia in a slightly exasperated tone, "but what you've asked me to do is very difficult."

"What could be so difficult about opening a restaurant two hours early?"

"Well, for one thing," said David like he was talking to a child, "there won't be any food there. Or at least it won't be cooked yet. There won't be any waiters. No maitre d'. No piano player. None of the stuff you like. Can't I make you a reservation for six o'clock, at the very *moment* it opens?"

"No, David, honey, you know that I'll be awake all night with heartburn if I eat after six. Ever since I've been living in Boca, I've been going to the early-bird specials for dinner. If I eat after six nowadays, I'll be in *torture* all night. You don't want that to happen, do you, dear?"

So take a freaking antacid, he thought, rolling his blue eyes heavenward.

"Tell you what. I'll call the chef. He gets in early. I'll tell him to make your favorite dish, or whatever you want. And I'll have the room-service guys send it up to your room. Don't worry about the tip, I'll tip them in advance."

"It's not the same," said the woman petulantly.

David started to give in a little. "You realize you'll be sitting there all alone?"

"I like eating alone. I prefer it. But that reminds me," she sensed her impending victory, "could you buy a *Cosmopolitan* magazine for me and have it sitting at my table? I like to read when I eat. Especially when I'm all by my lonesome."

She was really angling for David to join her at this four o'clock dinner. But she knew he could wriggle out of that one easily by saying he had another appointment. The bottom line for Mrs. Abramson was that she was lonely and the Villagio Hotel & Casino was the closest thing she had in life to a friend.

"Oh, and could you make sure Antoine is there? I really love Antoine."

Antoine was the handsome young maitre d' at the Villagio's steak house. He would be thrilled about coming in two hours early, thought David. "I'll see what I can do, Mrs. Abramson."

"Oh, you're so *sweet!*"

"Don't mention it," said David, "part of my job. I'll check in on you at some point to see how you're doing."

"Lovely! Perhaps we could have dessert together."

"We'll see, Mrs. Abramson," said David. "I have to go now. I'll see you later."

"Bye, David," she said and made a big *smack* into the telephone. "Mmmmwwwaaa!"

David instinctively wiped the lipstick off his cheek and looked disgustedly at his hand, as if it hadn't been merely a telephone kiss. The thought of this old crow kissing him, even on the cheek, made David's stomach turn. She was about seventy-five years old, with makeup caked on her face so thick it couldn't be removed with a jackhammer, and so much gold and diamond jewelry attached to her body in various ways that she looked like an Egyptian queen. Or mummy, more precisely, thought David.

But this old gal bet at least $500 a hand on blackjack. And she could sit at that blackjack table with the mind-numbing permanence of a steelworker sunk into his La-Z-Boy on a Sunday afternoon during the NFL playoffs. It was not unusual for Mrs. Abramson to put in ten solid hours at the blackjack table. At $500 a hand, roughly sixty hands an hour, that came to $300,000 in action per day. And she usually stayed at the Villagio for three days. Her husband, who died from a heart attack two years earlier—while playing craps at the Villagio, interestingly enough—had owned a fur factory in New York. Together they had amassed a fortune of some $30 million and Mrs. Abramson was furiously trying to spend it before she would be forced to leave it to her children, whom she despised. She was a lousy blackjack player and had no interest in improving. She liked to split tens—a stupid beginner's mistake—because she thought they looked "prettier" apart than they did together. She was, in short, a casino host's wet dream.

Open up the restaurant early for her? Hell, she could get Antoine to come up there and serve her dinner in the nude, thought David, if she only had the good sense to ask for it.

David didn't know why he sometimes made life difficult for himself by resisting these favors when he knew all along that he would eventually grant them. Perhaps it was a way of making them seem more valuable to the customer. Perhaps it was some tiny, vestigial bit of self-respect rearing its ugly head.

The job of a casino host had come a long way since the days when an aging Joe Louis was paid to glad-hand customers walking into the Caesars Palace in Las Vegas. But whether the job had gotten better during those years or worse, David wasn't so sure.

He was certainly paid well. Depending on the quality of the customers he attracted to the casino, David could earn upwards of $400,000 a year. He got the privilege of working in a casino, which was better by far than working in a meat-packing plant like his father. David was attracted to the gaming industry, which was a little like being a gangster without the gunshot wounds. Casinos were glamorous, with just a little touch of danger about them, and they allowed him to indulge his passion for expensive Italian silk suits.

David's rise at the Villagio had been nothing short of meteoric. He started out as a craps dealer. Then he became a craps boxman. Then a floorman. Then a pit boss. When the Villagio management talked to him about the possibility of moving "upstairs" to become an assistant casino shift manager, he told them that what he'd really like to do was become a host. From his vantage point in the craps pit, hosts looked like they had a sweet job. They hobnobbed with the rich and famous. They dressed in expensive designer suits. They got to eat in the steak house almost every night. They never seemed to be working too hard. When he saw them on the casino floor, they were doing nothing more than schmoozing with their clients. Word was, they knew every whore in town. And if you know every whore in town, you never know when you might get a free-bie. It looked damn good to him.

He was wrong.

Being a casino host was a nightmarish job that consisted of playing a never-ending power game against people who had more power than him. David spent his fourteen-hour days doing favors for his clients, not because they really wanted them done but because it was their way of endlessly asking, "How much am I worth to you?" "How much will you do for me?" "How important am I to you?" And the conclusion that David came to every night before he went to bed was that some clients were more important than others, but the only truly unimportant person in the whole equation was himself.

In this never-ending quest for validation, David was always amazed to see how much money people would gamble and lose in order to get a "comp" from the casino. He'd seen people who really couldn't afford it risk and lose $3,000 to get a hamburger from the coffee shop. He'd seen them lose $5,000 just to get two free tickets to *Flesh!*, which was a god-awful show that wouldn't impress anyone who'd ever seen a naked nipple before.

It was David's job to encourage this sort of weird behavior. His lower-end players—the names on his Rolodex ranged from $2,000-a-night players to $2-million-a-night players—were constantly asking him, "How much do I have to gamble to get X?" or "How long do I have to sit at the table to get Y?" And for the one millionth time, he would patiently explain to them how the casino complimentary system worked—without revealing the actual mathematical formulas, which were guarded like the blueprints for the atom bomb.

A casino complimentary was based on the player's expected loss at the tables. Not the actual loss, but the *expected* loss. It was all a matter of how much money you bet on each decision and how long you sat there and did it. The casino really didn't care (well, it tried not to care) how much you actually won or lost. From their point of view, you were entitled to your comps whether you beat them badly, lost a bundle, or broke even. Their philosophy was that if we don't getcha this time, we'll getcha later.

The details of the casino complimentary system were secret, but the fundamental rules were simple and widely known. Nevertheless, David spent approximately half his day explaining them to people, usually people he'd explained them to a hundred times before. And this put David in the peculiar position of telling his clients that they would have to spend $5,000 for a cheeseburger or $10,000 to get a hotel room that was no better than what they could get for $100 at a Holiday Inn.

Some of David's lower-end players actually courted *him*, which always made him slightly nauseous. They sent him little gifts, little "friendship" notes; they buttered him up in conversation. He lived in fear of running into one of these small potatoes in the casino someday when he wasn't wearing the stupid necktie they gave him for Christmas. (David wouldn't be caught dead in anything less than an Hermes tie.)

And why did they treat him so well?

Because they wanted that free hamburger! A free line pass to the buffet. A free *anything*, it didn't matter. They wanted to be told, "You're somebody. You're valuable to us. You're an important person."

The low rollers on David's Rolodex were like fleas, an annoyance more than anything else. But it was the *really* high rollers who drove him crazy. These were the ones the management called "whales" behind their backs. These were the ones that David was really paid to seek, solicit, and serve.

Whales were gamblers who made Danny Pellegrino look like a kid pitching pennies in the alley. Even Mrs. Abramson wasn't a whale; she was a tuna by comparison.

So what exactly *is* a whale?

David didn't witness this with his own eyes, but one of his colleagues told him about it after the fact . . .

One night at the Villagio, a high roller was playing baccarat for about $1,000 a hand. He was an oilman from Texas and he was a very good customer. But a whale entered the casino, flanked by several casino executives, sat down at the baccarat table with this guy, and announced that he'd prefer to play alone.

The executives went over to the oilman and whispered that they had another nice baccarat table for him and they would be much obliged if he would move.

The oilman went ballistic. "This is my fucking table. I was here first. I'm having good luck here. And you can move my sweet white ass to another table on the day hell freezes over."

Most of this tirade was directed right at the whale because the oilman knew who was really asking him to leave. But the whale just sat there impassively. Finally, the oilman got right in the whale's face and said, "Listen fatso, do you have any idea who the fuck I am? I own the biggest oil refinery in Texas. I'm worth a hundred million dollars!"

And the whale said: *"I'll flip you for it."*

That's a whale.

And David Invidia had a love/hate relationship with whales. He hated them because of the way they patronized him, jerked him around, pestered him for favors. But he loved them because of their . . . well, because of their money.

He envied it. He admired it. He craved it. He got a vicarious thrill just being *near* it. He'd seen whales bet $50,000 on a single hand of blackjack or baccarat and the excitement of watching that much money tossed around so carelessly never grew dim. It was like watching a baby bobbing up and down in a flash flood. You couldn't watch it, you couldn't *not* watch it. It was horrifying and exhilarating at the same time.

The bigger the whale David could harpoon and haul into the casino, the more money he was paid. But David's income was a double-edged sword. Every time he met a new whale, he was overcome with more jealousy and envy. And, of course, the bigger the whale, the more ass-kissing he would have to do. Would he ever meet a whale who *didn't* want his ass kissed? he wondered. David suspected that such a whale did not exist. The more money and power they had, the deeper they seemed to want your tongue.

Whales could get anything they wanted from the casino, *anything*, and it was his job to make sure they got it. Even securing prostitutes was not beyond the pale. David's Rolodex included the number of several escort services in Atlantic City known to be reliable and discreet. But heck, hiring whores was the easy part! There was no telling what kind of crap these guys would want. They were all creative geniuses when it came to asking for favors.

One businessman from Okinawa wanted to have sushi served to him in the bathtub by a waitress wearing a French maid's outfit with fishnet stockings and no panties. It would've been a fairly easy favor to grant if the customer had allowed David to call one of his escort services. But nothing was ever that easy with these guys. Mr. Kirashawa had a particular waitress in mind, one who had served him many times in the steak house. This thirty-eight-year-old woman (who, to be honest, wasn't all that attractive) had a husband and two kids at home and was extremely reluctant to go along with the program. But the promise of a $5,000 tip softened her up a bit.

"No sex, right, David?" she asked.

"No sex. Scout's honor. He's going to be in a bubble bath, so you won't even have to look at him. And you'll be fully dressed—except for the panties, of course." This last line was delivered with the deliberately innocent face that David had been using to persuade females since he was three years old. With his full lips, pale blue eyes, and curly black hair, he was just cherubic enough to pull it off.

"Why doesn't he want me to wear panties if he isn't gonna ask me to flash him or something?"

"I swear to God, he's not going to touch you. If he looks, he looks. But gee, Karen, doesn't every girl in the world know how to walk in a mini-skirt without giving guys a free peek?"

She checked with her husband, who loved the idea, and she did it. That was the strangest request David had gotten in at least a week.

In some ways, it wasn't the really big favors that got David's goat, it was the small ones. One whale asked to have white truffles shaved onto his scrambled eggs every morning. Easy enough. But he insisted that the truffles be hunted by dogs, not by pigs. He swore he could tell the difference and David didn't dare to challenge him on it. So David had to find a truffle-hunter in the Piemonte region of Italy who only sold dog-hunted truffles and who, of course, charged twice as much for them, which brought the cost of those scrambled eggs to approximately $270 per serving.

David longed for the big score so he could kiss his measly $400,000-a-year job goodbye and start swimming with the whales. He was constantly soliciting stock tips and investment opportunities from his clients. But on the handful of occasions when he actually invested money, he lost every penny. So now he was gun-shy about it.

David's major form of investment nowadays was buying a $1 New Jersey state lottery ticket with his morning coffee at a convenience store in May's Landing on his way to work. The jackpot was $140 million this week—just enough to become a (small) whale. He tucked the ticket into his wallet each morning and longed for the day when some poor schmuck like himself would be catering to his every whim, when *he* could be the one asking for the special favors, the expensive champagne, the beautiful girls, the dog-hunted truffles.

Danny Pellegrino was on David's mind today. Which was unusual. He was only a $10,000-per-visit player, so David didn't waste a lot of brain cells on Danny Pellegrino. He liked the guy. He made sure he got all the comps he was entitled to get. He liked the fact that Danny did not pester him with neckties the way his other small players did, nor ask him for too many favors. But it wasn't until the other night that David started paying close attention to Danny Pellegrino.

David was being a little disingenuous when he told Danny that he had "heard" he'd done well in the casino on Friday night. As soon as Danny got about $250,000 up, one of the pit managers placed a call to Invidia and said, "One of your clients is having some luck down here."

"Which one?"

"Pellegrino. First name, Dante."

"How much luck?"

"He's about a quarter mil up with no sign of slowing down."

"Well, he's not a bad guy. I've known him for years. Don't do anything stupid. Let him win, he's overdue for a nice win."

"I think he's playing some weird kind of system. He's been parlaying yo bets, if you can believe that."

"Well, then we're *guaranteed* to get our money back, aren't we?"

"I don't know," said the pit manager tentatively. Pit managers were, by nature, skittish and superstitious people. They knew that all systems were theoretically destined to lose, but they lived in fear of running into the one system that did not.

"Tell you what," said David. "I'll run up to the eye in a minute and take a look at it. Believe me, Pellegrino's not a cheater. You've got nothing to worry about."

The eye-in-the-sky was the control room located above the casino floor where casino management could watch what was happening below. Former casino cheaters who had paid their debt to society were hired to watch dozens of video monitors for any sign of wrongdoing. They did so with the help of a variety of sophisticated technology, including two-way mirrors, high-powered video cameras with zoom lenses, computer-imaging devices, and lots of other stuff even David didn't fully understand.

But David understood craps. Unlike most craps dealers, he had taken it upon himself to read everything he could get his hands on about it. He considered himself an expert on the subject, a true student of the game. There was almost nothing he didn't know about how craps was dealt and how it was played, including the many dozens of systems that had been used to try to beat it in the past.

But he'd never seen this system before. It seemed to involve alternating pass line and don't-pass bets in an apparently random fashion, occasionally hedging them with yo bets and whirl bets. These last two, David knew, were among the worst wagers on the table. But Danny Pellegrino was having an extraordinary streak of good luck with them. By the time David got up to the eye, Danny was up almost $500,000.

"That's strange," said David to himself. "He should be losing a bundle with this thing, not winning." In fact, David was just about to call the pit manager on the telephone to discuss it further when Danny suddenly *did* start to lose. He had changed his betting style to the somewhat cautious approach David had seen Danny use many times in the past. But the dice cooled off dramatically at the same time and Danny suddenly began to bleed money. He lost $200,000 in just fifteen minutes while David was watching him. So David placed that call to the pit manager after all and said:

"See? What'd I tell ya?" Then he hung up.

But the situation left a funny taste in David's mouth. Something was ever so slightly fishy. Whether he won or lost tonight, Pellegrino was almost certain to pay another visit to the Villagio soon. You couldn't feel what $500,000 of chips felt like in your hands without wanting to feel it again. It was like looking at Pamela Anderson's breasts; you didn't get tired of it.

So David made a mental note to keep an eye on Danny the next time he showed up. And sure enough, Danny's telephone call came only three days later.

Chapter 7

DIED AND GONE TO HEAVEN

HEN THE TELEPHONE RANG, Virgil Kirk was reclining in a deck chair by his swimming pool, wearing nothing but a Panerai wristwatch. Deeply engrossed in a pocket Bible, he glanced at his cellphone with some annoyance before he decided to reach over to the nearby table and pick it up.

The Panerai was Virgil's "swimming-and-diving" watch. He had more than two thousand vintage wristwatches in his collection and each one had a purpose. It was not uncommon for Virgil to change wristwatches five times a day depending on his activity or his mood.

Made in Italy, the Panerai was developed for use by submariners in the Italian Navy. In the days before underwater computer-guidance systems, Italian frogmen actually rode on top of the torpedoes, steering them toward their target until they reached point-blank range and then slipping off at the last minute before the explosion. To equip these kamikaze frogmen, the Navy needed an extremely accurate waterproof wristwatch which would function well at great depths and be clearly visible in the murky water with a luminescent dial and easy-to-read numerals. Even the slightest error in timing, after all, might mean that the torpedo would explode with the frogmen still on board. So in 1934 the Navy commissioned a well-respected watchmaker in Florence named Giuseppe Panerai to manufacture such a watch, and Virgil Kirk was wearing one of his original creations.

And nothing else.

Virgil liked to swim in the nude. Even though he was at least sixty years old (Virgil's exact age was hard to pin down), he still had the body for it. Long, lean, muscular, and deeply tanned, with flowing white hair tied back in a ponytail, he cut a dramatic figure by the swimming pool.

The twenty-five-year-old blonde girl sitting at the edge of the pool and dipping her toes in the water could not help but glance at him from time to time. She wasn't quite sure what to make of this handsome elderly man who had picked her up at a casino and invited her to come to his house for a swim . . . and who then showed up poolside stark naked and not the least bit shy about it. She herself had decided to remove her bikini top, but no more. At least not for now.

Virgil was particularly fond of the Panerai watch because it reminded him of the ocean, and the ocean had played a very important part in his life. In a strange sort of way, it was the reason he could while away the hours sitting naked beside the swimming pool behind his magnificent house located in the foothills outside of Las Vegas. The ocean was the source of his wealth.

Fifteen years earlier, Virgil had invented a machine for removing the salt from seawater and making it drinkable. Of course, such machines had been around for many years. But Virgil took advantage of a new technology to make his machine smaller and more economical than any of its predecessors. The "Kirk Desalinator" could also be operated on solar power, making it perfect for use on small boats, especially sailboats, where electrical power was at a premium. Kirk licensed his invention to a manufacturer of sailboating equipment and, in return, he received royalty payments totaling about $10 million per year.

The Desalinator was just one of his many inventions. Virgil was the kind of man who liked to tinker with things and figure out how they worked. (Small wonder he was attracted to collecting vintage wristwatches as a hobby.) His natural curiosity led him in many different directions, and it was not uncommon for him to spend a few months learning about some new scientific field or technology, come up with a simple invention that nobody had ever thought of before, and sell it for a few million dollars. In fact, that was precisely what had happened with *Win By Losing*.

Virgil had been reading widely in the field of particle physics and quantum mechanics (he was trying to figure out how the universe worked) when he encountered a little-known mathematical theory called "Parrondo's Paradox." The theory, which had been developed by a mathematics professor at the University of Madrid named Juan M. R. Parrondo, postulated that two "losing" games of chance could be *combined* into a single winning outcome. Parrondo's Paradox was being used by some physicists to explain the apparently random behavior of subatomic particles and by some biologists to explain certain inexplicable leaps of logic in the theory of evolution. But Virgil's first reaction upon hearing about Parrondo's Paradox was that it would make an excellent gambling system.

So Virgil sat down at his computer, and in the course of a single afternoon, he developed and wrote a system for beating the game of craps based on the principles of

Parrondo's Paradox. He called it *Win By Losing*, and to sell it, he took out a small classified ad in *The National Enquirer*. Then something strange happened:

Nothing.

No orders at all. Not a single one. And this was in spite of the fact that the ad quoted Samuel Johnson in promising "wealth beyond the dreams of avarice" for the price of a mere $10, plus postage and handling.

But Virgil's mistake was that while he had spent many hours reading about quantum mechanics, particle physics, mathematics, evolution, and game theory, he had neglected to learn anything about an even more complex science:

Mail-order marketing.

In fact, although he received no orders whatsoever, his mailbox was jammed with dozens of letters from direct-marketing companies and consultants who politely informed him that he was going about the process all wrong and that, for a small fee, they would gladly share the secrets of direct-mail marketing with him and help make his new venture successful. He threw out most of these letters unanswered. But one of them intrigued him.

It was postmarked Montblanc, New Jersey, which Virgil recognized as an extremely upscale suburb of New York City, and the return address said, "Pellegrino Enterprises."

"Why would a mineral-water company be writing me?" Virgil wondered out loud as he sliced open the envelope. Inside was a brief handwritten letter:

"Hey paisano, you're doing it all wrong. You've got a great concept here, but you can't sell it straight from a classified ad. You've got to use a two-step process. The classified ad should offer 'free information.' Then when the cafones write in for the free information, you send them a letter selling your system. That's how it

works. Believe me, I've made millions doing this. But I've got an even better idea for your booklet. Why don't you give me a buzz?"

P.S. Here's your first lesson in direct marketing: No one reading The National Enquirer *has a fucking clue who Dr. Johnson is—unless you're talking about the guy who makes the vibrators.*

The letter was signed "Danny Pellegrino" and it gave a phone number with the 201 area code of northern New Jersey. Mr. Pellegrino seemed like an amusing guy, so Virgil figured, what the hell, and he called him. At the very least, he'd be able to shed some light on what was meant by the word "cafones."

During that phone call they worked out a deal whereby Danny would write a direct-mail letter selling *Win By Losing* to his own in-house list of one million gambling book-buyers at the price of $40 per booklet. Danny offered to pay Virgil a royalty of $15 for every booklet sold. He estimated a 10 percent response rate, which is what he typically received when he mailed a promotion to his own list. If he turned out to be right, Virgil would earn approximately $1.5 million for his system. In other words, it was a typical afternoon's work for Virgil Kirk.

But that phone conversation had taken place months ago. Meanwhile, Virgil had moved onto other things. As he sat by the pool today, he was intently studying the Bible because he was working on a brand new theory. His life was so relentlessly sweet that he had come to believe he had died and gone to heaven. He was riffling through the pages of his pocket Bible for some indication that this might be true when the annoying ring of the cellular telephone interrupted him.

"Hello," said Virgil gruffly.

But there was no one on the other end. Just a steady roar, like the engine of an airplane. Virgil hung up. He put the phone back down on the little table next to his deck chair and picked up his Bible. The phone rang again.

"HELLO?" he shouted.

Danny Pellegrino's voice came crackling through on the other end through a lot of static and the steady airplane noise:

"Hello, Virgil? It's Danny Pellegrino."

Virgil only heard the last word clearly.

"You say you want a Pellegrino? Well, I suggest you call a restaurant. You've dialed the wrong number." Virgil started to set the phone down again when he recognized Danny's voice yelling into the phone.

"NO, IT'S DANNY PELLEGRINO. I'm the guy who bought the mail-order rights to *Win By Losing* from you. Remember?"

"Oh, yes, Mr. Pellegrino, the mail-order maestro. How are you, my friend. Are we rich yet?"

Both men were already quite rich. But the pleasure of making money never dimmed. The only thing more exciting than making your first million was making your second.

"Well, no, not yet. It's in the mail, but I haven't received any returns yet," he lied. "Pretty soon now, though."

Then, after a pause, he added, "I'm on my way to Atlantic City to try the system out in a real casino."

Virgil didn't hear this last sentence at all.

"I can barely hear you. Where are you calling from? You sound like you're at the bottom of a well and trying to dig your way out with a jackhammer."

"I'm in my Bonanza. Here, I'll cut the engine for a few minutes."

It suddenly got quiet on the line.

"I don't think that's a very good idea," said Virgil.

"To try the system out in a real casino?" asked Danny.

"No, to cut the engine. I was under the impression that a functioning engine was considered vital to the safe operation of a single-engine aircraft."

"Oh, it's no big deal. I do it all the time. We'll just glide for a moment here while we talk. I'll turn it back on in a few minutes."

"Well, you're the pilot," said Virgil noncommittally. "So you're going to Atlantic City to try out the system?"

"Yes, I am," said Danny, followed by a very long pause. Finally, Danny asked, "Did you ever do that?"

"Did I ever fly an airplane without an engine? No sir, I always make a point of asking the captain to keep the engine on whenever I fly."

"No," said Danny, somewhat exasperated with Virgil's peculiar brand of humor. "Did you ever try the *Win By Losing* system in a real casino?"

Virgil chuckled. "You know, it's funny, but that never occurred to me. I guess I was mostly interested in it from a theoretical standpoint. I rolled the dice a few times on my desk . . ." he chuckled again and switched gears in mid-sentence. "You know, now that you mention it, that's a damn good idea. Maybe I'll run by a casino this afternoon and give it a whirl."

Danny's "NO" was so loud that it could be heard at the far end of the pool where the blonde girl was doing a backstroke, her bare breasts glistening in the sunlight. She stopped swimming, stood up on the bottom of the pool, and looked at Virgil quizzically.

Virgil held the phone away from his ear and signaled to his young girlfriend that everything was okay. When he gingerly returned the phone to his ear, Danny was still saying no.

"No, no, no, don't bother. Nope, not necessary. Don't bother doing that. Don't waste your valuable time, Virgil. No, I'll try it out, and I'll let you know if I learn anything interesting. I mean, I'll let you know if I have any problems. You see, the reason I do this is just in case I get any questions from the customers. If people call me with questions, I like to sound like I know what I'm talking about, you know?" Danny was rambling like an idiot now.

"Well, that sounds like an excellent idea, Danny," said Kirk. "I can't believe I didn't think of that myself."

But the connection was lost.

Danny wasn't even supposed to be using a cell phone from an airplane. Doing so violated a dozen federal regulations on the books of both the FAA and the FCC. It was against the law because a cell phone at high altitude accessed many different cellular antennas at once. The call usually went through, but it meant that thousands of other calls in the immediate area would be blocked. Of course, Danny, who was one of the most self-centered human beings on the planet, did it all the time.

Virgil put the phone down on the table and chuckled again. He couldn't believe how careless he'd been not to give the system at least one try in a real casino. He picked up his cell phone and pocket Bible and stood up.

The blonde girl watched him from the other side of the pool. He was exceedingly tall, probably the tallest guy she'd ever seen naked. She glanced at his penis and smiled. It was true what they said about tall guys, she thought.

Virgil started to call out to her, but he couldn't remember her name. Oh, well, no problem.

"Hey, little pilgrim, I'm going over to the Miracolo for a few hours. Would you do me the great honor of accompanying me?"

"I WORK there, Virgil. Did you FORGET? I can't think of any place I'd rather go LESS on my day off than the Miracolo." She was in the habit of strongly emphasizing at least one word in every sentence.

"Oh, I forgot," Virgil mumbled. She was a cocktail waitress at the Miracolo casino. They'd just met the other day and Virgil invited her to come over and see his pool. It was one of those "infinite horizon" pools that look like the edge of the water disappears into the sky. His glowing description of it, plus the $100 tips he kept giving her, made it seem worth checking out.

"Can't I just CHILL by your pool 'til you get BACK?"

"Of course you can, pilgrim, stay as long as you want. I'll tell Anna-Maria to bring you any libation your little heart desires. Then maybe when I return, we'll go out to dinner."

"That would be LOVELY," she replied.

She blew him a kiss and then leaned back on the side of the swimming pool to bask in the sun. As she did so, Virgil noticed that her large breasts did not flop over to the side of her chest, but remained pointed straight up at the sky. It was the sure sign of a surgical breast job. But he made a mental note that he would have to confirm this diagnosis with a physical examination later on.

Yes, he thought, he had clearly died and gone to heaven. But he still couldn't figure out exactly how that was possible.

Chapter 8

TORTURE IS ITS OWN REWARD

IN HIS OFFICE AT the United States Postal Service, Richard Goldman turned the plain white envelope around in his hands and examined the return address. It said, "Pellegrino Enterprises" and it was postmarked in Montblanc, New Jersey. But it didn't look like the usual Danny Pellegrino special, thought Goldman. It didn't have the usual blaring headline, the usual bright yellow paper stock, none of the usual techniques Danny employed to make his envelopes jump out of the mailbox and grab the boxholder by the throat. It was just a plain business letter. Except that when Goldman opened the envelope, a dollar bill fell out.

"Due to unforeseen circumstances," said the letter, and that was all Richard needed to know it was a dry-test letter. Danny had apparently decided not to publish *Win By Losing* after all.

Richard didn't like dry tests, but they weren't illegal. They were just a sneaky way for mail-order companies to do consumer research at the consumer's expense. They stunk to high heaven though, in Richard's opinion, because they got some poor boxholder all wound up about buying a product that didn't really exist. Richard was always amazed at the large and reputable companies that thought nothing about running dry tests. He had even mentioned it to his boss on a few occasions, hoping that the USPS might lobby Congress to make the practice illegal.

"You've got your hands full with stuff that's *already* illegal," said his boss without looking up from his newspaper.

Dry tests were not uncommon, but this was the first one he could remember seeing from the Bard of Montblanc. It was all the excuse he needed to give Danny a little scare. He would send him a cease-and-desist letter. He would inform Danny that he was concerned about the promotion, even more concerned by the dry test, and he would ask him to cease all mailings on behalf of *Win By Losing* until he could launch an investigation.

Of course, he had no intention of launching an investigation, but Richard knew that cease-and-desist letters caused little beads of sweat to form on the foreheads of guys like Danny Pellegrino. And he couldn't resist sending out several of them a day.

Richard also knew that Danny would have to forward the letter to Lefkowitz and Lefkowitz would have to respond. You ignored cease-and-desist letters at your own peril. If you didn't at least write back and confirm that you had ceased and desisted, Richard might indeed start an investigation. Of course, it was also clear that Lefkowitz would probably charge Danny about $5,000 for writing a one-page reply that was automatically generated by his secretary's computer. That brought Richard a little pleasure, too. As far as Richard was concerned, using the power of the federal government to torture guys like Danny Pellegrino was like virtue itself—it was its own reward.

So Richard turned to his own computer and began printing out his own boilerplate letter that began, "It has come to the attention of the United States Postal Service . . .

Chapter 9

RICKY THREE PIGEONS

ARIA WAS SITTING AT Danny's big desk stuffing dollar bills into envelopes when she heard the doorbell ring. She was dressed very casually on this Wednesday evening, not planning to see anyone she knew. She wore a pair of tight-fitting jeans, a baggy Rutgers sweatshirt given to her by an ex-boyfriend, and considerably less makeup than usual—roughly the same amount most women would wear on their wedding day.

"Who can that be?" she said aloud.

Maybe Danny got home from Atlantic City early, she thought, and he locked himself out of the house again. But when she opened the front door she was surprised to see her boyfriend, Ricky Trepiccione. He was dressed in tan slacks and a black silk shirt under an Armani sports jacket. Only it wasn't really an Armani, it was an *Armini*. He'd purchased it for $150 at a discount men's store in Paramus.

"What's up, babe?" he said with the sparkling smile that had first caught Maria's eye.

"Ricky, what are you doing here? I told you I was busy tonight. I can't go out. I've got to stuff a million envelopes or Danny is going to kill me."

"I thought I could help you," he said disarmingly. What Ricky really thought was that he could get a blowjob while he sat there drinking Danny's beer and watching Maria work. Then after he got his rocks off, maybe he'd cruise some bars.

"Well, that's sweet of you," she said, genuinely touched. "Yeah, I guess you could help. All I'm doing is stuffing dollar bills into envelopes. You can handle that, right?"

"Dollar bills?" asked Ricky with interest.

When Maria led him into Danny's office, Ricky got his first look at the enormous pile of greenbacks sitting on Danny's desk. At first glance, it wasn't clear that they were merely $1 bills, so it looked like a magazine advertisement for the lottery.

"Holy shit," said Ricky.

"Don't even think about it, Ricky," said Maria, jumping five steps ahead of him—which was roughly how far she was always ahead of Ricky intellectually.

"How much is there?"

"About $20,000, minus the thousand or so that I've already stuffed into envelopes."

"What's he doing with all this cash in his office?"

"We're giving people a dollar to make up for the fact that we're not publishing some craps system. Danny checked it out in A.C. and said it was so bad he couldn't sell it."

"Maria . . ."

"I said no, Ricky! I'm not going to steal money from my own boss."

"Just think about it, Maria, think about it. How much does he pay you every year?"

"Well, about $20,000, I guess, but it's just a part-time job."

"So we can take this money and you wouldn't have to work for a whole year." This was Ricky's philosophy of employment in a nutshell.

"Ricky, I am NOT going to steal from Danny and I'm not going to let you steal from him. He's my boss. I like him. He trusted me with this money and I'm not going to steal it."

"I don't know, Maria, I could use the money. I'm awfully light this month."

Ricky was stupid, but he could be as persistent as a bull-dozer. And Maria knew that he could simply wear her down if she didn't try a different approach.

"Ricky, if you promise me you'll keep your hands off this money, I'll give you what you've been asking for."

"What have I been asking for?"

"You know."

"No, I don't. What?"

"Ricky, you've been *begging* me for it," she said, and to make it clear, she turned her back to him, thrust her butt out, and brushed it once against his crotch.

"A new pair of jeans?"

"No, you idiot!" She stuck out her butt again. But this time she slammed it back into his body.

"Oh," he said with a smile. "Tonight?"

"Yes, tonight."

"Here?"

"Yes, here, if you want. But you've got to wait until I finish today's mail. I've got about five hundred more envelopes to stuff. It'll go faster if you help."

"Naaah, I think I'll get a beer," and he walked to the kitchen thinking, I'll get some ass and after we're done, I'll take the money anyway.

"So are you going to help me?" Maria asked when Ricky came ambling back into the office after thirty minutes or so of playing on Danny's pool table.

"Why are you sending out these dollar bills anyway?"

"I already told you." She tossed him a copy of *Win By Losing.* "The boss sent out a big mailing selling this system. But then he tested the system at Villagio. It sucked so bad, he said they'd throw him in jail if he sold it. So we're sending these people a dollar to apologize for wasting their time."

Ricky plunked down in a big black leather chair near the desk and began leafing through the booklet. He fancied himself something of a student of the game of craps.

"Hey, it says here that it's based on the theories of some professor guy in Spain."

"Yeah, it's bullshit," said Maria, continuing to stuff dollar bills into envelopes.

"Hey, it says that you can take two losing bets and *combine* them into a winning bet."

"Pure bullshit," said Maria. Pure Danny, she thought, with an affectionate smile.

"What it says here is that if you alternate the pass-line bet with the don't-pass bet, you can lose money on both of them, but still come out ahead in the long run."

"Now just think about that one, Ricky, and you'll realize why we're not selling the system."

"You got any dice?"

"Well, this is going to come as a severe shock to you, Ricky, but I don't generally carry dice on my person. Danny probably has some around here, but I don't know where."

"Wait, I've got some." Ricky pulled out his car keys. They were attached to a keychain made of two large fuzzy dice. They wouldn't exactly give you the kind of precision roll demanded by the casinos, but Ricky figured they were probably good enough for his purposes. He started tossing the dice. Maria glanced at him and rolled her eyes.

"If you would help me with the envelopes, we could get to you-know-what sooner."

Ricky didn't respond. He was engrossed in the book.

Maria wriggled her butt in the chair in such a way that Ricky, that *any* man, would notice. She knew it was her best feature, and this wasn't the first time she'd used her butt to manipulate a man.

Funny thing about best features, she thought. The girls whose best feature was their face were lucky, because everyone paid attention to your face. The girls whose best feature was their chest were a little less lucky, because most of the time your chest was covered. And so on down the line. Until you got to the girls whose best feature was their soul. I bet nobody ever gets close enough to those girls to notice, she thought.

Ricky didn't notice her butt. He was busy with the dice.

"This thing seems to work," he said.

"Oh, puh-leeze," said Maria. "Believe me, if this system is too bad for Danny to sell, you don't want any part of it."

"So you say. But these dice are saying something different."

"Those are toy dice from a keychain, Ricky."

"Dice are dice. And these dice are telling me that this system works."

The more she tried to talk him out of it, the more enthusiastic he got, until finally he jumped out of the chair and announced, "I'm going to A.C. Wanna come?"

Atlantic City was approximately two hours and forty-five minutes away from Montblanc by car.

"Ricky, don't be ridiculous."

"I'm going. You can come with me or not."

"What about our . . . well, you know . . . what about what we were going to do?"

"We can do it later, babe." Ricky was a true craps player—even sex paled by comparison to the thrill of rolling dem bones.

"And I've got some more bad news for you," he said as he grabbed an empty mailbag from the corner of the office.

"What?"

"I'm taking the money."

"Ricky, no!" she shouted.

"I've got to, babe. I don't have enough money on me to give this system a good try." He started sweeping dollar bills off the desk and into the mailbag.

"No, Ricky!"

"Don't worry. I'm just borrowing it. I'll make some money with it for myself. Then I'll bring you back the twenty large. I'll even put it back into singles for you, how about that? I'm not stealing it. It's just a loan."

When she reached for his wrist as he was scooping dollar bills into the mailbag, Ricky lost his temper. He backhanded her, flush on the nose. He hit her so hard that she tipped back in the chair and fell on the ground, banging the back of her head in the process. Blood gushed from her nose and tears welled in her eyes. But she was too stunned to move or make a sound.

"Maybe we can do something together on Saturday night," said Ricky as he walked out of the room.

Maria was still lying on the ground sniffing blood and wiping away tears when she heard Ricky's used Corvette lay a patch of rubber on Danny's driveway.

Chapter 10

ROOM, FOOD & BEVERAGE

R. PELLEGRINO! MR. INVIDIA! How nice to see you both," said Antoine, the maitre d' of the steak house at the Villagio. That's funny, he thought. I see Pellegrino all the time and I see David every night, but I've never seen them together before. "Follow me, gentlemen." And he showed them to their table. It was a better table than Danny was used to getting from Antoine.

"I'm in the mood for a lobster tonight," said Danny as he sat down and unfolded his napkin with a flourish.

"Have one," said David matter-of-factly. "I've put you on full RFB for the trip." RFB stood for Room, Food, and Beverage, meaning that Danny wouldn't have to reach into his pocket for anything on this visit to the Villagio. Full RFB was rare for Danny, no matter how much he bet, because David had him tagged as a "tough" player. Tough players were gamblers who gave the casino a good run for their money. They always made bets with the lowest vig. Always locked up their profits when they were winning. Cut their losses when they were losing. Never chased their losing bets the way most gamblers did.

Tough players were the casino management's least favorite species. Even the "fleas"—the folks who came in to town on buses every day—were more desirable. A nickel slot player was considered a much better customer than a tough player as long as he kept shoving those nickels down the hole with reckless abandon. If a tough player put enough money into action, he'd get the comps to which he was entitled. No more, no less. But it was easier for a camel to jump through the eye of a needle than it was for a tough player to get RFB.

"Hi, Karen," said David when the waitress arrived. It was the same woman who had donned the French maid's outfit for the sushi shogun.

"Hi, Mr. Invidia, how are you tonight?" She was rather fond of David at the moment, because the sushi incident had gone off without a hitch. The Japanese man had been a perfect gentleman. He didn't even try to peek up her dress. He just sat in the tub and ate his sushi like a fat little Buddha. Scarcely even looked at her. Karen and her husband had used the $5,000 to make a down payment on a new car.

"A five-pound live Maine lobster for my hungry friend here, and I'll just have a shrimp cocktail. I've got two more dinners up here tonight."

When Karen left, Danny couldn't help needling Invidia a bit. "I've been coming here regularly for ten years, David. I've known you for eight of those years. But this is the first time you've ever invited me to dinner. What happened? Did I have a birthday I forgot about?"

Casino hosts were famous for remembering birthdays.

"Well, it's long overdue."

"It couldn't possibly have anything to do with the five hundred large I put into action the other night, could it?"

"Well, you put $5,000 into action, Danny. The five hundred large was our money." With that comment, David revealed that he was intimately familiar with everything that had happened at the craps table on Friday night.

"Action is action," said Danny, quoting one of David's favorite lines back at him.

"Yeah, well, your action had nothing to do with it. I just thought it was high time for us to have dinner together." Of course, it had everything to do with it. "So you're up quite a bit again today, I hear."

"About a hundred large," Danny lied. It was more like $250,000, but Danny wasn't sure how closely he was being watched. Danny felt he could've hit the Villagio for a full million by now, but he was still in a test mode. He didn't want to draw too much attention to himself. He figured he'd take the Villagio for the million after he nailed all the other casinos in Atlantic City where he wasn't as well-known.

"Well, you might want to count those chips again, *Dante*, because it looked more like $250,000 to me from the eye-in-the-sky." David had been watching Danny's play almost non-stop since he arrived.

"Oh, you've been watching," said Danny, apparently unconcerned, as he wiped his mouth with a napkin. "And you've learned my real name. How sweet."

"Mmmm-hmm," nodded David, pausing expectantly.

Karen arrived with the lobster. She tied a bib around Danny's neck and Danny expertly pulled the tender meat out of the tail with a fork. He dipped a big chunk of lobster meat into the melted butter and popped it into his mouth with relish.

"I think I know what you're doing," said David.

"I'm eating a lobster. What's it look like I'm doing?"

"No, I mean at the craps table."

"Yeah, I'm winning. I know you guys find that very annoying, but I'm allowed to do it."

"I think I know *how* you're winning."

A piece of lobster meat went down the wrong pipe and Danny started spitting and choking. Antoine, who had saved three lives with the Heimlich maneuver in his career, came rushing to the table, eager to add another notch to his belt. But Danny held his hand up like he was taking an oath and swallowed the meat. Then he took a sip of water.

"Oh really, how's that?" said Danny with remarkable composure, considering the paroxysm he had just undergone.

"You've got a system."

Danny laughed. Too loudly. "Don't look now, Davey boy, but everybody down there's got a system."

"The problem is, yours seems to work."

"I'm on a lucky streak."

"Too lucky."

"Oh, give me a freaking break," said Danny with as much self-righteous anger as he could muster. "I'm winning a few bucks and you're trying to make a federal case out of it. You've got to let people win sometimes, David. It's a casino. They won't come back if you don't toss them a bone every now and then."

David listened to this impassively, then said, "Why do you hedge your don't-pass bet with a whirl bet, when you and I know the whirl is one of the worst bets on the table?"

"I'm a complex guy," said Danny, "I contain multitudes."

David didn't recognize the Walt Whitman quote, so he just plowed on. "Why do you parlay your yo bets three times in a row?"

Danny was starting to feel a cold sweat on his forehead. He simply shrugged and smiled in answer to this last query, as if to say, "Silly me."

After about thirty minutes of these questions, Danny sat at the table with three-quarters of a cold lobster in front of him, the butter congealed into a yellow gunk, and he realized that David had pretty much figured out the system. He didn't have all of the details right, but he'd done a pretty good job for somebody who'd never cracked the cover of *Win By Losing*. Even more importantly, it was clear that he knew enough about the system to invalidate it by recommending some rule changes to his superiors.

"So what are you going to do about it?" Danny finally said with resignation.

"I figure we'll put up a little sign that says you can't alternate between pass line and don't-pass bets. You'll have to make up your mind which way you're going to bet before you come to the table. That's the way most people bet anyway. I doubt if anyone will give a damn."

"You're really stupid, aren't you?" said Danny, feeling a new wave of hope flush through his body.

"I thought I was being pretty smart."

"Well, let me ask you a question, smart guy. What do you think you'll get out of tattling to your boss about this? Another C-note in your paycheck?"

"More like a grand," said David, insulted. "But something like that, yes."

"So you're telling me that you've figured out how a craps system works—a craps system that I've proven to you can make upwards of $500,000 a day—and your idea is to tell Mommy about it because she'll put an extra cookie in your lunchbox? You're a real genius, David. It's an honor just to break bread with you."

David was taking a beating here, but, in fact, the conversation was going exactly the way he had hoped.

"What are you saying?" asked David innocently.

"I'm saying, why you don't tell the Villagio Hotel & Casino to go screw itself, while you and I go to Las Vegas and make some money with this system."

"I've got a better idea. Why don't *you* go screw yourself and *I'll* take the system to Las Vegas."

"Because you have part of it, David, but you don't have the whole thing. You're missing some key details. You might eventually figure those details out. You might not. But until you do, you're not going to make any money with this system."

Not all of this was true, but David couldn't know for sure if it was or not. David's understanding of the system was like Newton's understanding of gravity. He knew it worked. He had a pretty good idea *how* it worked (i.e., which bets to place and when). But he had no idea *why* it worked. Danny held the keys to that mystery and without those keys, it was unlikely David could make millions by himself.

"Tell you what," said Danny. "Why don't you ask your boss for a few days off. You and I can take a trip to Vegas, where you don't have to worry about any of your colleagues recognizing you. We'll make about $40 million with this system, and we'll split it down the middle. When we come back, you can tell your boss you've decided to move to Bimini."

This was exactly what David wanted to hear. But he said nothing, as if he were carefully weighing the pros and cons. "How we gettin' to Vegas?" he finally asked.

"In my airplane."

"Oh, no! You're not getting me in one of those tin cans!" David hated to fly and he really hated small planes. When he was forced to pick up a client in the Villagio's own jet—which was almost as big as an airliner—he had to swallow three valiums before he could strap himself into the seat.

"Don't be silly," said Danny. "It's a brand new Bonanza, state-of-the-art avionics, everything first class. I'm the safest pilot you've ever flown with. And besides, I've got this thing tied up in so many corporate tax schemes that I've got to get as much business use out of it as possible. If I don't, the IRS will figure out a way to take it away from me. It would break my heart to buy a commercial airline ticket right now."

"So break your damn heart."

"Remember, David, I'm the one with the system. You're welcome to take American Airlines to Vegas if you want, but when you get there you might forget how it works."

The truth was, neither one of these men wanted to let the other one out of their sight for more than a few hours.

"Do you have an extra parachute?" asked David in all seriousness.

"Parachutes are for skydivers," said Danny. "Unless you're shot out of the air by a missile, a good pilot can usually bring an airplane down safely. We don't encourage people to jump out the window," he added with a chuckle.

David looked somewhat pale, but they agreed to meet the next morning in the lobby for the long taxi ride to Atlantic City International. Danny hadn't landed at Bader Field this time; it had been too windy on Monday. ACI was farther away from the casinos, but a safer and easier place to land.

As Danny went to sleep that night, he found himself thinking about all the cheesy ways that hell had been dramatized in movies and on TV. So many of them took place in a casino. And the one thing that they all had in common was that the person in hell wasn't losing, he was winning. Playing hand after hand of blackjack. Winning every one. Doomed to do this throughout eternity.

Chapter 11

A FAMILY PLACE

AT ALMOST EXACTLY THE same moment that Danny was choking on a piece of lobster upstairs, Ricky "Three Pigeons" Trepiccione walked into the Villagio Casino with a mailbag slung over his shoulder looking like an Italian version of Santa Claus.

He knew that the boxman at the craps table wouldn't be thrilled with counting all these one-dollar bills, but there wasn't much he could do about it. He had spent a few minutes in the parking lot removing a hundred singles from the bag and arranging them into a neat pile with all the George Washingtons facing in the same direction. His plan was to start with $100 and see what happened. A copy of *Win By Losing* was jammed into his back pocket.

"Change only, no action," said Ricky as he dropped the wad of bills on the craps table. This meant he wanted his money exchanged for chips, but he was not yet ready to place a bet.

The boxman looked up at him disbelievingly and said, "A hundred one-dollar bills?"

"Yup," said Ricky.

"You've got to be kidding me."

"I don't kid nobody about nuthin,'" said Ricky, and he gave the boxman his best Mafia glower. He'd spent years practicing it in the mirror.

But the boxman, who probably saw fifty people a day pretending to be gangsters, was decidedly unimpressed.

"I don't freakin' believe it," he said, violating his own rule about saying "freakin'" at the table. But it was legal tender for all debts public and private, so he started counting.

Ricky turned his back from the table and took a peek at *Win By Losing*. The system spelled out everything for him. All he would have to do was follow directions.

"Give the gentleman $100 in chips," the boxman said to the dealer, then added to Ricky, "there you go, big spender."

Ricky placed $5 on the pass line and waited for the comeout roll.

"Seven, winner seven, front-line winner, pay the line, take the don'ts," said the stickman, and Ricky's $5 had turned into $10. So he took his $10 and moved it to the don't-pass line.

"Three craps, line away. Pay the don'ts. The dice are out." Now Ricky took his $20 and moved it back to the pass line, where after a few minutes, it won again.

It was going well. Very well. So well that Ricky had tripled his $100 stake within a half-hour. But what's three times a hundred? Ricky did the multiplication in his head. Three hundred dollars. Hell, that wasn't so much. You couldn't buy a line of coke for $300 nowadays. The system was working, but he needed more investment capital.

So Ricky picked up the mailbag that was straddled between his legs and dumped the entire contents onto the craps table.

"Now you've really got to be fucking kidding me," said the boxman as he faced the prospect of counting nearly twenty thousand one-dollar bills.

As the boxman was pondering his plight, the pit boss got on the telephone to the casino shift manager upstairs. "We've got a dry cleaner down here."

"How do you know?"

"Shows up with a bag of one-dollar bills. Empties them on the table. No Villagio card. Never seen him before."

Ricky usually played at the Trump Taj Mahal. But the Villagio was the first casino off the Atlantic City Expressway and he didn't want to waste a minute tonight.

"Is he winning?"

(This is the first question a casino executive would ever ask about any player exhibiting unusual behavior on the casino floor. The pit boss could've said someone at the craps table was stark naked except for a floor-length Indian headdress who was playing a tom-tom and smoking opium through a peace pipe and the question would invariably come back: "Is he winning?")

"He bought in for a hundred. Also dollar bills, by the way. He was about three hundred to the good when he dumped the whole bag on the table."

"How much?"

"At least $10,000, I'd say, maybe more."

The image of ten thousand one-dollar bills on a craps table made the shift manager laugh out loud.

"What do you want me to do about it?" said the pit boss, who wasn't quite as amused.

"Give him the chips for now. But keep an eye on him. If he loses, we'll be happy to take those dollar bills off his hands. We can always use more singles in the cashier's cage. But if he wins, we should ask him to go. We can't have money launderers at the Villagio Hotel & Casino. This is a family place."

"Okay, will do."

"Keep me posted," said the shift manager and hung up.

To speed up the process of counting the bills, the pit boss authorized the boxman to give Ricky $3,000 in chips—there was at least $3,000 in the pile, everyone agreed—and called a few women up from the counting room to handle the rest. The boxman was relieved.

But an hour later, the women had still not finished counting the dollar bills, and Ricky had turned his $3,000 into $30,000. That's when Ricky received a gentle tap on the shoulder.

He turned to see a man in a suit smiling at him. It was obviously a casino executive of some kind.

"No, I don't want any dinner right now," said Ricky, who thought he was being offered a comp, and he turned back to the table.

Another tap on the shoulder.

"Are you still here?" said Ricky. "What part of 'no' don't you understand? No dinners. No shows. No girls. I'm gambling here, for chrissakes."

"No, I don't think *you* understand, sir. May I speak with you for a moment away from the table? Don't worry about your chips, we'll watch them for you."

"Say whatever you have to say right here, mister," said Ricky who could not have been pried away from the table with a crowbar at this point.

"We'd like you to leave, sir."

"What?"

"Sir, we'll give you all your dollar bills back. And you can keep all the chips you've won. What is it, about thirty large?

But we've decided we don't want your craps action anymore. You're too lucky at craps."

"Too lucky? You're not allowed to ban me. This is Atlantic City, not Las Vegas. You can't ban people."

The executive winced a little and tried a different tactic.

"Look, sir, you came in here with a bag full of one-dollar bills. That's highly unusual. But we didn't ask any questions about it. That was our mistake. We're really supposed to notify the Casino Control Commission when someone walks in here with a pile of small bills." He nodded in the direction of the CCC, which actually had an office located just off the casino floor. A state employee was dozing at his desk.

" . . . because of all the drug problems these days, you know. Now, sir, I can rectify that mistake," he continued, "by walking over to the CCC and telling them about your bag of bills. Or you can simply put the bills back in the bag, take your $30,000 in chips, cash them in, and say good-bye. So how would you like to play it?"

Ricky knew he had lost. He was already on probation for various drug offenses. The last thing he wanted tonight was a conversation with somebody from the New Jersey state government. He had no card left to play but sheer bluster.

"You stupid motherfucker! Do you know who the fuck I am? Do you know who you're messing with? Let me give you a hint, asshole. You better wear your cowboy hat to bed tonight, fuckface, because you might wake up with a horse in your bed tomorrow morning, *if* you know what I mean."

"Should I take that to mean we don't have a deal?" said the executive impassively. Like the boxman, he, too, met several people a day who tried to intimidate him with their alleged mob connections. But so far he hadn't seen even a single horse's head in his bed.

"Give me the fucking money," said Ricky. "But sleep tight tonight, mister, sleep tight. Because I got lots of friends in this town. I got your fucking name, too." He fingered the name tag on the executive's lapel. "Mr. Stephen Parlavecchia of Absecon, New Jersey. They gotta lot of fishes in Absecon Bay, Steve? I hope you like 'em, 'cause you might be sleeping with them tonight."

"Yes, sir," said Parlavecchia, wondering, not for the first time, if guys like Ricky had seen any movie other than *The Godfather.*

But Ricky did indeed know someone in the Atlantic City mob. It was an older cousin of his—much more successful in organized crime than Ricky had ever been. And the *Godfather* quotations were appropriate, because this man had the highly unlikely name of Frank Pentangeli.

Chapter 12

THE THIRD CIRCLE

S URE, I CAN TALK to you, Ricky Three Pigeons. Come on over to the house and we'll split a sub."

Ricky knew his cousin well enough to know that the "house" didn't mean his large estate in May's Landing, it meant the White House Submarine Shop, which was only a few blocks away from the Villagio. And he knew that "splitting a sub" meant that he would sit there and watch his cousin eat nine-tenths of a two-foot-long submarine sandwich after offering a tiny slice to Ricky. Two things always impressed Ricky about his older cousin: how much he could eat and how much money he had.

Sure enough, by the time Ricky arrived at the White House ten minutes later, his cousin had already ordered a two-foot-long meatball sub and had shaved about two inches off the end. It was waiting for Ricky on a coffee saucer. Frank Pentangeli was so fat that he took up one entire side of a large booth at the back of the restaurant. Ricky slipped into the seat across from him.

"Here, I saved you a piece," said Pentangeli, pushing the saucer toward Ricky.

"Thanks, Frankie. You look good. You lost weight?" Pentangeli could lose three hundred pounds without anyone noticing, but Ricky knew that this particular compliment worked with Frankie for some reason.

"Yeah, I've been working out. Using some of the exercise equipment at our clubs, you know. The doctor says if I don't lose weight, I got five years to live. But on the street, I may only have five minutes, so who knows?"

Actually, nobody in the world wanted Pentangeli dead. He was a good earner for his superiors and a generous boss to his underlings. Plus, he had the kind of business you couldn't just muscle your way into. But Pentangeli liked to exaggerate the physical danger of being in the mob and he never went anywhere without a retinue of body guards and flunkies—three of whom were seated nearby at the lunch counter.

"So why did you come to me?" asked Pentangeli. "What did I do to deserve this generosity?" It was a line from *The Godfather*, the scene where Don Corleone first meets the drug-dealer Sollozzo. It was the way Pentangeli began nearly every meeting, no matter what it concerned.

Ricky looked at his cousin with an odd combination of disgust and admiration. He watched Pentangeli lift a big slice of sub to his mouth with fat, greasy hands adorned with gaudy diamond rings, then stared at the layer of grease covering his cousin's face—did the man have really oily skin or was it just the residue from his last meal?

For a moment Ricky hesitated to answer his cousin's question. Maybe he should just swallow his pride and go to another casino. He had a bankroll of $30,000 now; he didn't have to worry about showing up with a bag full of dollar bills anymore. What's to stop Frankie from taking this system from me, he thought. Nothing. The smart thing to do would be to have a nice dinner with his cousin and walk out in sole possession of the secret.

But in Ricky's world view, respect was more important than money. That casino executive, that Parlavecchia guy, had treated him with disrespect. Ricky wouldn't be able to show his face in the Villagio again until someone was punished for treating him so badly. Besides, Pentangeli had so much money that he couldn't possibly want more. He was the richest guy Ricky knew.

After going back and forth several times in his head, Ricky eventually decided that he would share the broad strokes of what had happened at the Villagio, but he would draw the line at actually revealing the system itself. So he started talking, while Frankie listened and chewed.

Frankie Pentangeli was known to the police and to local crime reporters as the Sultan of Suntans. He owned a chain of nearly thirty tanning salons located in shopping malls throughout central New Jersey and Philadelphia that worked something like this:

Men were charged $50 for a suntan, while women were on a permanent half-price special of $25. When a man walked into one of these salons, what happened next was as ritualized as Kabuki theater. He would hand his credit card to the receptionist, and she would say, "Your tanning consultant is named Kim, and she'll be with you in a moment. Please have a seat in the reception area."

A few minutes later, Kim would come out of the back room dressed in a white lab coat, a plain white skirt, white stockings, and sensible white shoes. She looked like a nurse. Or really more like a doctor, because she held a metal clipboard.

"Peter?" she inquired, referring to the clipboard. Always first names. "We're ready for you in the tanning area now."

From there, she would lead Peter into the men's locker room and spa area. This was a purgatorial never-never land located halfway between the drab reality of the reception room (which was kept purposefully plain so as to prevent unwanted attention) and the blinding light of the tanning rooms.

The men's locker rooms in Pentangeli's tanning salons were truly spectacular. They were as plush and luxurious as any spa in the world. Canyon Ranch would've been proud. There were gold-plated plumbing fixtures, plush carpeting, marble tile, row after row of complimentary toiletries. Pentangeli never spared any expense in these rooms, which he liked to decorate in a Japanese theme.

"Give me a geeshie look in this room," he'd say to his interior decorators, some of whom actually knew what he meant.

Once inside the men's locker room, the tanning consultant would tell the customer to take a shower, a sauna, and a Jacuzzi, too, if he wished, and "when you're ready, meet me in Tanning Room Five. Just put a towel around your waist and I'll be waiting for you there."

Most men were in too much of a hurry to get to the tanning room to take advantage of the sensual pleasures of the spa area. But some of the regulars came to think of the spa as their favorite part of the whole experience and would spend hours languishing there.

Back in the tanning room, the consultant had changed from her doctor's outfit into a bikini. When her customer arrived, her first line to him was carefully scripted: "Would you like me to apply the suntan lotion or would you like to do it yourself?"

Virtually every man said, "Well, I guess you'd better do it." Some justified the decision by adding, "You can get the spots I can't reach."

The consultant then asked him if he wanted a lotion of Sun Protection Factor 10, 20, or 30. Thirty meant the guy was going to walk out later with almost no tan at all, but that was still the most popular choice.

At this point, the consultant would tell the customer to lie face-down on the massage table and begin rubbing the lotion on every part of his body. When she got to his buttocks, she recited another scripted line. "Do you mind if we loosen the towel a little bit here? It will make it easier."

Most men didn't mind.

Discreetly and professionally, she would apply the suntan lotion to the man's buttocks without fully removing the towel. But she would always manage to get a fair amount of lotion into the crack of his butt, which is not normally an area that gets a lot of sun.

"Turn around and we'll do the front side," she'd say. And when the man complied, the loosened towel invariably slipped off.

"That's okay. Let's just get rid of this. You don't mind, do you? Believe me, in my line of work, I've seen it all before . . . although maybe not as nice as this one!"

That line was also fully scripted. And the compliment was appropriate, because at this point most guys were sporting a fairly substantial hard-on.

Now the consultant would continue to apply the lotion to the front part of the man's body, paying particular attention to the groin area. She would accidentally brush by his penis and testicles many times, although she didn't deliberately touch him there. But with that thing standing up and waving around like a flag in a stiff wind, it was hard not to bump into it with a forearm, or a wrist, or a breast from time to time.

At this point, the consultant would ask the climactic question, "Is there any other part of your body that you would like me to apply lotion to, any area that I might've missed?"

The vast majority of these guys would say, "Yeah, my cock," or words to that effect. Those few who did not were either so dumb they didn't know what to say, or they were actually there to get a suntan. In which case, they got exactly what they deserved—a suntan.

The others got a very sweet handjob. While she did so, the consultant would say, "You'll take care of me afterwards, right? You'll give me a nice tip, right?"

"Of course!" the guy would say with enthusiasm.

Most guys would ask their consultant to remove her bikini top, which she would willingly do after making a pitch for a bigger tip. Some men asked her to remove her bikini bottom too, and she would usually comply with this request after securing his assurance of an even larger tip.

When the man finally came, she would clean him up as professionally as a nurse and ask, "Do you still want the tan?"

About half the men did, half did not. But when the business of the tanning room was concluded, she'd say, "Get dressed and meet me in Post-Tan Consultation Room B."

Post-Tan Consultation Room B was pretty much the only way out of the joint. All the other doors were locked from the inside with the consultants in sole possession of the keys. The consultation room was very plain, with no furniture, no decorations, nothing but a fluorescent light hanging from the ceiling. It looked like the foyer of a public bathroom.

It was here that the consultant made her final pitch for a tip. She wanted $100, but she would accept as little as $50. If a guy offered her less than $50 and stonewalled it, she might accept, but she'd let him know she didn't want to see him again. Every now and then a guy would simply bolt out the door, but he would receive a visit from some of Pentangeli's associates a few days later, and he wouldn't make that mistake again.

Of course, regular customers just went with the program. Once a guy had become well-known and trusted at the salon, a lot of the rituals were dispensed with altogether. He'd simply pay his money and get his handjob. The consultant, usually a favorite girl whom he had requested in advance, would be waiting for him in the tanning room naked when he arrived. Very generous tippers might get a blowjob, or even intercourse, depending on how much the girl liked him.

The genius of this arrangement was threefold.

First, the girl always asked for the money *after* the sex. That was Pentangeli's original contribution to the art of prostitution in its storied five thousand-year history. Most prostitutes liked to get their money in advance, for obvious reasons. But Pentangeli's innovation made it very difficult for the police to bust the operation. The cops might send an undercover guy in, but once the subject of sex-for-money was even broached, the cop was bare-assed naked with his penis in the hands of a tanning consultant. He was hardly in a position to whip out his badge and make an arrest.

The second master stroke of the operation was largely financial. The girls were an unusual combination of paid staff and freelancers. As prostitutes, they were freelancers. Management pretended it didn't know what was going on in the tanning salons and didn't want to know. But as tanning consultants, they were paid employees. They were paid slightly more than minimum wage. State and federal taxes were withheld. Social Security was taken out. Every legal "i" was dotted and every financial "t" crossed. From the standpoint of Pentangeli's accountants and the Internal Revenue Service, it was clean as a whistle.

What the IRS didn't know—and what, in fact, Pentangeli's own accountants didn't know—was that each girl was expected to leave about $500 in cash in the office kitty at the end of a twelve-hour shift. If it was a slow day, management might cut the girls some slack. But if it was a busy day, they would be encouraged to leave even more money in what was euphemistically called "the coffee pool." The coffee at these salons was spectacularly good.

Pentangeli's third brilliant innovation was the manner in which the salon treated its female customers.

It bent over backwards for them. The "limited-time" 50 percent discount for women never came to an end. All the advertising and promotion was geared to women. (The only advertising the salons ever directed at men was that a few of Pentangeli's goons were encouraged to visit various bars, bowling alleys, and golf courses in the area to spread the word that "there's more than tanning going on there, if you know what I mean.")

Women were treated exceedingly well in the reception area and the spa area, where they were offered free manicures, free pedicures, free bikini waxes, and a variety of other pampering touches. Pentangeli loved nothing more than to see three or four women sitting in his waiting rooms.

Once in the tanning room, women were treated exactly like men—with a few minor differences. They were never asked if they wanted the consultant to apply the lotion. They were given the option of wearing freshly laundered bathing suits or they could bring their own suits from home. And once in the Post-Tan Consultation Room, they were never pressured for a tip. Instead, they received a pitch for a monthly membership at a price so absurdly low that the vast majority of women jumped at it.

Women found the whole experience so pleasant that they would often recommend the place to their husbands. And it was not unusual for a husband and wife to come together. (To arrive together, that is.) When this occurred, the expression on the husband's face as he waited in the reception area with his wife cannot be described in the English language.

It was a sweet operation. And with twenty of these salons around the area, it made a ton of money for Pentangeli—more than $250,000 a week in tax-free cash, after expenses.

But he was sick of it.

Running tanning salons wasn't like the old days in Atlantic City, before legalized gambling, when he used to help operate illicit gambling dens. How could you act like a big Mafia kingpin by hanging around tanning salons with a bunch of women, looking like you were waiting to get a permanent? The only real perk of the operation was that Pentangeli insisted on personally training most of the new consultants in the rituals of the tanning room. He was very meticulous and specific about this:

"Okay, once you got the guy on his back, you ask him if he minds if you remove the towel. Tell him that in your line of work, you've seen plenty of guys naked before. It doesn't bother you. He's usually going to have a big hard-on by now. Just like

the one I've got here. (Pentangeli's erection was barely visible in the folds of fat, but it was in there somewhere.) *So tell him he's got a nice cock. Guys love to hear that. Tell him it's the nicest one you've ever seen. He'll eat it up. It's important that you use that word. Because in a minute, you're going to want him to say the word 'cock.' And he may be too shy to say it unless he hears you say it first, you know what I mean? Let me hear you say it. Good girl. So you rub him all over with the lotion, and make sure you brush by his cock and his balls a few times. Real accidental-like. Try it. Yeah, just like that. That's perfect. But don't do him yet. First, you ask him if there's any place you missed that he'd like you to do. And he'll usually say, 'Yeah, do my cock,' or something like that. Make him say it out loud. Don't let him just point down there or look down there. Because a cop might be able to bust you if you're the first one to suggest it. So you do his cock. Yeah, honey, go ahead and do me. And after you've jerked his cock for a minute or two—not before—you ask him to give you a nice tip later on. After the tan. Don't stop, baby. Finish me up. And look, this is impor-tant. Do NOT give the guy a blowjob. Do NOT let him fuck you. Not unless you know the guy. Not unless you know he's a solid citizen and a good tipper. But you know me, right? So suck me off, Kimmy-san, and I'll tell you what comes next."*

Pentangeli called all of his consultants "Kimmy-san," "Cindy-san," "Karen-san," etc., which they might've found offensive, if only they had a clue what he was talking about. The majority of these girls were from Korea, Thailand, and the Philippines. Despite the Japanese decor, there were very few Japanese tanning consultants. The standard of living in Japan was such that few young women embarked on a pil-grimage to America to find their fortune in the field of prostitution. In fact, about 95 percent of the girls were

Korean and nearly half of those were named Kim. But rather than have six girls working at the same salon named Kim, they were given American names in a kind of baptismal rite on their first day at work. A new girl walked into the salon as Kim and walked out as Karen.

Pentangeli tended to call most of them Kim anyway, unless he knew otherwise, because he figured he had a pretty good shot at getting it right. He concluded each one of his training sessions by saying, "Kimmy-san, you're the best piece of ass I've ever had, and I've had it all over the world." It was another quote from *The Godfather*, the scene where Robert Duvall has dinner with the Hollywood producer.

Whenever a new girl was hired at any of the salons, Pentangeli would call the manager and say, "Give me a number on her." Which meant rate the girl on the universal scale of one to ten. If the manager said the girl was a six or a seven, Pentangeli would say, "Okay, you train her." If the manager said she was an eight, nine, or ten, Pentangeli would affect a world-weary tone and say, "Okay, I'll stop by tonight and break her in."

None of these girls was less than a six, but the managers quickly learned to make an extremely accurate appraisal of the girl's precise locus between six and ten. Two things could piss Pentangeli off about these training sessions: if a manager had given the girl a higher rating than she deserved, in which case he was fired on the spot; or if the girl didn't swallow, in which case *she* was fired on the spot.

But the managers were in a very dicey position, because if they rated the girl too low, they ran the risk of Pentangeli running into her later and wondering why he hadn't been given the opportunity to train her. Managers had been fired on the spot for that, too.

As a result, the managers were reluctant to make these evaluations by themselves. There was no accounting for taste, especially when it came to women. One man's seven is another man's eleven. So a manager would usually invite four or five other salon managers to come over and check out the new girl. They'd rate her independently and take a mathematical average of the result. It was not uncommon for a skittish manager to tell Pentangeli that he felt the new girl was "somewhere around a 6.023"—the more nervous the guy was, the further he'd carry out the number beyond the decimal point.

The other managers were sympathetic to the man on the hot seat. But as long as it wasn't them, they could be somewhat sanguine about it too. "Don't worry," they'd say, "the worst that can happen is that he'll fire you. He's not going to kill you for this. For other things, yeah, but not for this."

The managers put up with the situation, because it was a rather cushy way to get started in the mob, which a remarkable number of young men in New Jersey aspired to do.

Tonight, Pentangeli listened to Ricky's story, and when he finished his meatball sub, he stood up and said, "Let's go get some *galimar.*" That was Sicilian American dialect for calamari. He and Ricky (followed at a respectful distance by Pentangeli's retinue) walked around the block to Il Terzo Circolo, which was Pentangeli's favorite restaurant.

Il Terzo Circolo was an Italian restaurant of modest quality owned by a plump little man named Roberto Aragosta. Roberto had named the restaurant after the third circle of Hell, the circle of gluttony. He greeted Pentangeli warmly, as he did virtually every night, although he knew it meant he would have to stay open two or three hours after closing time.

Pentangeli sat down and ordered a plate of fried calamari with marinara sauce on the side. When it arrived, it looked to Ricky like enough squid to feed the United States Navy for a month. But Pentangeli glanced at it and said, "Bring some for my little cousin, too, wouldja honey?" The only thing bigger than this man's stomach is his wallet, thought Ricky.

Pentangeli was indeed feeling rather flush this evening, because he had recently come up with a new way to promote and expand his tanning empire. It was an ingenious new method for advertising to men.

Pentangeli had always been always bothered by the fact that women ate up the vast majority of his advertising budget and overhead expenses, while men were the true profit center. So he opened up a chain of smaller stores in suburban strip malls (no pun intended) that he called the Jack & Jill Tanning Salons. And here the promotion was entirely geared to men. Men were constantly on half-price special. A big sign in front of every salon said, "MEN WELCOME!" The chain advertised heavily in the sports section of local newspapers.

These salons were much smaller than the others. Much less capital investment. Much smaller staffs. In fact, two girls could run the whole operation. There was also much less security against the cops, because what went on in these salons was not illegal. Not really.

When a man entered a Jack & Jill salon, one of the girls would take his credit card and tell him to go into the tanning room, remove his clothes, put on a towel or bathing suit, whichever he preferred, and she would join him in a moment.

When the tanning consultant came back into the tanning room, fully and demurely dressed, she began by asking the following scripted question in a very conversational tone. "Are you married?"

The vast majority of them were.

If he answered "Yes," she'd say "Too bad!" It was a joke, but a suggestive one.

If he answered "No," she'd ask if he had a girlfriend and pick up the script from there. "Would you like me to model some swimsuits that you might be interested in buying for your wife? No pressure. You don't have to buy one, but you can if you like."

Most men thought this was a perfectly charming idea. A few of them went so far as to add that just by coincidence they happened to be in the market for a new swimsuit for their wives—although the number of men who bought bathing suits for women in America every year was infinitesimal.

Very few men declined this offer. Sitting there naked except for a terrycloth towel and hearing this provocative question from a beautiful girl was pretty much irresistible. And these girls were *very* good-looking. Pentangeli insisted that they all be eights or better and they weren't hard to find, because they didn't have to be prostitutes. Nor did he have to rely so heavily on Asians for this job. Plenty of pretty American girls were eager to work in the Jack & Jill salons.

So the girl would pop into the dressing room and come out wearing what is sometimes described as a dental-floss thong bikini. Pentangeli had bought a gross of bikinis with a fig-leaf design on the crotch for the girls in the Jack & Jill shops after seeing them on a mannequin in JC Penney's and thinking they were super-sexy.

"Shall we put some music on?" she would ask.

Another good idea, the man allowed. And she would proceed to half-dance, half-strut around the man like a runway model, taking care to brush by him very closely from time to time. Most men would reach out to touch her at some point. But even if they did not, she would eventually stop and say, "Honey, you can't touch me. And I'm not allowed to touch you. Although I'd really, *really* like to. Because it's against the law. This is a tanning salon, not a whorehouse. But there's no law against touching yourself."

A few guys sat there like idiots pretending to evaluate the bikini for future purchase. But the vast majority took off their towel or swimsuit and began masturbating. As she danced and modeled, the girl would keep up a running commentary on how attractive she found the man's penis. If it was over six inches long, she'd talk about how big it was. If it was under six inches, she'd talk about how handsome it was.

Either way, the guy ate it up. And as he sat there pumping away, she could be reasonably assured that he wasn't a cop. So she'd take off her top. Then her bottom. Or sometimes she'd merely change, in full view, into another suit. She would let the man be the one to suggest that she dispense with the suits altogether. The girls played this by ear, because some men liked total nudity, while others found it much sexier to watch them change in and out of bathing suits. The discarded suits were always handed to the man with the words, "Maybe you'd like to take a closer look at this one."

Most men gave the bikini a good sniff.

"Before you leave," she'd say at some point, "please remember that tipping is permissible."

"You bet!" he'd say.

Eventually, nature took its course and as the man cleaned up with a Kleenex—a box of Kleenex and a jar of body lotion were always nearby—she'd say, "Do you still want the tan?"

This too was a scripted line: the tanning bulbs wore out quickly and Pentangeli didn't want to buy any more of them than he absolutely had to. The men usually wanted to decline the tan anyway, because a sudden tan could be hard to explain to your wife—especially in the middle of a New Jersey winter.

Back in the reception area, the girl would hand the man a business card and say, "Now that you've had your first tanning experience, maybe you'd like to visit one of our bigger salons. They'll take *really* good care of you there." Repeat customers were not especially welcome at the Jack & Jill salons; the whole idea was to upgrade them.

So that was that. It was a self-sustaining form of advertising. The Jack & Jill shops made just enough money to stay in business. The girls made a nice tax-free living off the tips. The local gentry got their rocks off. And Pentangeli got a steady stream of new male customers for his larger salons. Everybody was happy.

But Pentangeli was growing tired of the whole business. The process of running an enterprise with that many employees and that many locations—even a legitimate business—was a giant headache that was only partially ameliorated by the occasional blowjob.

Pentangeli, in fact, wanted nothing more out of life than to retire. But his monthly nut was too big. For all the money he raked in each month from the tanning salons, it seemed like almost as much went out in various expenses. So he was stuck in what was basically a boring, dead-end job. And he compensated for this by submerging himself into the world of gangster movies.

Pentangeli owned videocassette and DVD copies of *Godfather I, Godfather II, Godfather III, Goodfellas, Casino,* and every season of *The Sopranos.* He had seen all of these hundreds, perhaps thousands, of times. And nearly every word out of his mouth was a quotation from one of them.

In talking with his cousin, Ricky always got the feeling Frank was constantly doing impressions. But the characters changed so quickly, Ricky was never sure who he was doing. One moment it would be Brando. Then DeNiro. Then Pacino. Then Gandolfini. Back to DeNiro. Pesci. Brando again. It was like watching a DVD with a misfiring memory chip. Pentangeli quoted from these movies the way evangelists quote from the Bible, finding little bits of wisdom to enlighten or illuminate virtually every possible situation that occurred in life. But it didn't stop there. Quite often, they weren't quotations at all, but part of the fabric of his conversation, the very matrix of his thought process. Pentangeli's subordinates found themselves praying that he would quote from some of the less violent scenes in these films. They knew that if he quoted from one of the more violent ones, there was a chance someone might die.

Pentangeli enjoyed *The Godfather* movies so much that when he was twenty-five years old, he did something unusual for a member of the Mafia, at least for one who has not yet entered the Witness Protection Program.

He changed his name.

He changed it to "Pentangeli" after the gravely voiced underboss in *Godfather II.* Pentangeli's birth name had been Frank Costello, which, not coincidentally, was also an important name in the history of organized crime. In fact, he had been named after the original Frank Costello, who was a distant relative. But Pentangeli could never get over the fact that Costello was both an Italian and an Irish name. It bugged the hell out of him to be mistaken for a mick, which happened occasionally. It disrupted his whole self-image, which was a delicate thing under the best of circumstances.

The only difference between the two names was a slight change of emphasis. The Irish put the accent on the first syllable, Cos'•tel•lo, while the Italians put the emphasis on the second-to-the-last syllable, Cos•tel'•lo. But not every Irish American of the second generation or later was aware of this distinction. In fact, the proper Irish pronunciation of the name was gradually disappearing altogether.

One time when he was in his early twenties, Frank was seated next to an Irish priest at a bar in Hell's Kitchen. When it came out in conversation that they were both named Costello, the priest, without waiting for further explanation, called out to the bartender, "Bring a drink fer me cousin from County Cork!"

Pentangeli cold-cocked him.

Sure, it was a sin to punch a priest. But it was better than having people think he was Irish. So that was the day that young Frank Costello decided to change his name. And given his affection for the *Godfather* movies, Frank Pentangeli was not only a reasonable choice, it was essentially the only one—since there were no other Franks in either movie.

After Ricky had finished telling his story, the waitress came by to clear off the empty plates of calamari. Pentangeli had eaten all of his own, and about half of Ricky's. But Pentangeli was still hungry and suggested that they order an entree.

"Try the veal," he said to Ricky, "it's the best in the city." It was a line from *Godfather I*, the scene where Sollozzo takes Michael to the restaurant in the Bronx.

But Ricky was quite full after one-tenth of a meatball sub and half a plate of calamari. So Pentangeli ordered a plate of buccatini carbonara and a piece of osso bucco. Then he had a few questions for Ricky.

"You got this crap system on you?"

"Yeah, I got it in my pocket."

"Can I see it?"

"Sure," said Ricky, reluctantly, but he had no choice.

He started to hand the booklet to Pentangeli, then changed his mind at the last moment. Too late. Pentangeli already had a firm grip on it. Then there followed a brief tug-of-war as Ricky tried to pull back the booklet and Pentangeli tried to wrest it out of his hands. But Pentangeli had the advantage of 475 pounds of leverage, and he won easily. Embarrassed by his behavior and completely at a loss to explain it, Ricky giggled and shrugged in a manner worthy of Gomer Pyle.

Pentangeli shot him an icy look, then looked down at the book. After no more than a minute of riffling through its pages, he said: "This'll never work. Alternating pass line and don't-pass bets? Hedging them with prop bets? That's a one-way ticket to Palookaville."

"Believe me, Frankie, it really works. I made $30,000 in less than an hour. I woulda made $300,000 if that *pezzono-vante* from the casino hadn't kicked me out. That's why I want him dead. I want justice."

"That's not justice. He didn't kill you."

"Well, I want him to pay for the way he disrespected me."

"Who else knows about this system?"

"Well, my girlfriend's boss obviously knows about it, Danny Pellegrino. Maria knows about it. I know about it. I doubt if this Virgil Kirk guy is for real. Maria told me that most of the time Danny writes these books himself and puts someone else's name on them. I guess that's it."

"What's the story on this Danny Pellegrino guy?"

"Real rich guy. Lives in Montblanc. He sells these gambling systems through the mail. Makes a ton of money doing it. Got his own airplane and everything. He's down here right now, Maria told me. Staying at the Villagio."

"What kind of airplane does he have?" Pentangeli asked casually.

"It's named after that old television show. The one with Hoss and Little Joe and you know. I can't remember the name." He started humming the theme. "Dum-de-de-dum-de-de-dum-de-de-dum-de-de-DUM-DUM."

"Bonanza?"

"Yeah, that's it. Maria took me by the airport to look at it a couple of weeks ago. Cool-looking airplane. It had a weird tail section on it, like a 'V.'"

"And how's Maria doing these days?"

"She's fine, real good. I was going to go out with her tonight, but she had to stay at Danny's and work. So I decided to come down here and try out this craps system."

Pentangeli took all this in while trying to feign disinterest. His ne'er-do-well cousin was finally bringing him something of value.

"Well, I tell you what, Ricky. I like you. I've always liked you." Pentangeli had always thought Ricky was a lazy bum. "I tell you what I'm going to do for you. I'm going to keep this booklet for now. See if it's as good as you say it is. But meanwhile, I'm going to straighten out your problems at the Villagio. I know this Parlavecchia guy. He's a regular at one of our salons. He's got a wife and kids. I'm going to explain to him why it would be in his best interest to let you come back. Gimme an hour or so to do that, and you'll be welcomed with open arms. We'll even get you a comp to spend the night. Meanwhile, you can play at another casino, okay?"

"Can I have the booklet back, Frankie?"

"You remember how to play the system, don't you?"

"I guess so."

"Well, leave the book with me tonight. Then, if you still want it in the morning, drop by the White House and I'll give it back to you."

"Okay, Frank," said Ricky, unsure whether he was getting the best part of this deal or not. "Thanks for all your help."

"Don't mention it."

When Ricky left, Pentangeli called one of his flunkies over from where he was perched at the bar. It was a young guy named Carlo Montagna who had just stepped up from tanning salon manager to bodyguard. Pentangeli reached for his wallet—no easy job for a man of his girth—and several plates and glasses on the table in front of him were disturbed in the process. Eventually, though, he succeeded in reaching his billfold and he pulled out ten fresh $100 bills. He handed Carlo the money and the booklet.

"You play craps, don't you, Carlo?" asked Pentangeli lightly.

"Every day, boss."

"I want you to take this money and try out the system in this booklet. It'll only take you ten minutes to read it. Go anywhere you want except for the Villagio. See if the system works, then give me a buzz on the cell phone." Like most gangsters, Pentangeli used pay phones for important business, but the cellular was okay for routine matters like this one.

When Carlo left, Pentangeli called another flunky over to his table.

"You know my cousin, Ricky Three Pigeons, the guy who was just sitting here?"

"Sure, boss, I seen him around."

"In about an hour, you'll find him at a crap table in the Villagio. Keep an eye on him for me. But don't let him see you. I'll call you later if I need you to do anything."

Then he made a brief telephone call to Steven Parlavecchia, the casino executive who had booted Ricky out of the Villagio.

"Mr. Parlavecchia, this is a courtesy call from the Jack & Jill Tanning Salons. My name is Frank Pentangeli. I'm the proprietor. We just wanted to let you know how much we appreciate your business at the salons."

"Oh."

"That young fella you kicked out of your casino this evening, Ricky Trepiccione, you remember him?"

"The one with the dollar bills?"

"Yeah, that's right. He's my cousin. And I'd consider it a personal favor if you'd let him back into the casino, maybe give him a comp for dinner, a room for the night. I would be greatly indebted to you if you'd do that."

"Well, he's a money launder—"

"Speaking of money, Mr. Parlavecchia, I've been going over your credit card receipts here from the tanning salon and I'd like to send a copy of these to your house, so you and your wife can go over them. To help with your household budgeting, you know."

After a long pause, "I understand, Mr. Pentangeli. Tell your cousin he's always welcome at the Villagio. That was a big misunderstanding earlier tonight. I'll straighten it out."

After he hung up, Pentangeli was finally ready to sit down and enjoy a decent meal. An hour or so later, as he was polishing off a cannoli with an espresso and sambuca, his cell phone rang.

"Hey, boss, it's Carlo. You're not going to believe it, but this system works like crazy. I turned your ten C-notes into five freakin' G's. What do you want me to do with it?"

"Bring it back to me, Carlo. And thanks for your help, you did a good job. Tell you what. You and I are going to check this thing out in Las Vegas. You're going to be my right-hand man in Vegas, Carlo. I have your airline ticket right here. So bring the booklet back to me. Don't show it to anyone else and keep your mouth shut about it. Just come back here, and I'll give you your ticket to Vegas."

Carlo hung up the payphone in the lobby of the Taj Mahal. He had a big smile on his face. He'd done something good for the boss and he was going to be rewarded with a trip to Las Vegas. He was proud of himself for not having run off with the system, a course of action he had carefully considered before making the call.

Unfortunately, Carlo had seen *The Godfather* only once in his life. He was not familiar enough with the dialogue to know that he had just received his death warrant.

Chapter 13

MURDER IN MONTBLANC

ONCE AGAIN, DANNY WAS awakened by a ray of light streaming through the blackout curtains in his hotel room. It happened in spite of the fact that he had closed the shades tight the night before and held them in place by pushing the little dinette table against them. The light always got in at the very top, so Danny had stacked two chairs on top of the dinette table in such a way that the back of the top chair was pressing against the uppermost part of the curtains. But when sunrise came at 5:45 a.m. over the Atlantic Ocean, one little beam of light still found its way directly into Danny Pellegrino's half-shut eyelid.

"Shit," he said.

It was his customary greeting for each new day that God had made. But again, Danny had requested a 6:15 wake-up call, so it barely made any difference. He showered and dressed quickly. When he packed his suitcase, he took special care to bury his only copy of *Win By Losing* at the bottom of a pile of dirty underwear so there was no chance David might get a look at it.

At 7:00 a.m., he walked out of the hotel room with his suitcase in hand and stepped over the complimentary newspaper that was already waiting for him outside the door. Danny never read the newspaper, but something made him glance down at this one. Perhaps it was seeing the name of his own hometown on one of the front-page headlines:

"GANGLAND MURDERS IN A.C. AND MONT-BLANC"

Gangland murders in Montblanc? he thought, as he picked up the newspaper and walked back into the room. Now that's unusual.

He knew there were two or three Mafia bigwigs who lived in Montblanc, or at least they were rumored to be Mafia bigwigs. But the chances of them being killed in their own homes were next to nil. So Danny started to read the article with some interest. His interest soon turned to horror.

The article told the story of three gangland-style murders that had taken place late the previous evening. The bullet-riddled bodies of two small-time hoods named Ricky "Three Pigeons" Trepiccione and Carlo Montagna had been found washed up on the shore after an apparently botched attempt to dump them off Atlantic City's Steel Pier weighted down with concrete blocks. The blocks were gone, but the frayed ropes were still tied to their ankles. Ricky's death didn't have much impact on Danny; he never liked the guy anyway. But reading about the third murder was devastating.

A twenty-eight-year-old woman named Maria Falcone was killed in Montblanc in what looked like a drive-by shooting. But police were highly suspicious. First of all, drive-by shootings didn't occur in Montblanc, New Jersey. It was the first one on record. Secondly, this shooting was performed with a fully automatic weapon—a machine gun, in other words—which was also unusual. Third, one of the organized-crime experts in the local police force knew that Maria Falcone was the current girlfriend of Ricky Trepiccione. It was too much of a coincidence that she should be killed in a drive-by shooting in Montblanc at the same time her boyfriend was being fitted for a cement swimsuit in Atlantic City. So the police figured the bullets that hit Maria were intended for Ricky. One of the windows in Ms. Falcone's Camaro was broken and had been covered with a plastic trash bag and duct tape. When it turned out that Ricky was not sitting in the passenger seat, the assassins apparently realized their mistake and went looking for Ricky elsewhere.

The tears gushed out of Danny's eyes like a flash flood. No sound. No choking. No sobbing. Just a steady rain coming out of his eyes and landing on the newspaper until the article was covered with a big wet stain.

For the first time, the full force of his affection for Maria hit him. All that nonsense about not wanting to "ruin a perfectly good secretary" and not wanting to "mess with a mobster's girlfriend" suddenly seemed like stupid, cowardly excuses. If he'd told Maria how he really felt about her, she'd still be alive. Danny would be flying to Las Vegas with *her* this morning instead of flying there with that prick David Invidia.

Danny wiped his forearm across his eyes and looked up from the paper. He needed to think. Something was wrong with this story. "Oh my God, could this have anything to do with the craps system?" he wondered aloud. Is it possible that Ricky got his hands on the system and somehow got them both killed over it?

"No, no, no," he said over and over again, as if to convince himself that it couldn't be true. He was being too paranoid, he decided. There was nothing like the prospect of winning $100 million to make a man paranoid. No, it couldn't be. It couldn't possibly have anything to do with the system. He was being obscenely self-centered, he told himself. That asshole Ricky had gotten himself into some kind of trouble with the mob and poor Maria got caught in the crossfire. That's all.

Danny put the newspaper down on the bed, stood up, and started to pace around the room.

"What should I do? What should I do?" he whined.

Would it be better to tell David to go to hell and rush to the aid of Maria's parents? Or better to put the memory of Maria behind him and go about his business?

He wanted to go to Maria's funeral. He owed her that much. He really loved her, after all. He could admit that to himself now. But no amount of love would bring her back to life. And this thing with David Invidia was too pressing. He couldn't let David out of his sight for a minute or he might piece together the rest of the system and start winning big in Las Vegas. Or he might change his mind about tattling to his bosses.

Maria would understand—wouldn't she?—how important this was to him. Maria would know that he'd been looking for a score like this his whole life. The big hit that would enable him to get out of the business of defrauding little old ladies once and for all and start living life the way he should.

It was a *tour de force* of self-persuasion and self-delusion—all dedicated to the dubious proposition that money is more important than love.

He had to stick with the plan, Danny decided. He had to fly to Vegas with Invidia. He would send a huge spray of flowers to Maria's parents for the funeral. When he got back, many millions of dollars richer, he'd give her parents a huge "death benefit" out of his own pocket. Maybe a million bucks. It wouldn't bring her back, but it would ease the pain.

That's what he would do, he decided. So he threw the newspaper in the wastebasket and proceeded out the door, almost as if he had never looked at it in the first place.

On the second page of the paper, however, there was a smaller, apparently unrelated story about how security had been breached the night before at Atlantic City International Airport. A careful inspection of all airliners revealed no signs of sabotage. But given that the two men were seen fleeing the general-aviation area, the owners of private aircraft were strongly advised to inspect their planes carefully before flying today.

When Danny got down to the lobby, David Invidia was waiting for him as planned. Already nervous about flying, his face was a ghostly shade of white.

Chapter 14

MAYDAY!

ENTANGELI'S MEN WERE SMART enough to figure out which was Danny's airplane. The distinctive "V"-tail and the fact that it was the only Bonanza in the general aviation area that evening was like a flashing neon sign that said, "SABOTAGE ME!"

They were also smart enough to know that a box of sugar dumped into the gas tank would give the airplane a severe case of heartburn.

It was a simple matter for these guys to pick the lock on the gas cap. It was similar to a car lock and both men had plenty of experience with those.

What they didn't know is that an airplane usually has *two* gas tanks. One in the left wing and one in the right. These two tanks are completely separate and the pilot, in fact, must make a conscious decision to switch from one tank to the other during flight. Many apparent "fuel-exhaustion" accidents have occurred over the years when pilots simply forgot to flip the switch.

Danny thought it might calm Invidia's nerves if he gave him a little flying lesson. Nothing complex. He decided to show Invidia how to do a pre-flight inspection to help convince him how safe it was to fly in a small plane. Maybe later when they were in the air, he'd let him hold the yoke for a while. Danny had flown with nervous passengers many times before and he'd always found this an excellent strategy for easing their fears.

After showing him how to untie the airplane and remove the wood block holding the tire in place, Danny demonstrated the technique for draining fuel and checking it for impurities underneath the left wing. Then he gave David the little plastic cup and said, "Okay, now you check it under the other wing."

David was starting to enjoy this. He crawled under the right wing and unscrewed the tiny release valve, just as Danny had showed him. He let an ounce of fuel drip into the cup, then he shut off the valve. He held up the fuel to the sun. It was mostly clear, except for some crystalline sediment at the bottom, which he assumed was normal.

"Is it clear?" asked Danny.

"You bet," said Invidia enthusiastically.

Danny almost went to look at it himself, but then thought better of it. The more responsibility he gave David, the more interested he'd get in flying. And the more interested he got in flying, the less frightened he'd be by it.

After a normal take-off, Danny set up his navigation and settled in for a long flight. They would probably get to Illinois by the end of the day, spend the night in a motel, and get into the Rockies the following day. Las Vegas might require a third day of flying, but it all depended on what kind of winds they encountered aloft. So far, the weather for the trip looked favorable.

After establishing his route, Danny let Invidia play with the yoke for a few minutes. Using the intercom on their headsets, he explained that pushing the yoke forward meant the plane would go down and pulling it back would make the plane go up. He showed him how to coordinate the rudder with the yoke to perform a simple turn. Invidia seemed to be enjoying it. He had relaxed considerably.

Danny wisely refrained from doing his customary engine-out drills and stall recoveries. He knew it would scare David to death and, besides, he was in a big hurry today. But he did have one related habit that he didn't bother to change.

Danny was in the habit of letting one gas tank go completely dry before switching to the other one. Most pilots switched back and forth every half-hour; it was safer and it helped keep the wings level. The rule of thumb was for the pilot to look at the big hand on his wristwatch. If the big hand was on the left side of the dial, he should be drawing from the left tank. If it was on the right side of the dial, he should draw from the right.

But Danny loved to run completely out of gas in one tank so that he could do his engine-out drill with more than the usual amount of verisimilitude. He liked to hear the engine sputter and die. He liked going through the engine-out checklist and all the other emergency procedures. He loved to set up for an off-airport landing. Then when he was just about ready to land in a cow pasture, he'd switch to the other tank and the engine would come roaring back to life.

He wouldn't do that to David today. But he did have a mischievous thought that he might do *some* of it. Maybe he'd let the engine go out and pretend to be frightened by it—just to see the look on Invidia's face. This asshole was in the process of costing him $50 million after all, so a cruel joke wasn't really out of line. Danny decided to leave the fuel selector set on the left tank and make a decision about the practical joke later. It meant that the left wing would get progressively lighter, rolling the aircraft over to the right. But he was used to that. In fact, the extra challenge of dealing with a heavy wing helped keep him awake and mentally engaged on long flights.

Several hours later, Danny had almost forgotten about his practical joke when he heard the engine sputter. David was asleep. That's no fun, Danny thought. So he nudged Invidia's shoulder and gestured for him to put his headset on again.

"Did you hear that?"

"No, what?"

"Listen."

"Listen to what?"

"The engine, you idiot. There, listen. Don't you hear that?"

The engine was sputtering and coughing noticeably now, and Invidia sat so bolt upright in his seat that the seatbelt dug into his stomach.

"What do you make of that?" asked Danny casually.

"What do *I* make of it?" Invidia shouted. "You're the fucking pilot! What do *you* make of it? What the hell's happening, Danny?"

"It's highly unusual," said Danny, stroking his chin, as the engine began to enter what sounded like its death throes.

"DO SOMETHING, GODDAMN IT!" shouted Invidia.

"Well, let me see," said Danny pensively. "There was something in my flight training about this, but I can't quite remember . . . what was it?"

"Oh, Jesus Christ, we're going to die!" Invidia was sobbing now.

"Oh, I remember!" said Danny, realizing the joke had gone on long enough. "You're supposed to switch to the other gas tank! Would you flip that switch right there from "L" to "R" for me, David?"

"Which one? Which one? Oh, Jesus Christ. Oh Jesus, Mary, and Joseph. This one? THIS ONE?"

"Yup, that's the one. I think."

"From 'L' to 'R'?"

"If I recall my training correctly, yes, I believe that's the proper move."

Invidia flipped the switch from left to right, and the engine instantly roared back to life. The propeller started to turn again, and the nose of the airplane began to rise.

"Oh, sweet Mary, mother of God," said Invidia over the blessedly loud noise of the re-started engine.

"I always forget that damn switch," said Danny. "You can go back to sleep now."

"I'm not going to sleep for the rest of the trip."

"Oh, don't be afraid. I was just having some fun with you."

"You mean you planned that?"

"Well, not really. I actually did forget about the switch," said Danny. "But I guess I might've delayed flipping it for a minute or two."

"You sonofabitch! You asshole! I'd fucking kill you if I didn't need you to land this airplane."

"Oh relax, David. That's just a little aviation humor. I'm teaching you how to be a pilot. Believe me, I wish I had a nickel for every time my instructor cut the engine on me. You weren't even flying the plane when the engine went out, David. You don't know what scared is, pal."

It was in the middle of this little speech that Danny heard the engine misfire again. So subtly this time that only Danny's practiced ear heard it. Invidia didn't notice at all.

"Oh, yeah, that's a great way to get me relaxed, asshole," said David. But now he couldn't help himself from smiling.

Danny, however, was not smiling. He had heard the engine misfire again while Invidia was talking and now he had one ear tilted toward the engine to see if he would hear it a third time. But the third time was more of a sputter. The fourth time sounded more like a cough. And the fifth time, Invidia heard it.

"Don't do it again, you prick."

"Be quiet for a second."

"I'm not kidding you, Danny," said David without lifting his head from the little pillow. "It was funny the first time. But I don't want to ride all the way to Las Vegas with some kind of a practical-joking maniac."

"Shut up!" said Danny with some urgency.

Again, Invidia sat bolt upright and again, the seatbelt dug into his gut.

"What is it?"

"I don't know yet. I'm not kidding this time. This doesn't sound right. And I just switched the tanks, we should still have a full tank of avgas."

Danny switched the tanks back to the left, but there was nothing there. The engine stopped. Then he switched back to the right tank. The engine came back to life.

"Good," said Invidia. "You fixed it!"

Then it started sputtering again. This is worse than fuel exhaustion, Danny thought. It's a different kind of sound. He checked the gauges on his instrument panel that had to do with the engine. OIL PRESSURE: Normal. ENGINE

TEMPERATURE: Normal. FUEL: Left tank empty; right tank full.

While he was checking the instruments, the engine coughed one last time and died. All fell silent. Danny feathered the prop, pulled out his engine-failure checklist, and proceeded to do for real what he had practiced so many thousands of times in the past. He was so calm, he was almost serene.

Invidia was not.

"Mother of God, what are you doing? The airplane is falling and you're reading!"

It occurred to Danny as he perused the checklist that he'd never noticed before how religious David seemed to be.

"Don't worry, David, it's not falling, it's gliding. We're going to go through this checklist to see if we can start up the engine again. If we can't, we're going to set up for a nice soft landing on one of those pretty farms down there. Nobody's gonna get hurt."

"It's falling, it's falling!" Invidia said, and the nose of the airplane did indeed seem to be dipping noticeably downward. The silence in the aircraft without the engine was also unnerving, although Danny always found it peaceful.

"You've got to pull it up, Danny!" said Invidia. "You've got to pull it up!"

"Don't even think about it. That's pretty much the last thing you want to do in this situation, David. Just tighten your seatbelt and I'll take care of everything."

The seatbelt was cutting into Invidia's skin so badly now, it was starting to bleed. But he gave it a sharp tug anyway.

"PULL THE AIRPLANE UP, DANNY, FOR THE LOVE OF JESUS CHRIST IN HEAVEN!"

I haven't heard this much Jesus talk since my confirmation, thought Danny, as he spotted a perfect landing field a few miles south of the aircraft's current position. As he turned the airplane toward it, he knew it would be a smooth landing.

But Invidia had grown tired of begging Danny to pull the aircraft up and decided to put his flight lesson of several hours ago to practical use. He grabbed the yoke on his side of the cockpit and pulled it all the way back to his chest.

The nose of the aircraft lifted so high and so suddenly that the view out the cockpit windshield resembled the view from the space shuttle on blast-off. Danny was a little taken aback by it. At first he didn't realize what had happened.

Invidia, on the other hand, was quite pleased with himself. He'd taken matters into his own hands and saved them both from imminent death. Maybe he could get into this flying thing after all, he thought. He seemed to have a natural talent for it. He was feeling very much in control, until he sensed the aircraft begin to slip backwards in the air—which was a *very* strange sensation indeed. It wasn't often that you were sitting in an airplane flying backwards. Even Danny had never felt it before.

Danny grabbed Invidia's forearms and ripped his hands off the yoke. Suddenly he remembered that even though he was a by-the-book pilot, he'd forgotten to do something important. He'd forgotten to give Invidia the customary lecture about safety in the cockpit—the one that said a passenger should never touch the controls without permission.

Actually, it happened all the time. Passengers *in extremis* were forever trying to grab the controls. It was human nature. Some passengers were too scared to do it. But many others were too scared *not* to do it. The instinct for self-preservation was too strong to sit there and do nothing.

"Don't EVER do that again," said Danny, as the aircraft gradually righted itself with no control input from either Danny or David. But having righted itself, the aircraft resumed a rather severe nose-down dive toward the ground.

So Invidia pulled back on the yoke again. And now with the additional airspeed from the dive, the aircraft whipped sharply upwards like a rodeo bronco rearing on its hind legs.

Again, Danny tried to rip Invidia's hands off the yoke by his forearms. But this time, Invidia's fingers had frozen to the wheel. He had a blank stare in his eyes, and it was clear that his fingers would remain locked on that yoke, pulling it back as far as it would go, until the moment they crashed into the ground.

To prevent Danny from prying his hands off, Invidia rotated his hands away from Danny by turning the yoke all the way to the right. This caused the airplane to roll to the right on its longitudinal axis as it simultaneously slipped backwards in a severe stall.

It occurred to Danny as he wrestled with Invidia that of all the thousands of stalls he'd performed over the years, this was the best . . . er, the worst one he'd ever seen. Talk about "recovering from unusual attitudes!" This was a beauty! Invidia's continuing backward pressure on the yoke had actually caused the aircraft to do a little loop, leaving them suspended upside down for a moment, until the airplane resumed its nose-down dive in a fully-developed clockwise spin. Out of the corner of his eye, Danny could see the view outside the cockpit windshield:

The planet Earth was spinning around like a top.

You couldn't *plan* a better spin entry than this! thought Danny with enthusiasm. He couldn't wait to begin working his way out of it. But first he had to do something about Invidia. After one more unsuccessful attempt to pry David's fingers off the yoke, Danny turned around in the seat, tried to get as much leverage as he could, drew back his right hand, and punched David flush in the cheek. So hard that it shattered the jaw and broke several bones in the nose and around the eyesocket. Invidia went out like a light and slumped onto the yoke, pressing it forward against the control panel. The airplane reacted in a weird way to this input, but Danny was so spatially disoriented now that he didn't have a clear mental picture of the aircraft's position or attitude.

When Danny pulled Invidia's slumping body off the yoke and finally took a moment to look out the window, he noticed that the aircraft had leveled off perfectly.

That was the good news.

The bad news was that it was in a flat spin. In other words, it was rotating around its vertical axis like Dorothy's house in *The Wizard of Oz*. Or like a dog chasing its tail. It occurred to Danny, in a remarkably calm way, that probably only one out of every ten thousand pilots who ever entered a flat spin lived to talk about the experience.

But there *was* a technique for getting out of flat spins. Correction: There was a technique for *trying* to get out of flat spins that Danny had read about in a book on emergency flight operations he'd purchased from Amazon.com three years earlier. The book was called, *I LOVE YOU, MOMMY! Techniques for Unusual Aviation Emergencies*. The title was derived from the fact that the National Transportation and Safety Board (NTSB) had done a study of black-box recordings revealing that these were the most common last words of pilots who were about to have an argument with the ground. (They were followed by "SWEET JESUS CHRIST!" and "OH, SHIT" on the NTSB's hit parade.)

Danny had a distinct memory of buying *I LOVE YOU, MOMMY!* It was number 3,025,977 on Amazon's list of best-selling titles. He had a distinct memory of its dust jacket, where there was a rather dramatic photo of a Cessna 172 sticking out of the roof of a barn. And fortunately, Danny also had a distinct memory of the book's advice for attempting a recovery from a flat spin.

It was more than a memory, really. The relevant text appeared in Danny's head with the luminescent clarity of a vision of the Blessed Virgin Mary. He didn't remember it so much as he *read* it right in front of his eyes. Position the yoke like so. Apply the rudder like this. Trim the elevator like that. All he had to do was follow the instructions printed in his head. And sure enough, in a few moments the aircraft eased out of the spin like a green colt who suddenly realizes it's easier to give the rider what he wants than it is to keep on resisting.

When he recovered, Danny was at five hundred feet above ground level, positioned perfectly in front of the same landing site he had selected from the air three terrifying minutes earlier. He had just enough time to tune his radio dial to the emergency frequency and report "Mayday, Mayday, Mayday," followed by his exact coordinates from the Global Positioning System. And while his landing was not quite as smooth as it would've been at Teterboro, it was remarkably gentle when you consider that it took place in a field of young soybean plants.

The soybean sprouts tugged the aircraft to a stop without any need for applying the brakes, and Danny popped out of the aircraft to inspect the damage. His heart was pounding. He felt exhilarated and exquisitely alive. The fresh clean air, the scent of the vegetation around him, the warm sun on his face . . . all of these things struck him as he stepped out of the cockpit as if he were experiencing such sensations for the first time in his life.

To his amazement, the airplane was undamaged. In fact, if it had had a working engine, he could've flown right back out. Danny cracked open the cowling to look at the power plant. It looked normal. There was no oil spewed about. No broken rods. Whatever had happened must have been something internal, he concluded, something deeper than his own knowledge of piston engines would take him. He'd have to wait for help.

For one fleeting moment, he considered the possibility that the same people who had killed Maria and Ricky were now trying to kill him, too. But again, he wrote it off as being absurdly paranoid. Plus, there was no sign that anyone had tampered with the engine.

David was still unconscious in the front seat. Danny took out a handkerchief and gently patted David's cheek until he was certain the bleeding had stopped. David was in no danger, he concluded; he had just gotten himself cold-cocked.

Danny stepped out of the cockpit again and looked around. He was truly in the middle of nowhere. Was it Ohio or Indiana? He hadn't been paying attention to his GPS or the section map. He'd given the coordinates on his Mayday call, but they were just numbers. He made a silent resolution, not for the first time, to start paying more attention to his navigation skills and less to his obsessive practicing of safety procedures.

I guess I'll just have to sit here and wait for help, he thought, as he plunked himself comfortably back into the pilot's seat.

But the more he thought about it, the more he realized that help was not what he wanted. If someone had heard the Mayday—and it was virtually certain someone had—the ambulances and fire engines would be showing up within an hour. The FAA and NTSB would be on the scene within two hours. He could cancel the Mayday—simply get back on the radio and tell the world that he had pulled off a miraculous recovery—but that wouldn't be fair to David. He knew David wasn't in serious danger, but he could use some medical help. It wouldn't be nice to make a man walk out of the woods with a broken jaw.

On the other hand, if the NTSB and the FAA showed up, he'd have a lot of splainin' to do. He hadn't broken any laws. It was a genuine emergency. But you didn't know the meaning of red tape until you've landed a fixed-wing aircraft someplace other than an airport. He would be cleaning up this mess for the next week, and he didn't have a week to spare.

Invidia might be so pissed that he'd tell his bosses about the craps system just out of spite. Or he might take off for Las Vegas on his own. The more Danny thought about it, the more he realized that he had to get to Las Vegas and get there fast. He had to make his big score in Vegas before Invidia realized which end was up. The idea of sharing the money was no longer operational. Now it was every man for himself, and Invidia's current lack of consciousness would give Danny a nice head start.

So Danny pulled his briefcase out of the baggage compartment, where he had stashed the $250,000 he had recently won at the Villagio. He opened his suitcase and pulled out a few pairs of clean underwear and socks, a shirt or two, and stuffed them into the briefcase with the money.

"Goodbye, old chum," he said to David, patting him once on the hand and gently rearranging his head so that any remaining blood would drain out of his mouth and nose normally. "The ambulance should get here in less than an hour."

David moaned, but he didn't wake up.

"And goodbye to you, sweetheart," he said, as he kissed the Bonanza on the fuselage near the numbers N345J. "You did good up there." Then he headed off in the direction where he thought he'd seen a paved road from the air.

The ambulances and the fire engines were the first to arrive on the site, as Danny had predicted, about an hour after he left. The FAA and NTSB representatives exceeded Danny's predictions, arriving only a few minutes later. By then Invidia had regained consciousness and he was walking around the airplane in a circle saying Hail Mary's.

"Are you the pilot, sir?"

" . . . full of grace, the Lord is with thee . . ."

"Is this your airplane, sir?"

" . . . art thou among women and blessed is the fruit of thy womb, Jesus . . ."

"Can we ask you to sit down, sir, so we can take a look at your face? It looks like you may have broken your nose on the landing."

" . . . pray for us sinners now and in the hour of our death, amen."

Only the B.V.M. herself knew how painful it must've been for David to say this prayer with a broken jaw. Eventually, the rescue workers got a hold of him and, when he wasn't looking, injected a mild tranquilizer into his arm. When he regained his composure, Invidia explained that he was not the pilot. The pilot was a man by the name of Danny Pellegrino who had disappeared. Probably gone to heaven. And that he, David Invidia, was grateful to God for sparing his own life.

"Enough casinos and whales," he said. "No more sushi in the bathtub. No more four o'clock dinners and stupid neck-ties. I'm going to get out of this dirty business and serve the Lord."

"That sounds like a good idea, sir," said the emergency medical technician, as he held up a vial, tapped it with the needle, and drew out a second, much larger dose of the tranquilizer.

Danny had gotten to the road in less than fifteen min-utes, but it took him another forty-five minutes to thumb a ride. So he stepped into the dusty black pickup truck at roughly the same time David was getting his first injection. He'd heard the ambulances and fire engines approaching the landing site from a different direction and he felt relieved to know David was getting help.

"Where you headed, mister?" asked the grizzled old farmer driving the truck.

"Well, my friend, that depends. Where's the nearest air-port? And I mean an airport big enough where I can get a jetliner to Las Vegas."

"Well, I reckon that would be Indianapolis, and I ain't going all the way to Indianapolis today. But I can take you most of the way."

"Take me as far as you can, and I'd be mighty obliged."

Mighty obliged? It was Danny's way of mirroring the culture of the people around him. By the end of this car ride, he'd probably be spitting tobacco and talking about how poor the soybean crop looked this year. But only twenty miles later, Danny saw a sign that changed his plans.

It was a billboard for an Indian casino located in a town called Brandton, Indiana. It was called the Broken Arrow Casino and the billboard promised a great time for the whole family.

"You ever been to the Broken Arrow Casino?" asked Danny.

"Oh, hell yes. Many times. My wife's damn near addicted to them video poker machines. I reckon we go there just about every weekend. And she'd go there every night if I let her. But we ain't got that kind of money to throw out the window."

"Tell me about it," said Danny knowingly. "What else they got there 'sides video poker?"

"Well, bingo's real big there. They got blackjack. Roulette."

Danny knew that craps was comparatively rare at Indian casinos, but he thought he'd take a shot anyway.

"They have that game with the dice? What is it? Craps?"

"Yes, sir, they do. I almost forgot about that one, because I never played it. Too complicated for me. I don't mind losing money, but I wanna know *why* I'm losing it!" The old man laughed so hard at his own joke that he had to roll down the window and let a big wad of brown phlegm fly out.

"Tell you what, my friend. Where's Brandton, about ten miles from here?"

"Yup."

"Why don't you just leave me off at the Broken Arrow Casino and I can get my own transportation to the airport from there. You've been right kindly to me, and I don't want to take advantage of your hospitality anymore."

Right kindly?

"Well, sir, if that's what you want, I'd be happy to drop you off there. It's just up this road apiece. I'll only do it on one condition, though."

"What's that?" asked Danny.

"If you see my wife playing them video poker machines, you tell her to get her fat ass back home!"

They both laughed and rolled down their windows to spit.

This seemed like a decent plan to Danny. It was a virtual certainty that the Broken Arrow had some kind of shuttle service between the casino and Indianapolis. He'd play some craps while he waited for the bus. Besides, hitting the Indian casinos in the Midwest was part of the overall plan, anyway. He'd take this joint for $250,000 or so, then he'd head to the airport with a nice half-million dollar bankroll for Las Vegas.

The man in the pick-up left Danny off right in front of a big sign at the end of Broken Arrow's entrance road. It read, **"How! You'll Win Heap Big Wampum at Broken Arrow!"**

"They don't know the half of it," Danny mumbled to himself.

WIN BY LOSING
SECTION TWO: MASTERY

"God does not shoot dice with the universe."
— *Albert Einstein*

How could a can of mixed nuts, a physics professor, an Otis elevator, and a self-winding wristwatch have anything to do with you making money in a casino? What if I told you that all of these things were proof that you could take two negative-expectation casino games and *combine* them in such a way that they produced a winning outcome?

Interested? Bear with me. The story you're about to hear may be the most important thing you've ever read about casino gambling.

But before I tell you that story, let me say a word about a very important subject: mastery. What you are about to read is a description of a craps system. It is no better or worse than any other craps system in the world. Which is to say that it wins sometimes and it loses sometimes. All you need to get rich playing this system is for it to win slightly more often than it loses. And how well you succeed at that will depend to a large extent on how thoroughly you master the system and the entire game of craps.

We live in a society nowadays where very little emphasis is placed on the concept of mastery. People want to get rich quick. Lose weight fast. Learn how to play golf overnight. And there is never any shortage of books, systems, programs, formulas, and self-help courses designed to help you do just that.

But it can't be done. The road to mastery, mastery of *anything* from playing chess to flying an airplane, is a long and arduous one. It is a road with many hills and valleys. Many twists and turns. Perhaps most frustrating of all, it is a road with many plateaus—long stretches of featureless terrain where it seems like you're going nowhere fast.

The road to mastery is littered with many people who have simply given up because the journey was too long, too difficult, too unrewarding. But the master stays on that road. Not because he is focused on getting to his destination, but because he finds satisfaction and fulfillment in the road itself. He likes the hills and the valleys. He enjoys the hard work that is sometimes required of him, and he learns from the many disappointments he suffers along the way. Most of all, he likes those long, empty stretches when he doesn't seem to be making any progress. Why? Because they are peaceful.

The master understands that he may never become the best chess player in the world or the best golfer in the world. And it bothers him not in the least. Because the joy of mastery is not in the attainment of your goal, but in the pursuit of it. So please keep that in mind as I tell you the strange story of the Spanish physics professor who discovered how to take two losing games and turn them into a single winning one.

It all began in a coffee shop in Madrid in 1997 when two prominent scientists met to discuss an interesting wrinkle in the relatively new scientific field of "game theory." Their names are Juan M. R. Parrondo, a physicist at the Universidad Complutense de Madrid in Spain, and Derek Abbott, a biological engineer from the University of Adelaide in Australia.

The rather esoteric study of game theory had risen to prominence in recent years due to its apparent relevance to some of the more ticklish problems in physics, mathematics, economics, sociology, and evolutionary biology. In physics, for example, game theory is used to help explain the random and chaotic movement of subatomic particles in the specialized field of nuclear physics known as "quantum mechanics." This was the same field that once inspired a skeptical and frustrated Albert Einstein to remark famously, "God does not shoot dice with the universe!"

The two scientists had met to discuss Parrondo's belief that two losing games could somehow be combined into a winning outcome. Although Parrondo had done most of the pioneering theoretical work in this area (the theory, after all, is named "Parrondo's Paradox"), it seems likely that Abbott and his partner Gregory Harmer were the ones who came up with a unique way of testing Parrondo's theory in real life.

Although the theory involves many complicated mathematical formulas, the best way for a layman to understand it is to visualize the image of two slopes and a pair of ball bearings. The first slope is smooth and flat. The second one has a jagged, saw-toothed surface. If you took a ball bearing to the top of each slope, the ball would slide down the first slope quickly. But on the second slope, it would bounce and jiggle down until it was "caught" in one of the notches.

Slope 1   **Slope 2**

The point of this game, however, is not to drop the balls from above. The point is to *flick* the balls upward from below.

Try flicking the ball up the first slope with your thumb and forefinger and it would rise a little, then slide right back down. Do the same with the second slope and it would scarcely go up at all, because the saw teeth would act as a barrier. Both games, in other words, are "losers" in the sense that it's impossible to get either ball to the top and keep it there. But if you could somehow *alternate* between the two slopes, "flashing" from one slope to the next, you might be able to use the notches of the second slope to slowly advance the ball uphill until it got to the top.

It's like a ratchet, a device that allows movement in one direction but not the other. Any child who has ever opened a can of mixed nuts is familiar with how a ratchet works. The heavy brazil nuts often settle to the bottom during shipping. But you can make the brazil nuts rise to the top simply by shaking the can. The smaller nuts, in effect, prevent the brazil nuts from moving downward and gradually push them toward the top.

Have you ever wondered why virtually every elevator in this country has the name "Otis" on it? Elisha Graves Otis did not invent the elevator, but he invented the ratchet that makes elevators safe and practical. To demonstrate his invention to a skeptical and fearful public, Otis used to stand on an open elevator platform and deliberately cut the cable with an ax. He didn't fall because his safety ratchet prevented downward movement.

Self-winding wristwatches are another example of how ratchets are used in everyday life. As you randomly move your hand and wrist throughout the day, any movement that contributes to winding the watch is utilized, while the movements that might otherwise contribute to *unwinding* it are ignored.

To test their theory about turning two losing games into a winner, Parrondo and Abbott created an experiment involving two coin-tossing games. In the first game (we'll call it Game A), a single coin is tossed and the player always bets on tails. But the coin has been slightly weighted so that heads will come up more often than tails. In other words, this game—like every game in the casino!—is designed to lose.

The second game (Game B) is more complicated. It involves tossing *two* coins. Again, the player always bets on tails. The first coin is slightly weighted to come up heads more often (another loser). But the second coin is slightly weighted to come up more often on tails—a winner. What gives Game B its overall negative expectation is the fact that you must toss the losing coin more often than the winning one.

Can you see how these games resemble the slopes I mentioned earlier? Game A is a smooth downward slope. But Game B is a downward slope that has saw-teeth or ratchets in it created by the one coin that is designed to win.

Both games have a built-in negative expectation, precisely like every game in the casino from keno to roulette. When you play each game separately for a hundred tosses each, you will steadily lose your bankroll until eventually you're left with nothing. But Parrondo and Abbott believed that if you *alternated* between the two games, playing two hands of Game A followed by two hands of Game B, your bankroll would steadily increase. Why?

Because of the ratchet effect created by the winning coin in Game B. Any winnings that come along in Game A are "trapped" by the switch to Game B before subsequent repetitions of the first game can gradually erode your capital. In other words, your money slowly moves uphill as it is trapped by the ratchets in Game B.

When Parrondo and Abbott tested their theory using real coins and real money, sure enough, it worked out exactly as they predicted. By alternating between the two losing games, their bankroll steadily increased! Interestingly, it worked whether they systematically alternated between the two games (i.e., two hands of one followed by two hands of the other) or *randomly* alternated between them. No matter how they played the two losing games, they kept making money!

Okay, by now I'm sure you think I'm crazy or that I'm making all this up, or both. So I invite you to take a little break here to go on the Internet and search under "Parrondo's Paradox," "Juan Parrondo," or "Brownian Ratchets," and I assume you'll find scads of references. The theory has been written up in such publications as *the New York Times, Nature, Science News,* and many other scientific and general-interest magazines in this country and around the world. These are real people. This is a real theory. And it really works.

Which leads us to the $64,000 question: can it be applied to craps?

Derek Abbott says no. He said in an interview that it cannot be applied to casino games, and his comment has been dutifully repeated by the *New York Times* and many other publications. But I'm not sure that anyone, including Abbott himself, has given the question a lot of thought.

The main problem, of course, is finding a casino game that will supply the winning component of Game B, since every game in the casino (and, in fact, every *bet* in the casino) carries a negative expectation. As a result, it's hard to assemble a ratchet of casino games that precisely resembles the Parrondo model.

But are we going to let that stop us from trying?

Hell no!

My first thought was simply to alternate between betting the pass line and the don't-pass line. A series of two bets on the front line followed by a series of two bets on the back line. But this doesn't really cut it, because in casino craps, both pass betting and don't-pass betting have a negative expectation.

Then I had an idea: what if you could somehow eliminate the seven and eleven (and possibly the twelve as well) from the comeout roll when playing the don't-pass line? If you could do that, betting the don't would become an *extremely* positive game. The odds of seeing the seven before you see any given point number repeat are very much in your favor.

Is there a single hedge bet that covers the seven, eleven, and twelve? Yes! It's called the whirl bet. (Some players call it the "world" bet.) It is an exotic proposition bet with odds so stacked against the player that most books on craps don't even bother to mention it.

A whirl bet requires five units and it covers the seven, eleven, two, three, and twelve. Like any multiple proposition bet, if you win one, you lose the others. So a $5 whirl bet would pay $26 on the two and twelve and $11 on the eleven and three, plus you get your one-dollar winning wager back. The seven basically results in a push. You get paid four-to-one on the seven, but you lose the other four bets.

So to construct a wagering system in craps that resembles Parrondo's coin-tossing games, we would bet two series on the pass line (similar to Parrondo's Game A) and we would bet two series on don't-pass line, *hedged* by a whirl bet on the comeout roll. The latter would resemble Parrondo's Game B in the sense that the whirl bet provides the "losing" coin and the don't-pass line would comprise the "winning" coin.

How does the don't-pass line become a winner? It becomes a winner if you don't have to worry about the seven, eleven, or twelve!

So on the first two-bet series, we would put a $25 chip on the pass line. What happens next depends on the outcome of the first two bets:

OUTCOME 1: Lose both bets, maintain $25 bet on the second series

OUTCOME 2: Win one, lose one, maintain $25 bet on the second series

OUTCOME 3: Win both bets, *press* the bet to $50 on the second series

On the second two-bet series, we would move to the don't-pass line and place a hedge bet on the whirl for the comeout. If we're at a $25 level, we'd place $20 on the don't-pass and $5 on the whirl. If we are betting at a $50 level, we would put $40 on the line and $10 on the whirl. Of course, we will lose the vast majority of our whirl bets, but that shouldn't bother us. Our betting strategy from here on out depends only on the outcome of our don't-pass bets:

OUTCOME 1: Lose both bets, drop down to $25 on the next series

OUTCOME 2: Win one, lose one, drop down to $25 bet on the next series

OUTCOME 3: Win both, pocket $80+ profit, and return to $25 bet on the next series (That's our ratchet!)

Never take your winnings from the don't-pass series and apply them to the pass-line series, because there's no ratchet on that side to trap them. You want to pocket those winnings, not parlay them. The idea is to capture your occasional pass-line winnings when you move to the positive expectation of the don't-pass line. Remember, the pass-line is the slippery slope and the don't-pass line with the whirl bet is the saw-toothed slope.

This is not an ideal adaptation of the Parrondo model. The hedge bets don't quite make up for the fact that the don't-pass line is not a positive-expectation game like the winning coin in Parrondo's Game B. But does my adaptation of Parrondo's Paradox work in actual casino play?

Well, yes and no. If the dice just happen to fall your way—i.e., if they're passing when you're on the pass line and sevening-out when you're on the don't—you'll make out like a bandit. Obviously.

But if the dice are slapping you in the face all day—if

they're passing when you're betting wrong and failing to pass when you're betting right—you will, in fact, lose money with this system.

But it's those "choppy" in-between times when Parrondo's Paradox seems to work exactly the way it's supposed to. Which is good news because, after all, the most common temperature of any craps table is neither red-hot nor ice-cold, but somewhere in between. This is when the ratchet effect kicks in. And instead of breaking even—as you would expect to do in this situation—you will make a nice profit as your money gradually ratchets upwards. So, theoretically, you could win two out of three sessions.

At the very least, you'll never look at a can of mixed nuts in the same way again!

Book Two
PURGATORIO

In which our hero manages to wriggle out of the unholy
mess that sin has caused in his life

Chapter 15

A FOOL'S PAIR OF DICE

DANNY HAD READ ABOUT Indian casinos in his gambling magazines for years, but this brief stop at the Broken Arrow Hotel & Casino would be his first visit to one.

As he walked down the manicured entrance road flanked by pine trees, he saw two enormous buildings in front of him. He came to a fork in the road and for a moment he was confused. Are there two casinos? he wondered. But then he saw the little signs: One said "Casino," and the other said "Residence." The residence must be the hotel, he figured. Although why anyone would want to build the hotel so far way from the casino was a mystery. He followed the road to the casino.

Once inside, Danny paused to admire the building's magnificent lobby. A soaring cathedral ceiling constructed of knotty pine overlooked a waterfall in the center of the main room. The waterfall splashed into a pool of sparkling blue water, from which several streams flowed in various directions. A cocktail bar was built underneath the waterfall and the cocktail tables were located streamside. The waitresses serving these tables wore a two-piece "squaw" outfit that consisted of a suede bikini top with beaded appliqué and a beaded belt around the waist from which two plain squares of suede leather fell, one in the back and one in the front. Each girl had a single eagle feather sticking out of her hair. But the effect was a little dissonant, as every waitress Danny saw was blonde and blue-eyed.

Speaking of blondes, when Danny was able to pull his eyes away from the waitresses, he began to admire an enormous full-length portrait of a man in full Indian regalia hanging prominently on one wall. This man, too, had blond hair and blue eyes. A gold plaque nearby said simply, "Our Beloved Chief."

When a cigarette girl walked by dressed in the same outfit as the cocktail waitresses, Danny caught her eye in a friendly way and started up a conversation.

"Who's this guy?" he asked, pointing at the painting.

"That's our chief!" said the girl proudly.

"What's his name?"

"Chief Anderson."

"Anderson, eh? Doesn't sound too Indian. What's his first name, Running Water? Flying Saucer?"

"Bill," she answered matter-of-factly.

"He doesn't look very Indian to me."

"He's one-thirty-second pure-blooded Poctaw," she said, "Same as me!"

If anything, this girl was even blonder and more blue-eyed than the chief. She looked like a Swedish movie star.

"Is he a good chief?"

"You better believe it! He gave me this!" She held out the back of her hand with her fingers curved slightly upwards to show off a diamond the size of a grape.

"Are you engaged to him?" Danny asked with a trace of disappointment in his voice that he didn't bother to disguise.

"Oh, no," she giggled. "He gave them to all the waitresses. I wouldn't mind being engaged to him, though. Did you see his house?"

"No."

"You must've seen it. That big house on the way in. You couldn't miss it."

"That was a house? I thought it was the hotel."

"No, the hotel rooms are in this building. That's Chief Anderson's house. It's the largest private home in the country next to Aaron Spelling's," she said proudly.

"What did the chief do before he got into the casino business?" Danny asked. "Sell beads and blankets?"

"No, he was a lawyer."

Danny felt he had taken up enough of this girl's time. She was supposed to be working, after all. So he decided to legitimize the conversation by purchasing a pack of Winstons.

"How much?" he asked.

"Dollar fifty."

"Fifty dollars?"

"No, silly! One dollar and fifty cents."

Danny hadn't paid $1.50 for a pack of cigarettes since 1979.

"Why so low?"

"We don't pay any taxes on the reservation. You can buy a carton in the store over there for $15. You oughta do that before you go."

Danny tipped her two dollars and said, "Thanks, hon, nice talking with you."

"How!" she said, raising her right hand. "Have a lucky day!" Then she gave him a sexy wink and walked away.

Danny couldn't help turning to watch the little leather patch dangling from her waist wiggle from side to side as she tip-toed down the stairs toward the bar.

Danny carried his briefcase into the casino, which looked pretty much like every other casino in the world, except there were fewer table games and more slot machines. There were just two craps tables, only one of which was operational on this late Thursday afternoon.

Danny had always wanted to walk into a casino and dump a briefcase full of large bills onto a craps table. He'd seen a guy do it once at Binion's Horseshoe in downtown Las Vegas, and it was one of the most impressive sights he'd ever witnessed.

Danny only had about one-fourth as much money with him today. But in a backwoods casino like this, he figured that would still cause quite a stir. So he walked up to the craps table, set his briefcase on the rail, clicked open the locks, told the dealer that he wanted "Change only, no action," and proceeded to dump the entire contents of the briefcase onto the table.

Two hundred and fifty thousand dollars, mostly in loose hundred-dollar bills, spilled out onto the green felt. So did five pairs of Jockey underpants, two pairs of rolled-up black socks, and a blue shirt.

"We'll need to count the money, sir," said the dealer dryly, "but we'll bet six briefs to your five that the dice don't pass."

"Just checking to see if you guys were paying attention," said Danny, trying to make the best of a bad situation as he scrambled to pick up the clothing and stuff it back into the briefcase.

As it happened, the dealers and pit managers were impressed with all the cash. But they were too busy giggling about the underpants to say anything. It was more money than anyone had ever brought to the Broken Arrow in its five-year history and it took them nearly an hour to count it. But in the meantime, they gave Danny $50,000 in chips to get started.

The scent of that much money in the air wafted through the casino, drawing various farmers and housewives off their slot-machine stools to the craps table like blood attracting sharks from distant waters. Unlike sharks, however, these folks just wanted to watch. To see $50,000 of chips on a dice table was an everyday occurrence in Las Vegas. But it was an extremely rare and wondrous sight at the Broken Arrow.

No point in pussyfooting around, thought Danny, and he decided to start off with a large bet. He put $5,000 on the pass line. There was a murmur of surprise from the little crowd behind him.

"Two craps, line away, pay the don'ts, the dice are out," said the stickman, as the dealer standing opposite him scooped up Danny's $5,000 in chips.

No problem, thought Danny, we'll just alternate to the don't-pass line.

"Seven, winner seven, front-line winner. Pay the line, take the don'ts. The dice are out."

Another $5,000 disappeared.

"Look, it don't even bother him," said a fat lady standing behind Danny in a voice that seemed to indicate she believed all high rollers were deaf.

It was bothering him a little bit.

Oh, I forgot the hedge bets, thought Danny, and he tossed the stickman two purple chips, saying, "Thousand dollar yo."

The stickman glanced at the boxman, who nodded slightly, and he said, "Thousand dollar yo it is." Meanwhile, Danny placed another $10,000 on the pass line.

"Three craps, ace deuce, line away, pay the don'ts. Your eleven is down, sir, back up?" said the dealer helpfully.

"I know it's down," Danny snapped. "Here, put $5,000 on the yo this time." It was a big yo bet, thought Danny, but he was just doing what *Win By Losing* called for. Or was he? He put another $10,000 on the don't-pass line this time. Again the stickman glanced at the boxman to secure permission for such a large proposition bet, but permission for such things was always granted willingly when the casino was winning.

"Seven winner seven, front-line winner, pay the line, take the don'ts. Sorry, sir," said the stickman as he pushed Danny's $5,000 yo bet toward the boxman and his $10,000 don't-pass bet toward the other dealer.

Now Danny was about $45,000 down and running out of chips, but the pit managers had finished counting his cash and authorized the boxman to pass him another $200,000.

"Better luck, sir," he said as he pushed the stack toward Danny.

I'm doing something wrong, thought Danny, as he wiped some sweat off his forehead. What is it? I'm alternating pass and don't-pass. I'm hedging with yo and whirl bets. What am I forgetting? I know what I'll do! I'll check the booklet.

He pulled the briefcase up to the railing again and snapped the locks. The dealers and boxman waited expectantly to see what would come out of the briefcase next. The stickman, in particular, had about five wisecracks in mind— most of them based on some variation of the idea that the casino wouldn't accept bras or panties as legal tender. But he wisely decided to say nothing. He had learned the hard way that you joked with losing gamblers at your own peril.

Danny opened the case and looked at the Jockeys and socks inside. But now he remembered that the booklet was not in the briefcase. It had never been in the briefcase. It was in his suitcase back in the airplane. Which, at the moment, was sitting in a soybean field somewhere in eastern Indiana. Danny wondered for a moment how many soybean fields there were in Indiana.

"You got any goddamned cocktail waitresses in this teepee, chief," he snapped at the boxman.

"Certainly, sir," said the boxman, who didn't take any offense at the Indian slurs. Why should he? He was Yugoslavian. "I'll call her."

And he proceeded to snap what looked like a castanet between his fingers. The cocktail waitresses in this casino, as they are in many casinos, had been trained using the same "clicker" technique that was currently popular for training dogs. One of the half-naked squaws was at Danny's side in an instant.

"What can I get for you, sir?"

"Double martini on the rocks with an olive, extra dry."

"I'll bring you one of our famous Broken Arrow martinis," she said.

"Whatever. Just don't take too long."

By the time the drink arrived five minutes later, Danny had lost another $40,000. He tossed the waitress a chip. He thought it was a one-dollar chip. It was a $1,000 chip.

"Thank you, sir!" she said and wiggled her little butt away. She made a mental note to ask him if he wanted another drink in two or three minutes.

Danny desperately needed to calm down. He'd never lost money at such a sickening rate before. He took a huge gulp of the martini and immediately spat it out all over the table. In fact, he choked on the drink so violently that he managed to spill the contents of the entire glass on the table.

The dealers stared at the wet stain, the ice cubes, and the olives on the green felt and wondered what this guy would do next.

"What *is* that?" said Danny, still coughing and spitting.

"A Broken Arrow martini," said the boxman.

"It tastes like a mixture of Sprite and 7-up with olives in it."

"Well, you've got some mighty smart taste buds, sir, because I think that's exactly how they make it."

"I ordered a fucking martini!"

There was an awkward moment of silence. The "F" word hadn't been said in the Broken Arrow by even the angriest gamblers in quite some time. It wasn't appreciated here.

"A *fucking* martini is made with *fucking* gin and *fucking* vermouth," Danny continued in a didactic tone.

"Now, sir, there's really no need for profanity," said a female pit manager who had decided to break into the conversation before it got out of hand. "We don't serve alcohol at the Broken Arrow. That's our policy. So our bartender makes what we call 'facsimile cocktails' out of soft drinks. You should've asked for a Manhattan. I swear you can't tell the difference between ours and the real thing."

"You don't serve alcohol here?" Danny asked incredulously.

"No, sir, we do not. Our policy is to combat the unfortunate stereotypes often leveled against people of Native

American descent with regard to their consumption of alcohol and other mind-altering drugs." She sounded like she was repeating from something she'd memorized. In fact, she was.

"You're telling me that because you injuns can't hold your firewater or stop sniffing glue, I can't get a freakin' martini in this dump?"

"Well, that's not the way we'd put it, sir, but that's the gist of it, yes."

"Okay, okay," said Danny as he put $30,000 on the pass line, which lost on the next roll of the dice. What was he doing wrong? He needed to look at that booklet. At the very least, he needed some sleep. But the more he lost, the more frustrated and angry he got. So he pressed his bets and chased his losses. Five hours later, it was nine o'clock and dark outside—far too late to try to find the airplane—and Danny had lost almost all of his $250,000. All but $38.

He looked at the female pit manager, who was regarding him with some pity, and he said, "I need a room."

"Wouldn't you really rather go home?" she asked in a motherly tone.

In thirty years of gambling in casinos, Danny had never heard a casino employee suggest to a gambler—especially one who was losing!—that he should go home.

"*What?* No, I don't want to go home. I need a room. My home is in New Jersey."

"Oh, I see. Well, welcome to Hoosier country!" she said with a big smile. "Yes, we have twenty-five fine guest rooms in this building."

Twenty-five rooms, thought Danny, what is this, a Motel 6? The MGM Grand in Las Vegas, by contrast, had five thousand rooms.

"Well, write me up for one, wouldya honey? I'm so tired I could spit." At the words "I could spit," the dealer closest to Danny flinched slightly.

"Write you up for one? No, I can't do that here. You have to go to the registration desk."

"I can't go to the registration desk unless you give me some paper here," said Danny with growing frustration.

"You don't need any paper, sir, you can walk right up to the desk. Just give them your credit card. They'll take very good care of you there."

The two of them were eyeing each other warily, and talking to each other slowly, as if they each had encountered the stupidest person in the world. The misunderstanding was based on the fact that Danny expected a comp, but the pit manager had no idea what a comp was. Well, she'd heard that such things existed in Las Vegas, but certainly not at the Broken Arrow.

Danny broke the stalemate.

"Sweetheart, I'm not amused. I just lost $250,000 here. If I'd lost that much money at the Trump Plaza I'd be able to sleep in Donald Trump's top bunk and fuck his wife in the morning. Now you write me a comp this minute, or I'm going to ask to see your supervisor."

"Oh, a complimentary!" The poor woman didn't know quite how to react. She was pleased that she had finally figured out what Danny was talking about, but horrified by the notion of him raping Donald Trump's wife.

"No, sir, we don't have complimentaries here. But the rooms only cost $29.95 a night. And they are luxury rooms. They were given five stars by the Citgo Travel Guide," she added proudly.

"I don't freakin' believe it," Danny muttered as he picked

up his briefcase and ambled off in the direction of the registration desk.

Was there any point in trying to find that airplane tonight? Was it even possible? Even in the daylight? He knew he'd driven about twenty miles with the farmer in the pickup truck. But he didn't have a clear picture in his mind of where he was on the road when the guy picked him up. Damn, he thought, there's no guarantee those bags are still in the plane anyway. David would've insisted on taking his own suitcase. The EMTs probably would've taken the other suitcase along, too. It's probably a fifty-fifty proposition as to whether that suitcase is still there or not, Danny figured.

But even if it *was* there, what good would it do him? He had no money to use for gambling! Thirty-eight dollars wouldn't be enough. If the dice turned cold for even a moment, he'd lose that much money in a heartbeat. If he could get to Las Vegas or back to Atlantic City, he could play on markers. But these hicks in Indiana wouldn't know what a marker was if you slapped them in the face with it. They didn't know what a comp was, for chrissakes!

Danny threw his MasterCard down on the registration desk and said, "Need a room for tonight."

"Yes, sir, we do have a vacancy tonight. Let me get you checked in." She took Danny's card and Danny studied her. She was dressed in a dark blue business suit, but she still had a lone Eagle feather stuck in her hair.

"Sir, this is not going through properly. Is there another card you could give me?"

He dropped her his Visa card. She put that in the machine, but again it failed to respond. Then he remembered. He had maxed out both of his credit cards just prior to going to Atlantic City for the first time. He was so financially strapped after putting the *Win By Losing* promotion in the mail that he had to tap one card to buy a high-definition television and another card to . . . well, he'd forgotten what he'd bought with that one. But there was no doubt, they were both maxed out. Under normal circumstances he would've noticed this on his second trip to Atlantic City, but David had given him full RFB so he didn't have to reach into his wallet for anything.

"Forget it," he said, "I'll just pay in cash. How much is it?"

"A standard luxury room is $29.95. It's a good deal. The rooms were given five stars by the Citgo Travel Guide."

"So I've heard," said Danny. When he opened his wallet to pull out the cash, he realized he was now down to his last five dollars.

The travel connoisseurs of Citgo notwithstanding, Danny was not impressed with the room. It was about the same quality you'd expect from a budget motel off the highway. But it didn't matter. He was dead tired. He fell on the bed and went to sleep. He didn't bother to undress, didn't even bother to build his black-out contraption with the curtains.

He awoke the next morning with the sunlight streaming into his eyes, but it didn't upset him this morning, because the light seemed to put an idea in his head. It was simplicity itself. It was a way to get back to Montblanc that wouldn't cost him a penny. And if he got back to Montblanc, he would get back to all those copies of *Win By Losing*. He'd get back to his checkbooks, and his banker, and his Porsche—not to mention the $20,000 in one-dollar bills sitting on his desk!—and he'd be able to whip his financial life back into shape . . . at least long enough to get himself to Las Vegas. Then once he got to Vegas with the booklet, he'd never have money problems again. All he had to do now was steal an airplane.

After showering and changing into a fresh pair of underwear, Danny made himself look as presentable as possible and went down to the hotel gift shop. He walked directly to the newsstand and found exactly what he needed.

It was a copy of *Flying* magazine. He was about to purchase the magazine when he remembered how little cash he had remaining. The cover price was $4.95. It would've left him with one nickel to his name.

But he didn't really need to buy it. Instead, he stood at the newsstand and pretended to peruse the magazine. He was looking for one particular advertisement, an advertisement sponsored by the Cessna company that offered a free flight lesson at participating airports around the country.

He found it. The free coupon, called a "bind-in" card in the direct marketing industry, could be removed from the magazine by tearing at the perforation. The loose cards that fall into your soup are called "blow-in" cards. Danny hated blow-in cards. Everyone did. But this was one occasion when he would've preferred a blow-in to a bind-in. It would've been easier to steal.

Danny let out a loud sneeze, and at the same time he ripped the perforation.

"God bless you," said the sales clerk, a grandmotherly lady who was dressed in a leather robe with a totem-pole design on it.

"Thank you," said Danny as he walked out of the gift shop.

Danny went up to the main entrance of the casino where there was a black bellhop wearing a feathered headdress loitering by the door. Danny had seen the same guy yesterday. The man had almost nothing to do since the casino attracted very few overnight guests.

"How, chief," Danny greeted the bellhop.

"How!" said the black man, instinctively raising his right hand.

"Is there an airport in this town, my friend?"

"Sure is. Brandton Municipal. We got two flights a day 'tween here and Indianapolis. Matter a fact, I'm just leaving in two minutes in the van to meet the first flight."

"You don't say? I wonder if I could catch a ride with you to the airport."

"I'd be mighty glad to have the company, sir. Just between you and me, things can get pretty boring in this job."

"I'm sorry I don't have any cash on me to give you a tip."

"No tip necessary, sir. The way I figure it, when the Lord introduces me to a new friend, that's all the reward I need."

Chapter 16

HOW TO STEAL AN AIRPLANE

THE AIRPORT WAS A typical small-town municipal airport. The casino was the only reason there were any commercial flights at all coming into this strip. The bellhop explained that each flight carried about twenty people, mostly folks from Indianapolis who were wealthy enough to take the plane and lazy enough to want to avoid driving ninety miles. Other than that, the airport was a typical FBO, or Fixed Base Operator. They took care of private aircraft, rented airplanes, provided fuel and repair work, and gave flying lessons.

Danny walked up to the reception desk in the FBO and slapped the bind-in card from *Flying* magazine down on the counter.

"I'm here for my free flight lesson," he announced.

The receptionist looked at the card and turned it over in her hands. She'd seen one other card like this in her brief career. But at least the other guy had shown the courtesy to make an appointment.

"Well, we have three flight instructors here, sir, and two of them are in the air. But let me check with the other one."

"Fine," said Danny.

The receptionist picked up her telephone. "Mike, there's a guy down here who wants one of the free Cessna lessons. He's got a coupon. Can you do it?"

"He'll be right down," she said to Danny.

"Excellent."

"I need you to read this and sign it."

She handed him a form that essentially said if Danny died a fiery death it wasn't anyone's fault but his own. He signed it without reading a word. The signature was just a scribble.

When the instructor came down the stairs, Danny thought he couldn't have been more than twenty-two years old. He held out his hand to Danny and said, "Hi, I'm Mike Stanfield, mister . . . ?"

"Seamans. Daniel Seamans," said Danny, remembering the name of an old schoolmate.

"Well, Mr. Seamans, I'm always looking for a good excuse to get up in the air—especially if the Cessna corporation wants to pay for it. So why don't you and I take this bird for a spin?"

"Great!"

"May I ask how much you know about flying already? Is this your first time in a general-aviation aircraft?"

"Yes it is, Mike," said Danny sincerely. "I don't know very much at all. I guess I know that pushing the yo . . . the steering wheel forward means down and pulling it back means up."

"That's right. That's good. We can build on that. But first, before you start pulling or pushing the yoke—and you were right, it is called a 'yoke,' by the way—you've got to do what we call a pre-flight inspection. Basically, what we're going to do is walk around the aircraft and make sure everything is functioning normally."

As they walked out on the tarmac toward the aircraft, Danny sized up the situation. Could he pull this off? The kid was young, but he was no dummy. He'd have to time it perfectly. And play it with a straight face. And get a little help from the man upstairs, too, he thought.

When they arrived at the airplane, a Cessna 172 trainer, Mike showed Danny how to remove the tie-down rope from the wheel assembly and pull out the chock blocks from the tires. Both very simple tasks.

"Okay, why don't you do the other side," said Mike.

"Great," said Danny with enthusiasm.

Next he showed Danny how to check the fuel tanks for impurities. But since the Cessna was a high-winged air-craft, the instructor didn't have to crawl on his hands and knees under the wing. As a result, he didn't notice that Danny had done a less than perfect job of removing the chock block from the right tire.

Once inside the cockpit, they put on their headsets and Mike gave Danny a long explanation of the flight controls, the panel instruments, the pre-flight checklist, and various other essentials. As is customary, Mike let Danny sit in the pilot's seat while he sat in the co-pilot's seat on the right. But since this was Danny's first lesson, a "demo" lesson at that, Mike pretty much ran through the checklist and started the aircraft by himself.

When the propeller was turning, Mike said, "Okay, I want you to release the brakes on the rudders by pressing down on them. Then I want you to very gently add power to the throttle, and we'll start to move forward."

Danny released the brakes and added power, but the plane didn't move. Or actually it did move slightly, but it sort of veered to the right a few feet.

"Did you release those brakes?" Mike asked.

"Yes, I did."

"Both of them?"

"Yes."

"Okay, once you've released the brakes, keep your feet off the rudder pedals," said Mike. "We don't want to turn just yet. I'll show you how to turn in a moment. But right now we just want to move straight ahead. Okay, add some more power to the throttle."

Danny added more power, but again, the plane refused to move forward. Instead, it pivoted to the right a few more feet.

"Was I supposed to move that wooden thingie from under the wheel?" Danny asked, ever so innocently.

"Oh, that's it! I thought I explained that. Don't worry about it, Mr. Seamans. I've made that same mistake a hundred times. Every pilot in the world has made that mistake. Tell you what. Pull back the throttle and I'll run out there and remove the chock block."

Mike took off his headset, opened the right door, and stepped out of the aircraft. Danny gave him about three seconds to remove the block before reaching over to lock the door. Then he added power to the throttle and began to roll out.

Mike was behind Danny as he pulled out, and since there is no rear window in a Cessna, he couldn't get a good look at him. But when Danny applied the left rudder to move onto the taxiway, he got an excellent view. Mike was hopping up and down and waving his hands back and forth like a man who was trying to get into the *Guinness Book of World Records* for doing the most jumping jacks. Danny could see his mouth moving, too. He assumed he was shouting, but he couldn't hear him. The engine was too loud.

Mike was still in the same position and still doing jumping jacks five minutes later when Danny began his takeoff roll. Once in the air, Danny briefly considered flying directly to Las Vegas—perhaps he could hook up with Virgil Kirk and work out what was wrong with the craps system—but then he realized that he didn't have enough money to pay for the extra fuel such a long trip would require. So he set his navigation equipment on a course for New Jersey and settled in for the long flight. The return trip would take longer, Danny realized, because this Cessna trainer was much slower than his souped-up Bonanza.

As he took one last glance at the runway far below and saw the tiny flight instructor still jumping up and down on the tarmac, it was exactly 9:00 a.m. on Saturday morning, December 24, 2000. Had this occurred nine months later, he would've been shot down by an F-14 by now. But in those innocent days before the attack on the World Trade Center, Danny would enjoy a pleasant and uneventful flight to New Jersey in his stolen Cessna.

Chapter 17

THE RETURN OF THE PRODIGAL SON

ICHARD GOLDMAN WAS THE first to arrive at the surprise party waiting for Danny at his home. Not because he'd received an invitation, but because of what he *hadn't* received—a response to his cease-and-desist letter. Danny had left town so quickly (and Maria had died so suddenly) that no one was watching the store at Pellegrino Enterprises when Goldman's letter arrived. So it never got faxed to Lefkowitz for a response. Richard hated to have his cease-and-desist letters ignored. It made him feel unimportant.

Perhaps even more significantly, some of the people who had ordered *Win By Losing* were getting antsy about why it hadn't arrived. Maria had only been able to mail out roughly a thousand dry-test letters with dollar bills before she was killed. The remaining nineteen thousand customers were sitting at home, fuming, waiting for the booklet to arrive. A few of them had placed calls or sent letters to the United States Postal Service, which were forwarded to—guess who?—Richard Goldman.

It still wasn't much in the way of wrongdoing, but when you consider how long Goldman had waged his increasingly personal vendetta against Danny, it was all he needed to take further steps. Specifically, he obtained a warrant to search Danny's office and to confiscate all existing copies of *Win By Losing*.

Richard and his assistant—both of whom were armed with handguns for the occasion—were snooping around Danny's office when the doorbell rang.

The next to arrive at the party was an investigator from the Federal Aviation Administration by the name of Donald Pierce. He, too, had a sidekick, a young black man named Jerome Phillips. Richard let them in the door and introduced himself. They each explained why they were there.

"I've had my eye on this guy for years," said Richard. "He already owns a fancy airplane. Why would he steal another one?"

"His own aircraft had an argument with the ground," replied Pierce, "so he borrowed one that didn't belong to him."

"I don't think so. This guy is a con man, not a thief. I can't see him stealing an airplane."

"Well, his aircraft goes down in a cow pasture near Brandton, Indiana, on Thursday. Early this morning someone matching his description and calling himself 'Daniel' shows up at the local FBO in Brandton asking for a flight lesson. When the instructor has his back turned, this guy takes off in the flight school's Cessna 172. Now you tell me, is that a coincidence? If it is, it's a mighty big one. And I don't like coincidences."

"Well, you're welcome to stay if you want, but as you can see, the perp isn't here," said Goldman. "I've got a search warrant that confines me to his office, not the residence itself, and I'm allowed to confiscate anything related to a certain mailing we're interested in. Unless you also have a warrant, you guys pretty much have to just sit here and wait for him to show up."

"That's okay with us," said Phillips. "That's what we were planning to do anyway. We figure that if he left Brandton at nine this morning, he should be turning up here within the next few hours. Assuming he's coming here."

The third group of guests to arrive at the party didn't bother to ring the doorbell. When they saw the two black sedans with government license plates parked in the drive-way, they decided it would be better to park in the street at a discreet distance. They were the two men sent by Pentangeli to sabotage Danny's airplane.

"Uh-oh, it looks like we got company," said Peter Peccati.

"Those are fed cars," said Rocco Mortale.

"Let's get the hell out of here."

"What for? We're clean. We got nothing to worry about. Park over here. They won't notice us."

"What do you mean we're clean? We dumped a whole box of sugar in the guy's gas tank!"

"Yeah, but evidently it didn't work, you asshole. That's why we're here. For the one millionth time, are you sure there were no airplane accidents in New Jersey yesterday?"

"I checked it a hundred different ways, Rocco. Nothing unusual happened with airplanes in the whole state yesterday."

"He couldn't have gotten out of the state, could he?" asked Peccati.

"With a whole box of sugar in his gas tank? He couldn't have gone more than five miles from Atlantic City."

"Well, let's just sit tight here for a while. We'll see what these Junior G-men are up to. Maybe Pellegrino will show up and we'll get this over with. We'll whack him on the way into the house and by the time these stupid feds realize what's going on, we'll be halfway to A.C."

Inside the house, Richard and his assistant had completed boxing up the copies of *Win By Losing,* the dry-test letters, the unopened orders, and all the other incidental papers related to the *Win By Losing* promotion. They were going to take Danny's computer with them, too, and they had finished disconnecting it from the various peripherals. With nothing much left to do, Goldman and his assistant wandered into the other room where Pierce and Phillips were playing with Danny's pool table.

"Quite a place he's got here, isn't it?" said Goldman.

"It's like what Hugh Hefner would have if he lived in Montblanc," Phillips replied.

But Hugh Hefner would have decorated the house with a lot more warmth. Danny's home looked like it had been furnished by a nineteen-year-old boy with a million dollars and nothing much in the way of taste or ingenuity. The walls and floors were so bare that the voices of the agents reverberated slightly whenever they spoke. There was remarkably little furniture. Most of the large items in each room were toys of some kind—an enormous billiard table, a ping-pong table, a foosball table, even a full-sized craps table! But the principal decorative motif of the house was consumer electronics. There were fourteen large color televisions, including one flat-screen high-definition TV hanging in a prominent place in the living room. There was an audiophile stereo system that consisted of two enormous speakers, an amplifier, a radio tuner, a CD player, a turntable, and various other components that Goldman didn't recognize. The set as a whole was worth close to $90,000. But Danny had only five Frank Sinatra, three Tony Bennett, and two Diana Krall records to play on it.

There were scads of old computers lying about. Computers became obsolete within a year and had to be replaced, but Danny hated to throw the old ones out. Some of them had data on their hard disks that Danny thought he might need someday and he didn't know how to transfer it to his current computer. Old computers were stacked up like unread magazines.

Everything in the house that wasn't actually a computer was *computerized.* There was a computerized chess game sitting on a coffee table. There was a computerized aquarium in the corner. The fish were automatically fed once a day by the computer, which also turned off the light at night. There was even a little robotic dog lying in front of the fireplace. The dog had a tag around its neck that said "Chip," and Chip was operated by a big black remote control with a long antenna. Agent Phillips had seen one of these dogs demonstrated in a store and he was showing the others how to make Chip sit, roll over, lie down, and beg. Richard's sidekick, USPS Inspector Jablonsky, was now at the billiard table, and Pierce was admiring the flat-screen high-definition television. But Goldman was simply strolling through the house and drinking it all in.

"Yup, it sure is a beautiful place," he said.

"You know, I've never seen a high-definition television in person before," said Pierce. "Do you suppose the picture is as good as everyone says?"

"Maybe we shouldn't be messing with his stuff," said Goldman.

"It's okay," said Phillips from the other room. "Our earliest scenario for him getting here in a Cessna 172 doesn't put him at the house for another forty-five minutes."

"I guess there's no harm if I just turn it on," said Pierce as he picked up the remote control and pushed the power button.

"Wow," he said. "It's just like a movie theater! Phillips, come in here, you've gotta see this."

All four agents were now standing in front of the HDTV screen and staring up at it like supplicants gazing at a crucifix behind the altar.

"Is it hooked up to a satellite dish?" asked Goldman.

"Yeah, that's the tuner over there," Phillips replied, pointing to an electronic instrument nearby.

"I hear the pornography on DIRECTV has gone hardcore recently. Cum shots and everything," said Pierce.

"Yeah, we've been working on it with the Joint Pornography Task Force that our department runs with the Justice Department," said Goldman. "But there's not a lot we can do about it. These aren't just low-life smut peddlers we're dealing with anymore. You're not busting some dirty old man with a Super-8 camera. Time Warner, Hilton Hotels . . . they're all tied up in it in one way or another. You go in to arrest Johnny Wadd and the next thing you know you're putting handcuffs on Ted Turner."

"Did you say they have cum shots on satellite television nowadays?" asked Agent Phillips, who was lagging behind the conversation a bit. "I can't believe that."

"Believe it, Mister," said Goldman.

"Twenty bucks says there are no cum shots on satellite television. That's just not possible."

Goldman didn't accept the bet, even though he knew he'd win. But Pierce didn't mind picking up an easy twenty bucks from his own subordinate.

"You're on, buddy. Where's the directory? What channel is the porn on?"

"638," said Goldman, and everyone looked at him. "Friend of mine has a dish. We watched it the other day."

They all eyed Goldman suspiciously.

"I don't even own a satellite dish!" he protested. It was the first time he was ever proud of not owning one.

The sound of moaning filled the room and all eyes turned back to the television set. But the actor and actress had just gotten started, and the cum shot, if it occurred at all, would be many minutes away. So the agents settled into various folding chairs set up around the television set—all except for Jablonsky, who was a devout Christian. He returned to the billiards table.

Meanwhile, Danny had landed safely at Teterboro. But with only $5 in his pocket, he was forced to take a city bus home. When he left home a few days earlier, he'd taken a limo service to the airport because Maria was using the Porsche. Danny hadn't been on a city bus in twenty-five years, and he wasn't too happy about it.

The bus wound up saving his life.

It dropped him off in the tiny village of Montblanc and he was forced to walk seven blocks home to his large house on the outskirts of town. Had he driven up quickly in his Porsche and stopped in the driveway, Pentangeli's men would've had plenty of time to recognize him and whack him. But on foot, Danny was able to size up the situation well in advance and approach the house with caution.

He noticed the black federal sedans first and had no doubt about what they meant. On the long flight from Indiana, Danny had plenty of time to think, and he realized that the FAA would know immediately who had stolen the airplane in Brandton. You couldn't land an airplane in a cow pasture, disappear from the scene, and steal an airplane from the same town the next morning without someone putting two and two together.

But it wasn't until he got closer to the house that he noticed the third car. It was parked across the street from his house, and two men were sitting inside smoking cigarettes. It looked like a stakeout. But there was something wrong. This was not a government car. Even unmarked government cars were not Cadillac Eldorados. Plus, why would two guys be staked-out in a car when the other agents were already inside the building? No, if anything, these guys looked like they were watching the federal officers inside. Then it dawned on him.

Maybe he had been right about Ricky and Maria after all. Maybe they were mixed up with the craps system somehow. Maybe somebody really *had* tried to sabotage his Bonanza. Maybe Ricky had let the system get into the hands of some mob guys, and now these guys were out to kill everyone else who knew about it.

He decided he was better off taking his chances with the devils inside than the ones outside. Sure, the feds would arrest him for stealing the airplane. But Lefkowitz could get him out on bail for that. Meanwhile, he could pick up a copy of *Win By Losing*. And when Lefkowitz bailed him out, he'd be on his way to Las Vegas. It seemed like a good plan, much better than being shot in the head by two goombahs in a Cadillac. So Danny walked around to the back of the house and let himself in through the sliding glass door off the living room.

Just before Danny opened the door, he heard one of the men inside shout, "HERE HE COMES! HERE HE COMES!" At first, Danny thought they were talking about him. But none of the men were looking in his direction. They were all facing the television set.

"There it is, baby! Look at that! Jesus!" shouted Pierce as Danny quietly slid open the door behind him. "You owe me twenty bucks, my friend."

"I can't believe it," said Agent Phillips. "All over her face and everything. I never thought I'd see that on over-the-air television. I mean, little kids could walk in on this, for chrissakes."

Danny cleared his throat.

All three men jumped and turned—except for Jablonsky, who was still playing pool in the other room. Phillips started to reach for his gun, but thought better of it.

"What the hell is going on here?" said Danny in a measured tone.

"Well, we . . ." Goldman stuttered.

"Who are you and what are you doing in my house?"

All three men reached for their identification badges at the same time. They did it in such perfect unison that it looked like a Motown dance step. There was a sharp *crack* from the other room as Jablonsky broke a new rack of balls on the pool table. The only other sound in the room was more moaning and groaning from the television set as the actress, having finished with the first of her gentlemen callers, turned her attention to the other three.

"I'm Inspector Goldman of the United States Postal . . ." started Goldman.

"Oh, so *you're* Goldman," said Danny with a sneer, as he suddenly remembered that nobody had been sending out dry-test letters for several days.

"I'm Criminal Investigator Pierce of the Federal Aviation Agency," said Pierce in an authoritative tone, hoping to regain control of the situation.

"Hey boss, I just ran five balls in a row!" shouted Jablonsky from the other room.

Danny sensed he had the upper hand at the moment, even though he was the only one in the room who didn't have a gun. "I don't care who the hell you are, Agent Lovelace, I'd like to know what you're doing in my house."

"We have a warrant to . . ." Goldman stammered.

"You have a warrant to come in here and play with my pool table? May I see the warrant? Does it specify eight-ball or straight pool? Because it sounds very much like the guy in the other room is playing eight-ball. And if that's not covered by your warrant, you're in violation, Inspector Goldman."

"We have a warrant to search the premises . . ." Goldman tried again.

"And you took that to mean you had a warrant to search my satellite dish for porn flicks? What kind of warrants are they giving you guys these days? Look, you've even been playing with my dog!" Danny said as he noticed Chip was in the center of the living room, not in his normal spot curled up by the fireplace. "If you've hurt Chip, I swear to God, I'll kill you." Danny was enjoying this now.

Jablonsky finally noticed the unidentified voice over the non-stop moaning from the television set and wandered into the room carrying a cuestick.

"Oh, look who's here! Minnesota Fats!" said Danny. "I

heard you ran five balls in a row."

"Seven altogether," said Jablonsky groggily, as if he'd just awakened from a long nap.

Danny figured that as long as he had the advantage, he might as well press it.

"Tell you what, boys. I know how much fun it is to play pool and watch porn on TV. That's why I have these things in *my* house. So I'm not going to press charges against you. If you'll just pack up your stuff and leave now, I'll let this go and I won't even bother to call my lawyer. How does that sound?"

Agent Phillips, who was deeply embarrassed about the whole thing, was about to say, "That sure is nice of you," when Investigator Pierce brought the United States Government to its collective senses.

"You're under arrest for stealing an airplane in Brandton, Indiana."

"What kind of an airplane?" asked Danny, who was still in a mischievous mood.

"A Cessna 172."

"I own a V-Tail Bonanza. Why in the world would I steal a Cessna 172?"

The two FAA agents, both of whom had their pilot's licenses, conceded mentally that Danny had a point. But then Pierce shook his head like a wet dog and came to his senses again.

"You crash-landed your Bonanza in a field near Brandton, then you stole the Cessna the next day."

"It wasn't a crash landing," said Danny, his feelings hurt. "It was a greaser. You try landing in a soybean field some-day, *Agent Janine,* and see if you can do it without putting a scratch on the fuselage."

"I've had enough of this crap," said Pierce, "Turn around." And he pulled out a pair of handcuffs.

"There's no need for handcuffs," said Goldman, "these are civil violations we're talking about here." Goldman never would've dreamed he'd be defending Danny Pellegrino about anything.

"Stealing an airplane isn't civil," said Pierce, "it's a Class A Felony."

And then there followed a big discussion among all four agents about civil versus criminal law, the use of handcuffs in civil cases, which agent should give the Miranda warning, whether a Miranda warning was even necessary in this case, which car Danny should ride in, and so on and so forth.

Through it all, Danny was smiling pleasantly and wondering how he could get into the office to pick up a copy of *Win By Losing*.

"Can I take a piss?" he asked.

"I'll go with you," said Goldman.

"I'm perfectly capable of doing it alone," said Danny.

"Give me your wrists," said Pierce. Danny presented his wrists and Pierce put the handcuffs on him. "There, now he can go to the bathroom alone. Assuming he can unzip his pants."

"You might want to think about zipping yours up, too, Johnny Wadd," said Danny, and Pierce immediately checked his zipper.

Danny walked toward the bathroom adjacent to his office, and once inside the office complex, he immediately began searching for a copy of *Win By Losing*.

"They were scattered all over this room a few days ago," he muttered, as he started opening desk drawers and filing cabinets. Then he noticed the boxes on the floor. Goldman must've confiscated them, he thought. He was tearing open one of the boxes with his teeth, when Goldman entered the room.

"Get your hands off that, Mr. Pellegrino," said Goldman. "That's federal property. We've confiscated everything in this office related to *Win By Losing*."

"Why?" said Danny, kneeling on the floor. It wasn't funny anymore.

"No response to my cease-and-desist letter. Complaints about unfulfilled orders. Promoting a product in the mail and then withdrawing it later for no good reason. Plus, there's the whole question of whether this gambling system even works, Danny."

"It works! It really works!" said Danny desperately.

"Oh, I'm sure it works beautifully. All your products work so well, Danny. My wife and I swear by them. Our house is full of them. I gave my daughter a piece of the Blarney Stone before she went off to college. Didn't you say in your ad that it would help students write term papers?"

"Can I just look at one copy of *Win By Losing*, Mr. Goldman? There's something in it I need to check." Tears were starting to form in Danny's eyes.

"No, you cannot. Get up and go to the bathroom, if you really need to. I'll be waiting outside. When you're done, we're taking a ride to Manhattan."

A few minutes later, as Danny walked out of the house surrounded by the four agents, he decided to try something that might give him a little extra margin of protection from the men in the Cadillac. He pulled his arm out of Agent Phillips's hands and pretended to make a run for it. Phillips tightened his grip and the other three men, as Danny had hoped, pulled out their service revolvers.

"They've got guns!" said Mortale.

"Get down!" said Peccati.

The two gangsters submerged themselves under the windows of the Cadillac like crocodiles sinking below the water line. By the time they surfaced again, Danny and the agents were long gone.

At the federal building, Danny asked for permission to make his one telephone call, and Sol Lefkowitz showed up less than ten minutes later. Once Lefkowitz had arrived, Danny's legal problems were essentially over. Lefkowitz started shouting, spitting, cajoling, pleading, sweet-talking, double-talking, trash-talking, filibustering, arguing, lecturing, pontificating, whining, and wailing in such a way that the federal agents didn't know which end was up. It was a virtuoso performance of vocal and legal artistry.

By the time Lefkowitz finally took a breath, he had Pierce convinced that he didn't have enough evidence to hold Danny for stealing an airplane. That even if he *did* steal it, it was just a joyride, Danny was a first-time offender, and he'd promise to turn himself in—if and when Pierce had anything with which to charge him.

In Lefkowitz's opinion, the postal service had even less on his client than the FAA. He cited a dozen cases off the top of his head proving that dry tests were not illegal. He laughed at Goldman's charge that there were unfulfilled orders, simply because there had not been enough time to fulfill them. Danny was allowed at least six weeks from the date of the first order to get the booklet in the hands of his customers. So far, it had been scarcely seven days. And with regard to the allegedly "false and misleading" statements in the letter, Lefkowitz pointed out that all of Goldman's charges were based on the assumption that the craps system didn't work.

"But the craps system *does* work," Lefkowitz insisted, "and what's more, my client will demonstrate that it works in a court of law." Both Lefkowitz and Goldman knew that this case would never see the inside of a courtroom.

The only point Lefkowitz lost with Goldman was getting the booklets back, which, ironically, was the only thing Danny cared about. Danny gladly would've gone to jail for a few days in exchange for one of those booklets. But Goldman insisted he needed to hold them for evidence and he would release them when he was damn good and ready.

"We've got to toss the bastard a bone," Lefkowitz whispered into Danny's ear.

"How am I supposed to fulfill the orders without the booklets?" Danny asked Goldman directly.

"I thought you were going to withdraw the offer and do a dry test," said Goldman. And Danny was stumped by that.

When all was said and done, Danny was released on his own recognizance after promising to stay in town and cooperate fully with any future investigations. But when Danny and Lefkowitz got into a cab outside of the federal building, Danny startled Lefkowitz by turning to the driver and saying, "Take us to Kennedy Airport."

"Where are you going, Danny?"

"Las Vegas."

"I promised them you'd stay in town."

"Was it an official condition of my release or was it just a courtesy?"

"The latter, I suppose."

"Well, there you go. I've got to get to Las Vegas right away. And I've got some more bad news for you. You're buying my ticket."

"Me?" Danny was a good client, but not *that* good.

"Yeah, I'm tapioca." Tapioca was casino jargon for "tapped," out of money.

"And you want me to buy you a ticket to Las Vegas? You know I'll just bill you for it next month with a 20 percent markup. Why do you need to go to Las Vegas in such a hurry?"

Danny had his reasons, but he wasn't going to share them with Lefkowitz. The way Danny figured it, there were only four copies of *Win By Losing* in the world right now. Goldman had one of them and he wasn't parting with it. (Actually, Goldman had twenty thousand of them, but that was immaterial.) Another one was sitting in the baggage compartment of a Bonanza parked in a soybean field in Brandton, Indiana. Some gangster—probably in Atlantic City where Ricky was killed—had the third one. And the fourth booklet was undoubtedly in the possession of one Mr. Virgil Kirk of Las Vegas, Nevada, the author of *Win By Losing*. Even if Kirk hadn't saved a copy for himself, he would remember how it worked. Once Kirk explained to Danny what he was doing wrong, he could start making money again. Danny had a line of credit at virtually all the big hotels on the Strip and he could play on markers anywhere in Las Vegas.

But Lefkowitz's question still hung in the air.

"I always go to Las Vegas for Christmas," Danny replied.

Chapter 18

EXECUTIVE ORDERS AT THE WHITE HOUSE

SIX SHOTS IN THE back and he's still alive, HE'S STILL ALIVE!" exclaimed Pentangeli.

"No, you don't understand, boss," said Peter Peccati. "We weren't able to get any shots off at all. He was surrounded by federal agents."

"They had guns," Mortale added helpfully.

Pentangeli was sitting in his favorite booth at the White House Submarine Shop in Atlantic City. Peter Peccati and Rocco Mortale, the gang that couldn't spill sugar straight, were seated across from him. These two were a mismatched set of salt-and-pepper shakers. Peccati was short and fat. Mortale was tall and thin.

"Well, that's bad luck for me, and even worse luck for you if you can't get this done."

"We'll get it done, boss. But we're not sure where he is now. After the feds took him, we stayed at his house. I called my guy in the federal building, and he said they released him on his own recog. We figured he'd come back to the house. But so far he hasn't showed up yet. We've got two guys sitting out there now just in case he does."

"So why'd you come to me? What did I do to deserve this generosity?"

Peccati and Mortale looked at each other blankly. After a long pause, Peccati spoke up.

"Well, we thought maybe you could give us some ideas about what to do next. We can keep sitting on his house, but it looks like the guy's on the lam. We thought maybe you'd know where he was likely to turn up. We don't really know this guy or where he hangs out. Man, this job is impossible," Peccati added under his breath in exasperation.

"Impossible? You surprise me, Peccati. If history has taught us one thing, if we've learned one thing down through the years, it's that you can kill anyone. What do you think, Rocco?"

"Difficult, not impossible."

Pentangeli smiled. It wasn't often that his subordinates were able to reply to one of his quotations with the very next line of dialogue from the movie. The fact that both the character in the film and his own real-life employee were named Rocco was icing on the cake. Pentangeli knew it would be a good day.

"What did the feds want with him anyway?"

"My guy in the federal building said they pinched him for stealing an airplane in Indiana."

"I thought you jokers were going to do some preventive maintenance on his airplane here in Atlantic City."

"We did, boss! But somehow it didn't kick in until he got to Indiana."

Pentangeli thought about his next move. He had tried the craps system a few times since Ricky gave it to him and it worked. It worked beautifully. But just like Danny and David Invidia before him, Pentangeli knew enough about craps to know that the system could be invalidated in a heartbeat with a simple rule change. If he was going to make a big score with this system, he'd have to do it under the radar. And when it came to Frank Pentangeli, the radar in Atlantic City was very powerful indeed.

The thing to do, he decided, was to go to Las Vegas and hit as many casinos as possible in a short amount of time. He wasn't as well-known in Vegas, and he might be able to pull it off without anyone recognizing him.

But Danny Pellegrino was still the fly in the ointment. If Pellegrino got to Las Vegas first—and Pentangeli assumed that's where he was going, given that he was headed west when his airplane went down—then Pellegrino would be the one to make the big score and the rules would be changed by the time Frank got there.

"My guess is that he's going to Las Vegas," he said.

Peccati and Mortale looked at each other and smiled. There was nothing better in the life of a small-time hood than a business trip to Las Vegas.

"I want his plane met there."

Chapter 19

XMAS IN VEGAS

ANNY'S BIGGEST PROBLEM AS he walked down to the baggage-claim area was how to get a hold of Virgil Kirk. Even money wasn't much of a problem anymore. Lefkowitz had given him a hundred dollars for pocket money, and now Danny was in the land of casino markers. He had about $100,000 worth of available credit at ten casinos around town.

It wasn't true, as Danny had told Lefkowitz, that he *always* spent Christmas in Las Vegas. But he had spent many Christmases there. It was his favorite time of year in Vegas. The crowds were always extremely light during the week before the holiday. Room rates were at their lowest level of the year. It was easy to get a cab. Easy to make show reservations. Easy to get into the best restaurants. It was even easy to find an open dice table or blackjack table, which had been getting increasingly difficult in recent years.

But it was more than that. Danny loved the cognitive dissonance of celebrating the birth of innocence in a city that was dedicated to sin. To Danny there was nothing more amusing than sitting at a $3 blackjack table in one of the sleazy downtown casinos next to a couple of degenerate gamblers in dirty raincoats while Bing Crosby sang "White Christmas" on the Muzak. It was so relentlessly depressing it actually gave Danny an emotional lift.

Christmas in Las Vegas always reminded Danny of the Pottersville segment in *It's a Wonderful Life*—that short portion of the movie that portrays the town of Bedford Falls as it would've been if George Bailey had never lived. The city is blanketed by a pristine layer of white snow on Christmas Eve, but underneath the snow it's a rat's nest of bitterness, anger, and sin. At Martini's Bar, a group of hard-drinking men ridicule and humiliate an old drunk. In town, the local cinema is playing X-rated movies. The village green is surrounded with casinos and dance halls. One of George's high-school girlfriends has become a prostitute. Even Donna Reed, the spinster librarian, hurries home along the sidewalk as if she were afraid of being mugged. The Pottersville segment was Danny's favorite part of the movie.

On one memorable Christmas Eve in Las Vegas, Danny was staying at the Bellagio and dining alone at one of the restaurants in the front of the hotel when it suddenly began to snow. He looked out the window at the snowflakes falling on the artificial lake and on all the casinos up and down the Strip as far as his eye could see. His eyes began to moisten with sentimental tears.

"Pottersville," he said wistfully.

Near the baggage-claim area at McCarran Airport, Danny found a bank of pay telephones and dialed 411. He was in luck. Virgil Kirk was not unlisted as he had feared. He started to dial the number . . . then hung up and stepped back from the phone. He needed to think about this.

He made a little praying gesture with his hands and rested his nose lightly on his fingertips. He couldn't just come out and say, "Hey, your system isn't working. Why don't you explain it to me again?" Virgil would wonder why he didn't just pick up the booklet and read it. What's more, Virgil knew that the mailing had gone out by now and he would be curious about the returns. He wasn't quite sure how he was going to wrest the necessary information out of Virgil, but he knew he couldn't do it on the phone. He'd have to suggest that they meet in person and then he could play it by ear.

As Danny stood there in front of the pay phone in the posture of a priest before the altar, he heard two men with New Jersey accents talking loudly behind him as they waited for their baggage on the carousel. There was a tall, skinny one and a short, fat one—like Mutt and Jeff.

"Which hotel should we stay at?" asked Mutt.

"Wherever he hangs out, I guess," said Jeff.

"Where's that?"

"How the hell should I know?"

"Well then how the hell are we going to find him?"

"I got lots of friends who work in the casinos around town. I'll make a few calls. Find out where he likes to play. Don't worry, we'll find him."

Danny turned around and stared at the two men, but their backs were turned to him. From the rear they looked vaguely familiar, but he couldn't place them. He was too preoccupied with Virgil Kirk to worry about it anyway. So he stepped up to the phone and redialed the number. It was ringing.

"May the peace of the Lord be with you on this Christmas Eve," said the voice on the other line.

Danny started to hang up. He thought he had a wrong number. It sounded like an answering machine at a church.

On second thought, it also sounded like a live voice.

"Hello?" said Danny tentatively.

"Hello. Virgil Kirk here. How may I be of service to you, sir?"

"It's Danny."

Kirk misunderstood him. "You say it's Dante?"

"Yes, that's exactly right!" said Danny, wondering if he'd accidentally used his real name.

"Well, correct me if I'm wrong, sir, but you've been dead for close to seven hundred years. Is this a long-distance call?"

"No, *Danny*. Pellegrino. From New Jersey. I'm the guy who bought the mail-order rights to *Win By Losing* from you."

"Oh, yes, of course, I've been waiting to hear from you! Have we received any orders yet? I tried to call you a couple of times yesterday, but there was no answer. I thought you'd skipped out on me."

"No, no, no, the mailing is doing great. It's a real winner. But there are some things I need to discuss with you. I was wondering if we could meet."

"When?"

"Now."

"*Now?* Where?"

"You tell me," said Danny, "I'll meet you wherever you want."

"Well, I'd suggest we meet in Kansas City, because it's about halfway between Nevada and New Jersey. But I can't get there for at least four hours, even if I hurry."

Danny was so distracted it took a moment for this to sink in. "No, I'm in town. I'm here in Vegas. I'm at McCarran."

"Oh, I see. Well that sheds a whole new light on the problem, doesn't it? Tell you the truth, I was just on my way out the door to go to Caligula's. You wanna meet me there?"

"The topless bar on Paradise Road?"

"That's the one."

"Twenty minutes?"

"I'll be there."

"How will I recognize you?" asked Danny.

"I'll be wearing a Stetson and ostrich boots. I'm a tall, lanky fella. Long gray hair in a pony tail. But if you don't recognize me, you'll surely recognize the dancer I'll be sitting with."

"How?"

"She looks like heaven."

In the cab over to Caligula's, Danny plotted his strategy for this peculiar meeting. He still couldn't quite figure out why Virgil Kirk had parted with this system in the first place. But the guy was obviously some kind of fruitcake and it didn't really matter now. He had to figure out a way to get the information from Kirk without letting him know the enormous value of the system. He couldn't simply ask for a copy of the booklet, because Kirk would know something was suspicious. Kirk would assume that Danny had thousands of copies sitting around. No, he had to tell Kirk that he'd been getting questions from his customers about how to use the system and he wasn't sure how to answer them. He would suggest that they go to a casino to play the system together. That way they could "work out the kinks," and Danny could find out what he'd been doing wrong.

Caligula's was very upscale by the standards of most topless bars. In fact, it was the only establishment in Las Vegas other than Le Cirque, the French restaurant at the Bellagio that required men to wear jackets and ties. An exception was made for "Nevada Formal," however, which was how Virgil Kirk was attired this evening. A cowboy hat, a bejeweled denim jacket, a bolo string tie, and expensive cowboy boots were good enough to get by the doorman at Caligula's. When Danny arrived in a plain white shirt and slacks, however, the maitre d' gave him one of the bar's jackets and ties to wear. Danny ducked into the men's room to change.

When Danny walked into the main showroom, he blinked his eyes to adjust them to the semi-darkness. Like Caesars Palace nearby, Caligula's was decorated with a Roman theme. But Caligula's did Caesars one better—the waitresses and dancers were not only dressed in sexy Roman slave-girl costumes, they were topless. Almost bottomless, too. The girls wore a diaphanous see-through bottom that made it look at first glance like you could see everything. You couldn't, of course; they also wore what amounted to a "crotch pasty" over the critical area. For an extra added note of surrealism, all the dancers and waitresses were wearing red-and-white Santa Claus caps this evening in celebration of Christmas Eve. The effect was rather like walking into the middle of a *Playboy* pictorial of Santa's workshop.

The slave-girl outfits were just the tip of the iceberg when it came to the Roman theme at Caligula's, however. There was enough phony classical statuary and architectural decoration to keep a marble quarry busy for years—assuming they were really made of marble, which, of course, they weren't. The main stage was set off by Ionic columns and had a triangular frieze at the top, where a dozen male and female figures performed various sex acts on each other, ostensibly a Roman orgy of some kind. There were three private lap dance salons located off the main room and neon signs in Roman lettering above each doorway identified them as "The Academy," "The Lyceum," and "The Forum."

Even someone whose knowledge of antiquity was as meager as Danny's would notice that there seemed to be a great deal of confusion at Caligula's about the difference between ancient Rome and ancient Greece . . . with a few ancient Egyptian elements thrown in for good measure. The guiding principle seemed to be that if it had to do with the pre-Christian world and the costumes were sufficiently skimpy, the statuary sufficiently bawdy, it would find a home at Caligula's.

Kirk was not hard to spot. He was as tall and lanky as advertised, with a prominent Adam's apple and a big nose. His hair was pulled back and arranged in a long ponytail. He actually had that sort of lean and hungry look you often see in ex-convicts and various other species of male trailer trash, particularly in the West.

But as Danny took a closer look at Virgil, there were signs that this man was anything but trailer trash. He wore a handmade Patek Philippe watch on his left wrist. Kirk's boots were obviously made from the leather of some exotic animal. Had he said they were ostrich? Whatever they were, they screamed money. The diamond ring on Virgil's right pinkie finger was the largest stone he'd ever seen on a man. And, yes, the dancer who was with Virgil did indeed look like heaven.

Virgil suggested that the three of them retire to the Lyceum where they could have some privacy and some relief from the loud music in the main showroom. Although it was customary for two men to retain the services of *two* dancers when entering the lap dance salon, this was just the first of several occasions this evening when it would become apparent that Virgil operated by his own set of rules at Caligula's.

Without going into too much detail, Danny told Virgil how he'd been getting some questions from customers that he couldn't answer. He suggested that after a few drinks at Caligula's, he and Virgil should go to a nearby casino and play the system together. Then maybe Danny could ask Virgil some questions about how the system worked. Virgil thought that sounded like a fine idea.

"Which casino would you like to go to?" asked Virgil.

Danny simply picked the closest one.

"How about the Miracolo?"

"Excellent! The Miracolo! The lions. The zebras. The live piranha in the moat. You couldn't possibly have come up with a better choice. I salute you, sir!"

They clinked glasses in a toast. Tiffany joined them. It was an odd collection of glassware. Tiffany was drinking champagne from a flute, Danny was drinking Campari and soda from a tumbler, and Virgil was drinking tequila from a shot glass. (Danny had decided to forego his usual martini this evening in order to keep his mind clear for this conversation.) Tiffany resumed her gyrations on Virgil's knee. As the evening wore on she would dance for one song, then sit out the next two songs while she smoked a cigarette and pretended to listen to the conversation.

"Well," said Danny, gulping down the rest of his drink, "shall we go?"

"What's your hurry?"

"Oh, no hurry. I just got off a transcontinental flight. I'm a little tired. I'd like to hit the sack early tonight."

"Shall we do it tomorrow morning?"

"NO! I mean, no, tomorrow doesn't really work for me, because . . ." Danny tried to come up with a good reason, but he couldn't. All he knew was that time was running out. It was now or never. He couldn't let Virgil out of his sight until he regained possession of the secret.

"Oh, wait, I can't do it in the morning anyway," said Virgil. "I've got to go to church. And I volunteered to work in the soup kitchen afterwards. One thing or another, I'll be there most of the day."

"You go to church?"

"Yes."

"Which church do you go to?"

"Flamingo Road Presbyterian."

"Ha! I can't believe you're a Presbyterian."

"I'm Scottish. What church do you want me to go to? Russian Orthodox?"

"No, I mean I didn't have you figured for a religious person at all," said Danny. "I mean, we're meeting in a freakin' topless bar here at your suggestion."

"God is in topless bars. God is everywhere. Did you happen to notice the attendant in the men's room?"

"The old black guy? That's God?"

"No, he's a Baptist minister."

"You're kidding me."

"No, I'm not. Go ask him. Ask him why he hangs out in the bathroom of a topless joint, and he'll tell you that's where God thinks he'll do the most good. Believe me, I've had a lot of conversations with that guy. Say hello to him the next time you go in there. It'll change your life."

Danny hesitated to ask the next question, which he knew could launch a very long discussion and that was the last thing he wanted right now. But his curiosity got the best of him.

"So you believe in God?"

"I do."

"Why?"

"Well, let me answer that with a question of my own. Do you know anything about quantum mechanics?"

Danny glanced at his watch before answering.

"You catching a train?" asked Virgil.

"No, no, it's just that . . ." Again, Danny couldn't think of a reasonable excuse for his anxious behavior. He wanted to grab Virgil by the throat and say, "Shut up and tell me how the craps system works!" But he realized the key to getting the secret out of Virgil would be to remain calm. So he took a deep breath and answered Virgil's question.

"It's nuclear physics. It has to do with the parts of an atom, as I recall."

"Exactly right. Those parts of an atom are called 'sub-atomic particles,' and quantum mechanics is the study of how they move, how they change, what they're made of, and so on. The only problem is, quantum mechanics was developed about eighty years ago, and scientists don't have a much better understanding of those particles today than they did then."

"Why not?"

"Well, you see, these so-called 'particles' don't behave like particles at all. They don't behave like tiny specks of matter should. They don't respond to gravity, or to electro-magnetic force, or to anything at all in quite the way they're supposed to. They bounce all over the place with no apparent pattern or predictability. Have you ever heard of the Heisenberg Uncertainty Principle?"

"It sounds familiar."

"Well, that's what old Heisenberg was saying. These particles are slippery little devils and you're never quite sure where they are or what they're up to. The more certain you are of their location, the less certain you are of their velocity. And vice versa. It's like, 'Now you see them, now you don't!' Subatomic sleight of hand. It's completely random, and many of the early particle physicists said the process was a lot like shooting dice. That used to drive Einstein crazy.

"You see," Virgil continued, "Einstein was still around back in the twenties and thirties when all this was happening in physics. After he finished the theory of relativity, he lived another fifty years and watched as the world of nuclear physics pretty much passed him by. Fighting it all the way, of course.

"But Einstein really hated the notion that subatomic particles behave in a random fashion. 'God does not shoot dice with the universe!' was his famous quote."

"Oh yes, I've heard that," said Danny. "But I wasn't sure what he was referring to."

"Well, now you know, pilgrim! He was referring to those subatomic particles."

Danny almost asked why Virgil had just called him "pilgrim," but he figured he was doing some kind of John Wayne impression. It fit with the cowboy hat and the boots. Although now that he'd mentioned being Scottish, Danny also noticed a slight Scottish burr in his voice. What a strange guy, Danny thought. Under other circumstances, he'd find this conversation interesting. But not tonight. He wiped some sweat off his forehead and deliberately fixed his face in an expression of interest. But he couldn't help but glance at his watch again.

"You're interested in time, aren't you?" Virgil asked.

"No, I, uh–"

"No, that's good. I've always believed that understanding time is very important. The person who finally figures out how time works will have figured out how everything works. I have one of the largest vintage wristwatch collections in America, you know."

"No, er, I didn't—"

"A watch is really mankind's attempt to replicate the universe on his wrist," Virgil continued without pausing. "Old-fashioned mechanical watches like my Patek Philippe here," Virgil pulled back his sleeve to reveal the vintage timepiece on his wrist, "represent the Newtonian universe as we understood it a century ago. Modern quartz watches like yours, however, are based on some of the same atomic principles we've been discussing this evening." Virgil nodded in the direction of Danny's wrist and added, "Your Rolex is a fake, by the way."

"I paid ten thousand . . ."

"Do you see how your second-hand jumps from one second to the next? That's the sign of a quartz watch. Rolex doesn't make quartz watches, pilgrim. I'm sorry."

Danny was temporarily dumbfounded by this. Had one of the world's greatest con men been conned by a watch dealer on 46th Street in Manhattan? Not for the first time, Danny was struck by the thought that the people who conned and the people who *got* conned were essentially the same kind of person. They were people who *wanted* to believe that what they were saying, or what they were being told, was true—despite all the evidence to the contrary. They were also the kind of people who wanted the easy way out in life. The quick money. The big score. The simple answers.

The old expression "you can't con a con man" wasn't true. They were the easiest people to con in the world.

He sat there pondering this in silence. So Virgil continued.

"Well, back to Einstein. You see, as brilliant as he was, Einstein was still looking at the world through Isaac Newton's eyes. He wanted those subatomic particles to behave just like billiard balls, or marbles, or planets—the kinds of objects he was familiar with in the Newtonian world. But those little devils refused to comply!"

"Even a guy like Einstein gets outsmarted at some point," Danny mused, still trying to figure out how he could've fallen for a fake watch.

"Afraid so. At any rate, these physicists just kept delving deeper and deeper into the atom and kept coming up with smaller and smaller 'bits' of matter. But the deeper they got into these particles, the less they started to look like particles at all. They started to look more like . . . well, like information."

"Information?"

"Yes, they started to look like ideas, concepts, programs, formulas. Not like 'things' at all. So what is the world made of?" Virgil asked rhetorically.

Danny shrugged.

"It's *not* made of hard little particles. It's made of wispy evanescent streams of information."

This entire conversation was taking place between mouthfuls of human flesh, so to speak, because Virgil was in the habit of shaking some salt on Tiffany's forearm or shoulder, licking it up with a loud smack of his lips, knocking back a shot of tequila, and biting into a lemon wedge. It was sort of an R-rated version of something that had come to be known in youthful circles as a body shot. Meanwhile, every five minutes or so he'd hand Tiffany a twenty-dollar bill, as if they were as worthless as Mardi Gras beads.

"It's awfully nice of her to let you do body shots like that," said Danny. "I don't believe I've ever seen that service offered in a lap dance before."

"We're not supposed to do it," said Tiffany, eager to join in the conversation on a subject where she had some expertise. "But I slip the manager a few bucks and he lets me do it for Virgil. As long as the owner isn't here, it's okay."

"We kick a few dollars upstairs to middle-management," Virgil summarized.

"So you're not really licking her arm," said Danny. "You're licking a wispy evangelical stream of information that *looks* like her arm."

"You've got it! Well, I said 'evanescent,' not 'evangelical,' but you've got the gist of it."

"Bullshit!" said Danny.

"Why?"

Danny slammed his fist hard on the little cocktail table in front of him, almost spilling his drink in the process.

"You call that information? I call it solid mahogany!"

"I'm not denying that it's solid," said Virgil patiently. "But at the subatomic level, it's still made up of information. Look at it this way. Have you ever seen a science fiction movie like *Star Trek* where there was something called a 'force field'?"

"Yeah, I've seen that a million times."

"Well, the force field is invisible, right? You can see right through it. But you *can't* put your fist through it. It's as hard as a rock."

"Yeah, so?"

"Well, that's what your cocktail table is. It's a particular kind of atomic force field that we happen to call 'wood.'"

Danny pondered this for a moment. Again, he looked at his watch. How long had it been since he'd suggested they leave? Ten minutes? He'd let another five minutes pass before he made the suggestion again. Meanwhile, he had no choice but to play along. "What's all this got to do with your believing in God?" he asked.

"Well, back in the 1930s when the scientists were doing all this pioneering work in particle physics, they didn't really know what they had on their hands. Nothing in their experience, or even their imagination, could account for a world made of information. But nowadays, a world of information is not only easy to imagine, it's downright commonplace."

"How so?"

"Do you have any computer games at home?"

"Yeah, I've got a lot of 'em. I don't play them very often. There's a golf game I like, though."

"That's a perfect example. You've got a little golfer there, right? He's on a golf course with trees and grass and lakes. There's usually a little bird singing in the background. And when your golfer hits the ball, it acts just like a real golf ball. It responds to the laws of gravity and aerodynamics. It's a whole world right in your computer. And what's it made of? Just bits and bytes of information."

"Oh, I see," said Danny. "You're saying that the world is a computer program, like in *The Matrix*."

"Something like that. Only the virtual world in *The Matrix* was a comparatively limited thing. People had plugs in their heads and they were being fed a computer program that was designed to *look* like reality. What I'm talking about goes much deeper than that. I'm saying the entire universe is *made* of information. It's not an alternate reality. It *is* reality. At least it's our reality."

"No, that's not possible," said Danny. "Because a computer program like my golf game only has two dimensions. The universe has three dimensions."

"The universe has *four* dimensions, pilgrim, if you count time. But all four of them are illusions. When you look at your golf game, for example, it looks like it's in two dimensions because you're watching it on a flat monitor. But to the golfers inside the program, it may very well look like three dimensions. The fact of the matter is that a computer program is neither two-dimensional nor three-dimensional. It's *non-dimensional.* At its most fundamental level, it consists only of numbers and ideas.

"Plato understood this very well, by the way. It's not the thing itself that's real, he said, it's the concept behind the thing. A triangle drawn on a blackboard is not a real triangle. It's only a pale reflection of the 'idea' of a triangle that exists inside your head. Plato said that what we consider the real world may only be a reflection, like shadows on the wall, of the underlying mathematical reality of the universe. Plato was born about three thousand years before the first computer, but he had it just about right."

Virgil wanted to give Danny a few moments to absorb this. So he took another body shot from Tiffany and handed her another twenty. Then he reached into his pocket and pulled out a pair of casino dice. He put one of them on the table in front of Danny with the number three showing on top.

"The nature of reality is really three-fold, Danny. At its most fundamental, subatomic level, this die is made of information—bits and bytes. At the physical level, it's a hard little plastic cube. That's the level that people commonly refer to as 'reality.' But at its highest level, it signifies the number three.

"In other words," Virgil continued, "information is what it's *made of.* A plastic cube is what it *is.* And three is what it *means.*"

Danny stared down at the die blankly like a man noticing a spot on his necktie. Tiffany continued to dance dreamily in her chair.

"The same can be said of you, pilgrim. At the subatomic level, you are made of bits and bytes—pure information. At the physical level, you are a human being. And at the highest level, you are the spirit and soul of Danny Pellegrino.

"You can view your entire life as a movement from information to meaning," Virgil went on. "When your Daddy's sperm unlocked the secrets of your Mommy's egg, you embarked upon a journey from pure information to a physical being. But your purpose in life is to move from being a physical being to one of pure meaning. Pure truth. Pure beauty. And God wants to help you do that."

Let it go at that, thought Danny, let it go at that. You're running out of time. But he just couldn't resist.

"So who or what is God?" he asked.

Virgil took a deep drag from his cigarette and paused to consider his answer.

Chapter 20

OVER THE HILL

HERE TO?" SAID THE cab driver, glancing in his rearview mirror at the two rather disreputable-looking characters in his back seat.

Peccati and Mortale stared at each other blankly. After twenty minutes of waiting in the cabstand line outside of McCarran Airport, they hadn't managed to resolve this rather important issue. In fact, they hadn't even discussed it. They had been arguing about whether it was the proper move in blackjack to hit a soft eighteen against the dealer's ten.

"Let's go to the Miracolo," said Peccati.

"No way," said Mortale. "That place gives me the creeps. I don't like the freakin' man-eating fish in the moat. I don't like the lions. I don't like anything about it. How about Paris?"

"After the way they treated us when we saved their asses in the war? Not on your life."

"It's a *casino,* for Chrissakes. Those aren't real French people. They put a beret on their heads and teach them how to say 'bonjour.' Get real."

"Still, I don't like it," said Peccati petulantly. He tapped the driver on the back and said, "Take us to Bellagio. They're Italian."

"They aren't any more Italian than the people at Paris are French. What the fuck is the matter with you?" Mortale waggled his hands up and down at the wrists in a very Italian gesture of impatience. He tapped the driver on the back and said, "Take us to Caesars Palace."

"Yes, sir," said the driver, adding under his breath, "Forty thousand cabs in this city and I gotta wind up with Abbott and Costello."

It really didn't matter much to the cabbie. He was driving slowly west on Tropicana Avenue toward the Strip while they made up their minds. From McCarran Airport, virtually all the hotels in Las Vegas were in the same direction. Driving a cab in Las Vegas was like driving a bus in most cities: you went down one street and made lots of stops. But then the conversation in the back seat suddenly took a turn that made the driver prick up his ears.

"It's too early to check into a hotel anyway," said Mortale. "We gotta figure out where Pellegrino's staying. Maybe we should go to a bar, have a couple of drinks while I make some phone calls and find out where he likes to play."

"Topless, topless!" said Peccati enthusiastically. He hadn't been in Las Vegas in more than a year, and he'd heard that several new topless bars—establishments that made Sodom and Gomorrah seem like a church social— had recently opened.

"You know any nice topless joints not too far from the airport?" Mortale asked the driver.

"Caligula's on Paradise Road is real nice." He glanced at them in the rearview mirror again. "You gotta wear a coat and tie. But they'll give you one at the door, no problem."

"Sounds good, take us there," said Peccati.

The cab driver was like a fisherman who was watching his bobber jiggle up and down while a big ol' bass nibbled at the worm. He knew from the moment that two single middle-aged men stepped into his cab that he had a couple of live ones on the line. Now it was time to set the hook.

"Maybe you boys would like to go over the hill?"

"Are you saying we're old?" asked Peccati, who couldn't remember the last time somebody insulted him to his face. One look at Peccati's face and you'd only insult him if you wanted to commit suicide and were fresh out of sleeping pills and bullets.

"No, no, no," said the driver, backpedaling fast. "Over the hill. Over the mountain. That's what we call it when we take a fare out to Nye County. Prostitution's legal out there, you know. In fact, it's legal in every county in Nevada, except this one. I know a real nice place I can take you to. They'll treat you boys real good out there."

"Oh yeah, I heard about that," said Peccati thoughtfully.

To the cabbie this was more than just a friendly suggestion. Not only was it a $100 cab ride out to the county line, but the brothel paid him $50 cash for every customer he delivered. A "yes" from Peccati and Mortale would mean a $200 bonus for the night and a delightful two-hour break from the tedium of driving a cab in Vegas, which consists mostly of waiting in long cab lines for the privilege of picking up four drunks who want to be driven three hundred yards to the next hotel. A good night for a cabdriver in Las Vegas was any night when no one threw up in the back seat of your car.

"Sounds pretty good," said Peccati.

Mortale batted him once on the ear and said, "Are you out of your fucking mind? We got work to do tonight."

"Oh yeah, I forgot."

"What kind of work do you boys do?" asked the cab driver, unwilling to let the subject drop so easily.

"Sanitation," said Peccati reflexively.

"You've got sanitation work to do in Las Vegas at eleven o'clock on a Friday night?" asked the driver.

"Shut the fuck up and drive to Caligula's, asshole," said Mortale in a tone that would allow no further argument. But then his cell phone went off. The ringer was set on "La Traviata."

"Talk to me," said Mortale into the headset, his customary salutation.

Frank Pentangeli did not believe in salutations when he was placing a call. He just started talking. Everybody he called knew exactly who he was.

"You two jokers taken care of that business yet?"

"We just landed, boss! We're in the freakin' cab. Besides, we got a problem."

"So what else is new?"

"We don't know where he hangs out. We don't know this guy. I figured I'd make some calls to some of the pit bosses I know in town and see if we can find out where he likes to play."

"Don't bother, I already did that," said Pentangeli. "I called around. He's got credit at a bunch of places. But the two he hangs out at most are the Villagio Las Vegas and the Miracolo."

"We're passing the Miracolo right now," said Mortale.

"Well then, genius, why don't you start looking there? And Mortale . . ."

"Yes?"

"I'm coming out to Vegas myself in the morning. But I don't want to see you again until this is done, *capisci?*"

"Si, capisco." Both Pentangeli and Mortale were pleased to end the call at this point because they'd each used up their entire inventory of Italian words.

"Turn in here," said Mortale to the driver, pointing at the Miracolo.

"Looks like you're going to have to face those lions after all," Peccati chuckled.

"Shut the fuck up," said Mortale, as he stared anxiously at a large billboard featuring Boris & Ivan, the famous magicians and lion-tamers at the Miracolo.

"Don't worry," said Peccati. "They keep them behind bars. Most of the time."

Chapter 21

THE SECRET OF THE UNIVERSE

IRGIL SET HIS DRINK down on the table and stared at Danny hard, as if trying to determine if he was ready to receive this information. Finally, he spoke. "God is the programmer of the universe."

Danny was unimpressed. "You're telling me that God sat down at his computer one day and created a giant video game called 'The Universe,' and that I'm a part of that program?"

"Well, I don't think it's helpful to visualize a nerdy kid sitting in front of his Dell, but you've got the gist of it."

"Why'd he do that?"

"Why did who do what?"

"Why did God create the universe?"

"I'll answer that question with a question again. What is a computer? What exactly is it for?"

"Word-processing. Spreadsheets."

"Give me a more general answer," Virgil continued didactically.

"Well, it's a machine for . . . er, computing. For doing calculations."

"That's right. Would it be fair to summarize by saying that a computer is a machine for solving problems?"

"That would be very fair."

"So if God was using a computer to create the universe, isn't it also fair to say he must've been trying to solve some kind of problem?"

"What problem?"

"That's the $64,000 question, pilgrim! Your guess is as good as mine. But *my* guess is that he was wondering if he could create life. Not a facsimile of life, like your golf game, but real, independent, intelligent life with a mind of its own and the free will to exercise it.

"Then I imagine God was asking himself that if he *could* create that kind of life, what would it do? Would it just eat and drink and fart? Or would it eventually come looking for Him? And if it came looking for Him, would it eventually succeed?

"I think God *wants* us to find Him," Virgil concluded. "That's why he keeps sending us so many messages and leaving so many clues. He sent messages through Moses and Noah, all the Old Testament prophets. He sent messages through scientists and philosophers and artists and holy men like Buddha and Mohammed. Then, of course, two thousand years ago, he sent the big message. The ultimate email. He sent us *Himself.*"

"Jesus?" asked Danny.

"That's the guy. I think there came a time when God was getting a little frustrated that his messages weren't getting through. He'd given us all the information we needed in the Old Testament, but we were still figuring out ways to screw it up. So he decided to plug himself into the program.

"And here your analogy to *The Matrix* is more apt," Virgil continued. "I don't know whether he stuck a wire in his head or not, but somehow God put himself into the program. He ate our food. He breathed our air. He felt our pain.

When he died on the cross, believe me, it hurt. It didn't feel like a computer game to him. No more than it would feel like a game if you stuck your finger in that candle." Virgil nodded at the little candle flickering on the cocktail table.

"So God is the programmer of the universe," said Danny. "He put himself into the program in the form of Jesus Christ. Where does that leave the Holy Spirit?" After twelve years of Catholic school, Danny was a confirmed Trinitarian—even if he was also an atheist.

"The Holy Spirit is inside you," said Virgil. "It's that part of your DNA, or maybe your soul, that recognizes the truth when you see it. Have you ever wrestled with a problem for hours only to have the answer suddenly pop into your head?"

"Many times," said Danny.

"Didn't you get the feeling that the answer was staring you in the face the whole time? Wasn't it more a feeling of *recognition* rather than revelation?"

"Yes, that's true."

"The truth always looks familiar to you, pilgrim. Because the truth has been inside you all along. That's a gift from God. It's the Holy Spirit, the part of God that's always inside you. You might think of it as God's latent fingerprint on your creation."

"You sound like you believe in the literal truth of the Bible," said Danny skeptically.

"What's not to believe?"

"Oh, all those ridiculous fairy tales. The water into wine. The fishes and the loaves. The burning bush. The guy who spent three days in a whale."

"Think about it, Danny. If you view the world in this context, the miracles that Jesus performed and all the miracles of the Old Testament don't seem so impossible after all. Do you think it would be so hard for God to alter the program in such a way that Jonah would have to spend a few days chilling out in the stomach of a whale? Why, that's no more difficult than programming Pac-Man to swallow an electronic dot. A burning bush? Child's play. Walking on water? Nothing to it. Feeding the multitudes with five fishes? He could've fed them with a tadpole if he'd wanted to.

"So you don't have to go through the Bible anymore picking and choosing what you'll believe in and what you won't," Virgil continued. "You don't have to select what you'll believe based on what's plausible, what's scientific, what's historical, what's possible, or whether you can cobble together some kind of rational explanation for it. You don't even have to decide whether something is literally true or metaphorically true. It's all true! Every word of it! It all happened exactly the way it's described in the Good Book." Virgil took a tiny Bible out of the breast pocket of his jacket and slammed it down on the cocktail table. The candle jumped.

"Don't question it, pilgrim, accept it as fact!" Virgil was shouting now. "Don't waste your brainpower trying to figure out if it's true or not. Assume that it's true and use your brainpower to figure out what it *means!* That's what God wants you to do. Those miracles are God's messages to you. You perceive them as miracles because he was trying to get your attention. Now it's your job to figure out what He was saying."

Danny decided to fight back.

"If this God of yours is so concerned with humanity, if he spends all his time conjuring up miracles and sending us messages, let me ask you this . . ."

"Fire away," said Virgil with an expectant smile.

"Why did he put us out here on this speck of dust? The third planet out from an ordinary star. Just one star among billions in the Milky Way. Just one galaxy among billions of galaxies in the universe. Why create this huge universe if God was only interested in human beings? No, my friend, whoever created this universe obviously didn't give a rat's ass about us. Or he wouldn't have stuffed us in the attic."

"Oh, that's an easy one," said Virgil. "You disappoint me. Let me ask you this. What are you made of?"

"What am I made of? Well, until I met you I would've said I was made of atoms."

"You're absolutely right. I don't dispute the existence of atoms. But what kind of atoms in particular?"

"Well, mostly carbon, so I'm told. Calcium for bones. Iron for blood. Oh, and lots of water."

"And what is water made of?"

"Hydrogen and oxygen."

"Good. You weren't asleep during biology class. But now let's see if you were awake in chemistry class. So far we've got carbon, calcium, iron, hydrogen, and oxygen. Which, as a group, are known as what?"

"Elements."

"Excellent! And where do elements come from?"

"How the hell should I know?"

"They come from the stars, pilgrim! You are made of stardust. God had to create a universe filled with stars, because they make the clay from which you and I were sculpted. To make human beings without first making stars would be like trying to make paper hats without first planting trees."

Danny was still eager to get going, but he saw an opening here to try a different tack. If he could somehow get the conversation back to craps, he could maneuver it toward why the system wasn't working. Maybe then they wouldn't even have to go to a casino after all. The gambit was worth a try.

"But wait a second. Does God shoot craps or not? You never answered that question."

"He does," Virgil answered. "But He's a rhythmic roller."

The phrase "rhythmic roller" was used in the literature of craps to describe a player who attempts to influence the outcome of the game by tossing the dice exactly the same way each time. The idea was that if you threw a six, for example, and then picked up the dice *exactly* as you did before and tossed them against the wall *exactly* as you did the last time, you couldn't help but throw another six. It was controversial, to say the least. But the theory helped sell a lot of craps systems, and Danny was intimately familiar with it. "You mean He controls the dice?"

"He does indeed."

"How?"

"By algorithms, for the most part. Have you ever heard of 'cellular automata'?"

"Enlighten me."

"Well, to put it simply, cellular automata are algorithmic instructions that enable a software program to take on a life of its own. It's sort of like telling your computer, 'Go ahead and do whatever you want, but make sure you follow these fundamental rules.' So what you get is a kind of controlled random behavior."

"Sounds like an oxymoron," said Danny.

"It is! That's what's so great about it! It's like a computerized version of yin and yang. Completely random, totally controlled. Both passive and active at the same time. Some computer programmers have used cellular automata to compose music and create abstract pictures. They're very beautiful. But they're even more intriguing than they are beautiful. Because they pose a mind-boggling question: '*Could you use the same technique to create an entire universe?*'"

"Well, that's all very interesting," said Danny, who didn't think it was interesting at all, "but why don't we talk about it on the way to the Miracolo?"

Virgil showed no sign of budging.

"So you're an atheist, I take it," he said.

"Well, I was raised a Catholic, but I fell away from it. So, yes, I guess you could say I'm an atheist."

"And where, may I ask, do you turn for guidance on moral behavior? On the right way to live your life? On the purpose of your life and the meaning of it?"

"Well, you don't have to believe in God in order to be a good person," Danny protested.

"Really? Well, if there is no God, it means you came from nothing and you'll wind up nothing. So why not just cheat, steal, and fornicate your way through life?"

Of course, this was pretty much the way Danny *had* lived his life. But he felt obliged to argue against the proposition anyway. "Well there's something to be said for being an ethical person," he replied, "regardless of whether or not there's a God."

"Really? What exactly is there to be said for it?"

"To make a better world. To improve the human condition. To reduce human suffering," said Danny, listing three things he'd never given a damn about before tonight.

"Oh, so you're a hedonist?"

"You're drinking tequila from a naked girl's arm and you're calling *me* a hedonist?"

"Philosophically, yes. You're more of a hedonist than I am. You just told me that the entire point of human life is to minimize human suffering and maximize human happiness."

"No, not exactly. I'm telling you that the point of human life is to make the world a better place."

"And what, pray tell, is the purpose of that? Even your most atheistic scientist admits that eventually the world will come to an end. It's going to happen in a few trillion years and there's not a damn thing we can do about it. So I ask you again: What is the point of making the world a better place if it's eventually going to be destroyed? That's rather like rearranging the deck chairs on the *Titanic*, isn't it?"

Danny was so stumped by this that he was forced to lash out with a counterpunch based on the well-if-you're-so-smart argument.

"So what do *you* think is the point of life?"

"It's simple," said Virgil. "To find our way home to God."

"And where is that?"

"In heaven, of course."

"You mean to tell me you believe in an actual heaven and an actual hell?"

"Actually, I do."

"With clouds and halos and harps?"

"I imagine it's a different place for everyone, Danny. If you're into harps, you'll get a harp. Everyone will get the kind of heaven they want, the kind they deserve, and the kind they can handle.

"Truly good and holy people, like the saints, may wind up very close to God. Because that's exactly where they always wanted to be. They might even help God in some way, acting as angels to do His work on Earth, for example.

"But ordinary schmucks like you and me will probably just be given a nice piece of real estate in heaven that makes us happy. I might find my heaven in a place like Caligula's, because I've always loved it here." Virgil gave Tiffany a warm smile, but she was gazing off into the distance and chewing gum. Even in this trashy pose, she looked like an angel.

"I may not be in your heaven," Virgil continued, "and you may not be in mine. But if there are people whom you love on Earth, you almost certainly will see them again in heaven. I'm sure I'll see Tiff in my heaven, for example," he added loudly.

"I'm your heaven right now, baby," she said absently.

"How does this jibe with your computer-program theory?"

"I suspect that if God decides you deserve to go to heaven, he'll stash you in some corner of the program that has been custom-made for your happiness. A 'subroutine,' I believe the computer geeks call it. Then you'll be on an endless loop of peace and joy throughout eternity.

"The only trouble I have with heaven," concluded Virgil in a reflective tone, "is that I can't figure out how it could be better than Earth."

As Danny sat there watching this man with a cigarette in one hand and a tequila in the other, a $200,000 watch on his left wrist and the Hope Freakin' Diamond on his right pinkie, plus a mouthful of one of the prettiest women Danny had seen in his life, he had to admit the guy had a point.

Danny stared at his watch again. He didn't even bother to politely disguise it this time. In fact, he hoped Virgil would take the hint.

"Are you upset about your Rolex?" Virgil asked.

"No, it's just that—"

"You can't figure out how time works by staring at your watch," said Virgil. "Believe me, I've tried it. It doesn't work. A clock is just the way we measure the passage of time. It's not time itself. Better you should sit back and try to hang on to one moment. Especially a moment when you're happy. That's what heaven really is, you know. It's a happy moment that lasts forever."

"So who gets to go to heaven?" Danny asked, his curiosity aroused.

"I believe that everyone goes to heaven eventually," said Virgil pensively, as if he'd given the matter a great deal of thought, but had come to no firm conclusions. "The question is, do you want to go the hard way or the easy way? Do you want to take the shortcut or the scenic route?

"People who don't put their faith in God may have some splainin' to do up there. You might have to wait in a long line to see St. Peter. Once you get to the head of the line, you might have to tell him that even though you screwed your sister and shot your brother, you're basically a good person who means well. He may or may not buy it. But you're always welcome to go in the side door."

"The side door?" Danny asked.

"Well, maybe I shouldn't call it the side door," Virgil mused. "Maybe I should call it the VIP entrance. You see, it's just like here in Las Vegas. The dumb tourists from Podunk wait in long lines for shows and restaurants. But the casino players get a line pass from their host and they waltz right in. Well, in heaven the VIP entrance has a sign on the door that says, 'ENTER HERE IF YOU BELIEVE IN GOD.'"

"What happens to the others?" asked Danny softly.

"Old Saint Pete may let some of them in. I imagine that crack babies with AIDS and kids who die of cancer won't have to wait any longer in line than Cindy Crawford has to wait to get into a trendy nightclub.

"Others may need some—how shall I put this?—*re-education*. They may need to do some time in hell or purgatory to ponder their sins and pray for redemption."

"It sounds awfully cruel for a so-called loving God," said Danny, putting sarcastic emphasis on the word "loving."

"It's your choice, pilgrim. It's actually the easiest choice you'll ever make in life. It's a no-brainer. You can make the choice right here at Caligula's. The minister in the men's room will even baptize you in the sink. I've seen him do it a dozen times."

"What's the difference between hell and purgatory?" asked Danny, who had silently narrowed down his options to those two.

"Hell is painful. Purgatory is just disappointing. At least that's my take on it."

"So even those who are condemned to hell eventually make it to heaven?" asked Danny with a trace of hope.

"It may take a few trillion years in the frying pan for a guy like Hitler to get into heaven, but yes, even the worst bastard eventually makes it. After all, little Adolph was a child of God, too."

Then Danny asked a question that came totally out of the blue. "Are there dogs in heaven?"

Danny didn't even own a dog, unless you counted Chip. He hadn't owned a dog since his family's beloved Irish Setter, Satan, died when Danny was twelve.

"Will I see my old dog Satan there?"

"That I can tell you for sure," said Virgil. "There *are* dogs in heaven. For the simple reason that it wouldn't be heaven without them. It's a tautological certainty. So yes, Danny, Satan is definitely in heaven. But whether you get there to see him or not is another story. If you don't grow out of your adolescent atheism, Satan may be catching someone else's Frisbee for a while—if you know what I mean."

Tiffany got up to go to the ladies room. This was part of the ritual of the lap dance. Theoretically, a lap dance was just a private agreement between the customer and the dancer. For a tip of $20, the customer got a much closer and more intimate view of the girl than he would get if she were on stage. That's why the dancers not only didn't receive a salary at Caligula's, they actually paid the club for the privilege of working there.

But the management hated to see all this cash change hands without getting an opportunity to dip their beaks in it. So the price of going into one of the lap dance rooms—the Academy, the Forum, or the Lyceum—was that you had to buy your dancer an expensive bottle of champagne.

Only it wasn't really champagne. Because if it was, the dancer would soon be flat on her back. So the champagne was made of carbonated grape juice. The only two things this fluid had in common with champagne was that it was made of grapes and it cost a lot of money—about $100 a bottle.

Approximately once every half-hour—scratch that, *exactly* once every half-hour—a sleazy-looking guy who worked for the club would arrive to ask Virgil if he'd like to purchase another bottle of champagne "for the lady." Which was a polite way of saying, "If you want to keep sitting here with a half-naked girl riding your hard-on for another thirty minutes, you've got to cough up a C-note."

Of course, to Virgil this was no problem at all. But one of the unfortunate side effects of this ritual was that the dancer was forced to guzzle the grape juice at a prodigious rate, which, in turn, meant she had to empty her bladder frequently.

While Tiffany was in the ladies room, another dancer cruised through the Lyceum like a cheetah looking for wounded antelope. She saw Virgil and Danny sitting alone and she stalked their table from behind. Reaching around Danny's neck with both arms, she said, "Would you boys like some company?"

"No," said Virgil pleasantly, "we're fine."

Danny tried to say something, but he couldn't. He felt the girl's hard nipple scrape against the three-day stubble on his cheek when she hugged him, and the sensation left him temporarily mute.

"Are you sure about that, boys? You haven't had a lap dance until you've had one from me. Satisfaction guaranteed."

Danny looked up at her. He had used that phrase so many times in his career. Was she a direct-mail copywriter? he wondered.

Tiffany came walking into the room daintily placing one foot in front of the other, which is the secret, known to all attractive women, for making your butt wiggle back and forth suggestively. But when she saw what was going on, she came to a stop with her feet planted wide apart in the pose of a traffic cop asking for license and registration.

"GET THE HELL OUT OF HERE, CINDY, THESE ARE MY REGULARS!"

Once an exotic dancer had found a good customer—a "regular," as they were called back in the dressing room—

they could be as jealously protective as a fat housewife with five toddlers and a handsome husband. (Danny wasn't a regular, of course, but as long he was with Virgil, who was the mother of all regulars, Danny was a regular by association.) For some of these girls, it was their only experience with the emotion of jealousy. It was not something that came up often in your personal life when you were an eleven on a scale of one to ten.

Cindy fluttered out of the room like a flushed quail and Tiffany resumed her seat on Virgil's knee with the exaggerated dignity of a princess sitting on the throne. She put her arms around Virgil's head and pulled it tenderly into the nook between her bare breasts. Then she pressed her own biceps against her breasts in such a way that Virgil's cheeks were snuggled tightly inside, and she kissed him sweetly on the top of his head. It smelled like perfume in there, and Virgil was in no hurry to remove himself.

But Danny's patience had finally come to the breaking point. He abruptly stood up and shouted, "Let's go!"

"I'm comfortable here," said Virgil, his voice muffled by Tiffany's chest.

"I really think we should go now," said Danny. "You've got that soup kitchen thing in the morning, remember? You don't want to be tired for that."

"Oh, okay," said Virgil, like a child being told it was past his bedtime. He kissed Tiffany on her collarbone and slowly stretched himself out to a standing position. He was even taller than Danny had guessed—maybe six foot seven or more. He picked up his little Bible and put it back in the breast pocket of his denim jacket. Kissing Tiffany again—on the tip of her nose this time—he handed her a fistful of hundred-dollar bills. She gave him a tender hug in reply.

Then Danny and Virgil marched out of ancient Rome like centurions on the road to battle, passing a bust of Constantine on the way.

Chapter 22

CREATIONISM FOR NERDS

T WAS A THREE-MINUTE cab ride from Caligula's to the Miracolo. But on a Saturday night at eleven o'clock, it would take at least half an hour. On weekend nights Las Vegas has some of the worst traffic in the world.

Danny was impatient, but he tried to settle in for what he knew would be a frustratingly long ride. He actually liked Las Vegas cabs. Most of them were minivans, so they were roomy and comfortable. And the drivers were often amusing characters. On their second or third careers—transplanted from California or somewhere back East—they liked to talk and they usually had a good story to tell. It seemed to Danny that they were like New York cabbies used to be fifty years ago, before they all became foreign maniacs screaming gibberish into their radios. He thought at least half of the cabdrivers in Las Vegas were recovering alcoholics or gambling addicts. The other half, he figured, hadn't recovered yet.

But this particular driver was a woman in her forties, with a sort of rough-edged Western look to her, like she'd been left alone with too many babies by too many drunken husbands in too many trailer parks over the years. She was preoccupied with her own thoughts. And Danny could only let the silence hang uncomfortably in the air for a few minutes before he felt he had no choice but to continue his philosophical conversation with Virgil.

"What about evolution?" he asked.

"What about it?" replied Virgil gruffly.

"Well, I know the Bible is full of crap, because it flies in the face of evolution. And the theory of evolution is a proven fact."

"Did you hear what you just said?"

"What?"

"You said the *theory* of evolution is a proven *fact.*"

"Yeah, well, I know they call it a theory. But they call that Pythagorean thingie with the triangles a theory too, and nobody doubts it's a fact."

"Well, there's a difference between a theory and a theorem, pilgrim. But if you honestly think the theory of evolution is a proven fact, then you don't know enough about evolutionary science to be allowed to have an opinion on it."

This was as close as Virgil had gotten during the entire argument to an insult, and Danny straightened up in his seat. But Virgil kept pressing.

"Look," continued Virgil as he warmed to the topic, "around the age of seven or so, kids start to wonder where they came from, who made them, how they were created. At that point, one of their parents, or a teacher, or an older friend sits them down and explains the basics of Darwinism to them. Natural selection, random mutation, survival of the fittest, and so on. The kid says to himself, 'Gee, that makes a lot of sense.' So it becomes a part of his permanent belief structure. And you know what?"

"What?" said Danny, not wanting to play along.

"That's the last time he ever thinks about it again! In other words, most of us are walking around with a philosophy in our heads about the single most important metaphysical question in the universe—namely, where did we come from?—and it's basically the philosophy of a seven-year-old kid."

"Well, Darwin wasn't seven years old when he came up with it. He was an adult."

"Yeah, and Kant was an adult when he came up with transcendental idealism, but try explaining *that* to a seven-year-old. My own feeling is that if your cosmology is popular with the teeny-bopper set, you deserve points for simplicity. But you may want to revisit your theories with a more critical eye."

"So cut to the chase," said Danny. "Did God create man and all the animals. Or did man evolve from the animals?"

"A little of both, I believe."

"A little of both?"

"I believe the process worked a lot like Darwin said it worked, until it hit a snag. Then God had to help it along a bit. It's like a revised program. When Word 5.0 develops a few glitches, Microsoft has to come out with Word 5.1.

"Consider this," Virgil continued. "When the dinosaurs disappeared from the face of the Earth, the only mammal on the planet was a little mouse-like creature similar to a tree shrew. Now, are you telling me that in the intervening two hundred million years or so, that mouse has evolved into everything from a human being, to an elephant, to a blue whale, to a tiger, to a dolphin, to an Irish Water Spaniel?

"And are you telling me that it did all that by virtue of random mutation, natural selection, and survival of the fittest?

"Are you telling me that what caused that mouse to evolve into an elephant is that one day, quite by accident, a mouse was born with a longer nose than usual, and this longer nose enabled him to sniff out food better than most of his mousey friends, and quite by accident, he ran into a little girl mouse who also had a long nose, and together they had baby mice who had *really* long noses, and so on, until one day the descendant of that mouse just happened to be born an elephant . . . *is that what you're telling me?*"

"Well," said Danny, "I can see it happening."

"Heck, I can see it happening, too. But it wouldn't take two hundred million years. It would take two hundred *trillion* years. How often do we see mutations in the human population? Not very often, right?"

Danny shrugged.

"And the ones we do see usually involve some kind of flaw. We see a certain number of people born without toes, for example. But we don't often see someone born with 20/10 eyesight, or the ability to hear high-frequency noises, or even a sixteen-inch penis for that matter."

The driver glanced in her rearview mirror. But this was not the most provocative thing she'd ever heard from the back seat of her cab—not even the most provocative thing she'd heard from there tonight.

"So yeah, I can see it happening," Virgil continued. "I can also see the infinite number of monkeys eventually typing out the complete works of Shakespeare. But I'm not holding my breath waiting for the last act of *Coriolanus!*

"Look, pilgrim," Virgil concluded, "the theory of evolution is just like the Big Bang Theory. It's creationism for nerds. These assholes don't have the *guts* to believe in God, so they come up with these pseudo-scientific fairy tales.

Because they know that if the Bible really is true, if there really is a God, then they're in a heap of trouble if they don't get down on their knees and repent!"

Danny was silent for a while. Then he asked a very perceptive question.

"But wouldn't evolution have happened much faster if all the random mutations that *contributed* to improvements in the species were utilized, while all the mutations that did *not* contribute were ignored?"

"You mean two losing propositions that combine into a single winning outcome?" Virgil asked with a sly smile.

"Yes, exactly."

"Well, we'll find out if your theory works in a moment, won't we?"

"How so?"

"Because, my good man, you have just described Parrondo's Paradox."

Startled, Danny looked up. At last, he was fully engaged by the conversation. But it came too late. Their destination had finally come into view.

"Look," said Danny. "It's the Miracolo!"

Chapter 23

A MIXTURE MADE IN HEAVEN

ORTALE AND PECCATI SPENT about fifteen minutes exploring the Miracolo in search of Danny until the siren song of the blackjack tables became too intense and they were forced to sit down. They played for about an hour, during which time the situation they had been arguing about at the airport came up twice: should you hit or stand when you're holding an ace and a seven while the dealer is holding a ten?

Mortale thought the answer was to stand—he was wrong—and when the situation arose, he signaled the dealer that he did not want another card. The dealer went on to bust her own hand, so Mortale won, and this only served to solidify his conviction that he was right.

"See what I'm talking about?" he said to Peccati. "I stuck on the soft eighteen and I won, so I was right."

"No, you were wrong. You just got lucky."

"That wasn't luck, my friend. That was skill."

"You're an idiot. The book says you're supposed to hit the soft eighteen against a ten. That doesn't mean that you're gonna win every freakin' time, but that's how the book says you're supposed to play it."

"What book? People are always talking about 'the book'? Where's this fucking book? How come I've never seen it?"

"Because you've never seen a book in your life, you *cafone!*"

And so it continued in this vein for several minutes until, unfortunately, Peccati was dealt and an ace and a seven, while the dealer gave herself a ten.

"So what are you gonna do now, wiseguy?" asked Mortale.

"Hit me," said Peccati to the dealer.

She dealt him an eight, which was pretty much the worst card he could get in this situation.

Peccati sighed and said, "Hit me again."

She dealt him a ten. Twenty-six. Busted.

"What the fuck did I tell you, asshole! Where's your freakin' book now?"

There's nothing more frustrating in life than doing everything right and having it all turn out wrong. So Peccati angrily snatched up his remaining chips and said, "Let's go look for Pellegrino."

"I forgot what he looks like. Lemme see the picture again."

"Not here, you idiot, let's go to the bar."

There was a bar right in the center of Miracolo's casino that looked something like a cabana on a beach in Tahiti. Peccati and Morale commandeered a small cocktail table on the periphery and ordered two double martinis. Peccati pulled out a sheet of paper from his back pocket.

As it turned out, Danny had been officially processed when he was taken to the federal building in Manhattan, complete with mug shot, fingerprints, the works. Peccati's informant in the federal building had managed to smuggle him a photocopy of the mug shot, and Peccati put it on the cocktail table and ironed-out the wrinkles with the palms of his hands.

"Nice looking guy," said Mortale.

"He looks like DeNiro, don't you think?"

"Oh, shit! Don't ask me to shoot DeNiro. That would be like shooting Jesus! I couldn't do it."

"Shut up about shooting, for chrissakes!" Peccati glanced up at the bartender to see if he had heard anything, and sure enough, he was looking at their table somewhat quizzically.

"We need some tequila shooters over here, *paisano*," said Peccati.

The bartender nodded and went to work preparing the lemon wedges, salt shakers, and shot glasses, thinking it was the first time that he'd ever seen anyone order tequila shooters to wash down double martinis.

"He looks more like Pacino to me," Peccati said thoughtfully.

"Oh, no! That's worse! I couldn't shoot Michael Corleone. I'd rather whack my own grandmother."

By the time they finished their martinis and several tequila shots, they had found some aspect of the photo to remind them of every major male Italian performer from Dean Martin to Joe Mantegna.

"Wait, wait," said Mortale, "I got it, I got it." He was slurring his words now. "It's that guy in *Midnight Run*. The guy who used to be a Chicago cop."

"There was no cop in *Midnight Run*. Those guys were bounty hunters."

"No, I mean the actor used to be a Chicago cop. Dennis . . . Dennis *Farina*, that's who!"

"Yeah, you're right," said Peccati quietly. Then he folded up the paper, put it back in his pocket, and said,

"The boss says he also hangs out at the Villagio. Let's go find him."

"Let's see the lions first."

"No, I told you I don't want to see the freakin' lions."

"C'mon," said Mortale, "what are you scared of? They're behind glass for chrissakes. What are you, a big baby?"

"Look who's calling me a baby. You're whining that you've gotta see the lions, you gotta see the lions."

"C'mon, it'll take five minutes. I always stop and see the lions when I come to the Miracolo. They know me."

So Peccati and Mortale stumbled off in the direction of the lion habitat, the outlines of their handguns just barely visible under their sport coats.

Martinis, tequila, guns, and lions. It was a mixture made in heaven.

Chapter 24

PRAYING FOR A HARD FOUR

ANNY AND VIRGIL WALKED through the main doors and into the jungle-like setting of the Miracolo casino. The craps pit was the first part of the casino they entered, and even though this was Christmas Eve, it was surprisingly busy. But a pit manager who knew both men saw them coming and asked some players to make room at the table for them.

"Mr. K! Mr. P! Good to see you both! I didn't even know you fellas knew each other."

"Well, I just had the honor of making this fine gentleman's acquaintance tonight," said Virgil.

"We're working on some business together," said Danny.

"Well, it's a pleasure to see you both. Can I draw up some markers for you gentlemen?"

Both Virgil and Danny held the fingers of both hands open quickly to signify the number ten. They each handed the pit manager a Miracolo VIP card, which he checked briefly in his computer before tapping the boxman on the shoulder and saying, "Ten large for both Mr. P and Mr. K." The boxman pushed the chips to the dealer standing to his left, who counted them into two piles of $10,000 each, then pushed them across to Danny and Virgil, saying, "Good luck, gentlemen."

Danny was so accustomed to playing in Atlantic City, it never ceased to amaze him how quickly he got his chips in Las Vegas. He didn't have to sign a thing. In a few moments, the pit manager would bring him a marker to sign, but in Las Vegas he got the money *before* that happened. In Atlantic City the process was more like closing on a house or adopting a child.

"If you'll just sign here for me, sir," said the pit manager when he brought over the marker. "Say, Mr. P, I've got a buddy who's a pit manager over at the Villagio Las Vegas. He told me a funny story about you. He said you actually drew a marker using your health-insurance card over there once. Is that true?"

"Yeah," said Danny distractedly. He was concentrating on the dice, which weren't behaving properly.

"But he said nobody tells that story better than you do, Mr. P," said the pit manager expectantly.

"I'd rather not talk about it now," said Danny.

By the time Danny signed his marker, he'd already lost a substantial sum of money. Virgil had already won a large sum. Danny and Virgil both were playing the *Win By Losing* system, but they happened to be on the opposite side of the dice. Whenever Danny was on the pass line, Virgil was on the don't. As the system dictated, they alternated back and forth. But they were always betting against each other, and they were getting dramatically different results.

As Danny watched his own pile of chips in the racks in front of him gradually diminish, he saw the pile in front of Virgil grow exponentially. Virgil seemed to be in an otherworldly state. His eyes were often closed, or if open, he was staring up at the ceiling.

"Are you looking at this?" Danny said, nudging Virgil with his elbow.

"Am I looking at what?"

"Are you watching the way I'm playing? This is what I was talking about. I want you to watch me carefully and tell me if I'm playing the system correctly. Because I'm not getting . . . my customers are not getting the results they want, and they're asking lots of questions."

"It looks fine to me so far," said Virgil.

"Well, keep watching."

But Virgil looked back up at the ceiling and his pile of chips continued to grow. Meanwhile, Danny was down to about half of his original bankroll.

Was Virgil cheating? Danny wondered. He keeps looking at the ceiling like he's checking out the two-way mirrors. Maybe he thinks they're watching him upstairs. He was carrying those dice in his pocket at Caligula's, Danny thought. Maybe he slipped a pair of loaded dice into the game.

"Check those dice," said Danny to the boxman. Danny didn't really want to get his new friend in trouble, but there wasn't much point in this exercise if they were playing with loaded dice.

Both Virgil and the boxman looked at Danny like he'd lost his mind. It was highly unusual, to say the least, for a player to ask for the dice to be checked. But the boxman complied anyway. Boxmen were always looking for any excuse to check the dice.

The boxman held each die one at a time between his thumb and forefinger and blew on them to make them spin around like a top. Casino dice are so perfectly engineered that they spin like gyroscopes if you do this just right. If the dice are loaded, however, they wobble. These dice checked out fine.

"Looks good to me," said the boxman to Danny.

"Yeah, well, give me a new pair anyway."

Danny tossed the new pair of dice at the back wall of the craps table and immediately lost another $1,000.

"Look at that!" Danny shouted, poking Virgil with his elbow again.

"Look at what?"

"Look at my chips. I bought in for ten large and I'm down to about two. What's happening? What am I doing wrong?"

"Bad run of the dice," said Virgil as he scooped in another $2,000 of winnings from the pass line.

By the time Danny ran completely out of chips, Virgil was up about $30,000. The pit manager circled around the table behind Danny and whispered into his ear.

"Can I draw you another marker, Mr. P?"

"No, not right now. Color up my friend here, we're going to take a break for a while."

"Color me up?" said Virgil. "Who said I wanted to leave? I'm winning here."

"We've got to talk," said Danny urgently.

"You don't have to leave if you don't want to, Mr. K," said the pit manager, who hated to see any player walk away from the table with more than a dollar of the casino's money.

Danny shot Virgil an insistent look.

"No, it's okay. He's right. We'll take a break and come back in a few minutes. Color me up." This was casino jargon for "change the color of my chips," or change all of the smaller denominations into a few large ones. The Miracolo actually carried $10,000-denomination chips, so Virgil's enormous pile of green and black chips would be exchanged for just three of those.

"Let's get a cup of coffee," said Danny, as he literally took Virgil by the arm and pulled him in the direction of the coffee shop. But they started talking along the way and they never got near the coffee shop. Instead, they came to a stop near a bank of slot machines and talked face-to-face.

"So what is it?" said Danny. "What am I doing wrong?"

"It didn't look to me like you were doing anything wrong."

"You weren't paying attention."

"Yes, I was. I was watching you very closely. You seemed to be playing the system perfectly. So what's your question?"

"What's my question?"

"Yes, what's your question? You said you had a question."

"My question is . . ." Danny looked around before he said the next sentence, because he knew it would be very loud and very profane. "WHY THE FUCK AM I LOSING?"

"What do you mean, 'why are you losing'?"

"What do you mean, 'what do you mean'? I wanna know why the system is losing if I'm playing it correctly."

"It loses a lot," said Virgil.

"It loses a lot?"

"Sure, it's a gambling system. It wins sometimes and it loses sometimes."

"But I thought it was a winning system."

Virgil laughed at this. "You think I'd sell you a winning system?"

"Yes," said Danny petulantly.

Virgil looked at Danny like he was seeing him for the first time.

"It's a gambling system," Virgil said again, but much more slowly this time, as if he were talking to a small child. "It wins sometimes and it loses sometimes. In the long run, it probably will lose more often than it wins. That's how they can afford to have volcanoes outside, pilgrim. Volcanoes aren't cheap. Believe me, I looked into putting one in my back yard once," he joked. But Danny didn't laugh.

"I thought it was a winning system," repeated Danny softly.

"Were you born yesterday? Maybe this is my mistake. I didn't realize I was doing business with a retarded person. Perhaps I should've explained it to you more carefully. I wanted you to sell the system in a direct-mail campaign so that we could both make some money on it. I was under the impression that this is what you did for a living. In fact, as I recall, you sent me some of the other booklets you've sold in the past and some of the direct-mail letters you've written. Were those winning systems?"

"No," said Danny wanly.

"No, I didn't think so. Maybe I should've tried them out in the casino to make sure. But I was laughing so hard at some of them, I never got around to it. You see, Danny, I wanted you to sell these booklets. I didn't want you to plant them in the ground like Jack and the Beanstalk, hoping you'd find some golden goose in heaven."

"But what about Professor Parrondo? The guy from Madrid? What about the ratchets? The Brownian Ratchet Theory?"

"It's all true," said Virgil in the gentle tone a parent uses when it's time to come clean with your kid about Santa Claus. "But Parrondo himself said the system probably doesn't apply to casino games. Heck, even the book says so!"

"But *you* were winning with the system just now," protested Danny weakly.

"Yes, I was."

"Well, how were you doing it?"

"That's simple. I was praying."

Danny let out a sharp, nasty laugh. It was his turn to be patronizing now. "You'd pray to God to give you a hard four?"

"Sure, why not?"

"Well, it's rather trivial, don't you think?"

"From God's point of view, everything we pray about is trivial. We pray for a better job. We pray for a better marriage. How many times have you watched a boxing match and when it's over the announcer asks the winner how he managed to beat the other guy into a senseless pile of jelly. The answer is always the same: 'Jesus helped me do it!' It's all absurdly trivial to God. But He answers many of our prayers anyway."

"We pray to spare our loved ones from cancer," said Danny. "That's not trivial."

Danny was thinking back to the last time he'd ever prayed seriously. He was twelve years old and his grandmother, who lived with Danny's parents at the time and doted on Danny, was dying of bone cancer. This was back in the days when Danny's parents were still taking him to church, and he prayed like a maniac on his grandmother's behalf for months. Lighting candles. Saying novenas. Asking the Virgin Mary to intercede. In fact, that was the reason Danny had *stopped* praying, because his prayers weren't answered. She died an excruciatingly painful death.

Suddenly, a memory flashed across Danny's mind, something he hadn't thought about for years. He had actually been on his knees in front of his bed when his mother walked softly into the room to break the news that her husband's mother had finally passed away. Danny slowly got up from his knees and said, "That's the last time I'm ever praying to God. What's the point? There is no God."

"Don't say that, Danny. You don't really mean that. It's just that God doesn't always answer our prayers."

"But this was *important!*" Danny cried out petulantly.

"Even the important ones," his mother said softly as she gently tried to tuck him back into bed.

Now, forty years later, Danny was having essentially the same conversation with some stranger in a casino with slot machines chiming and clanging in the background. The sound of Virgil's laughter snapped him out of his reverie.

"That's the most trivial prayer of all," Virgil laughed.

"How so?"

"From God's point of view, when you pray to spare a loved one from cancer, you're praying to delay that person's arrival in heaven. That's not only trivial, it's downright laughable from God's perspective."

"What about all the suffering? Does God find that laughable, too?"

"No, of course not. But again, look at it from His perspective. What is an instant of suffering when measured against an eternity of happiness?"

Danny thought about this for a moment.

"Does it work?" he finally asked.

"Does what work?"

"When you pray for a hard four?"

"I'm not much of a hardways player, to tell you the truth."

"You know what I mean. Does it work when you pray for the dice to pass, or not to pass, or whatever the hell you're praying for?"

"Sometimes it works and sometimes it doesn't. It worked just now, though, didn't it?" Virgil took his three $10,000 chips out of his pocket and waved them gleefully in Danny's face.

"It did for you," said Danny sourly.

"I really think it depends on what kind of mood God is in," Virgil continued. "Or how strong my faith is on any given day. Or more likely, it depends on things I have no understanding of. Maybe God is busy with other things when I pray to him. Maybe he has stepped away from the computer to order in some Chinese food. Like I said, it's all trivial to him. But I suspect he's more interested in whether or not it's trivial to *me.*"

"What do you mean?"

"I think He knows that if it's trivial to me, like getting a seven on the comeout roll, I'll probably only pray about it once or twice. But if it's important to me, like getting rid of a brain tumor, I'll keep pestering him about it until He does something. Or until I die, whichever comes first. Whether or not God answers our prayers is not the important thing, pilgrim. The important thing is that we keep praying. About everything. Because praying brings us closer to God."

"What's the point of being closer to God if He won't answer your prayers?" asked Danny with a trace of bitterness.

"Don't expect God to do tricks for you, Danny. He's not a trained seal. He's more like those lions over there." Virgil nodded in the direction of the lion habitat, toward which they were slowly walking.

"God can *bite*, pilgrim."

Chapter 25

MIRACLE AT THE MIRACOLO

S THEY WALKED OUT OF the casino toward the side entrance where the lion habitat was located behind large Plexiglas windows, Danny was kicking himself mentally.

He'd made the same stupid mistake that all of his mail-order customers had made down through the years. He wanted so badly to believe that he'd let himself believe. He let himself believe that the system really worked, even though he knew that no one had ever invented a gambling system that really worked. He'd fallen for his own manipulative and deceptive copy. He was a sucker. Just like all those millions of suckers who had paid for his airplanes, his pool tables, and his satellite dishes over the years. He felt like an idiot.

What's more, he was an idiot with problems—especially money problems. He had come to Las Vegas thinking that his money problems would soon be over, but now they were worse than ever. His credit cards were tapped out. His cash in the bank was at its lowest level ever. Lefkowitz was going to send him an enormous bill this month for keeping him out of jail. The Bonanza bills would keep coming. It would cost a bundle to get the Bonanza repaired and get it back to New

Jersey. If they nabbed him on the Cessna deal, he'd have to pay even more money in fines and restitution. He had just spent $300,000 on a direct-mail campaign that would now yield zero revenue. It was the worst mess of his life. Plus, there was one other problem in Danny's life, but he couldn't remember what it was. It had something to do with Maria. Poor sweet Maria. He'd never be able to pay for her funeral or give any money to her parents now. But that wasn't the problem. It was something else. What was it? He racked his mind. But then he thought, What, I don't have enough problems now without trying to remember another one?

As they stepped into the hallway just outside the casino, Danny noticed a little girl sitting on the floor cross-legged and playing with what appeared to be her baby brother. The girl was maybe twelve years old, the boy about three. Danny had never been interested in children before, but something about this girl called to him. She had dark skin and dark hair. She looked Italian. She looked, in fact, like all the little angels he'd seen so many times in Renaissance paintings on his many visits to Italy. Perhaps this was why he stopped and talked to her. Virgil watched.

"What's your name, little girl?"

"Beatriz," she said. She gave it the Spanish pronunciation, so it came out sounding like "Bay-uh-trees." She was Mexican, it turned out, not Italian.

"Oh, like Beatrice, huh? Like 'Ant Bea' of Mayberry?"

"I guess so."

"What's your little brother's name?"

"DeJesus." Again, she gave this name a Spanish pronunciation, so it sounded like "Duh-hay-soos." Had Danny seen this name on paper, he would've understood it to mean "of Jesus," or "Jesus's person." But the way she said it, it didn't sound familiar at all. It was not the first time Danny had heard Jesus's name without recognizing it.

"Where are your Mom and Dad?"

"Playing the slots."

"When are they coming back?"

"They said about ten minutes."

"How long ago was that?"

"About an hour."

"And they didn't come back yet?"

"No, but it's okay, mister. We're okay. They'll be back soon. They always come back."

"Wait here," said Danny, "I'll be back in a minute."

Danny had seen this a million times in casinos before. Parents abandoning their children at the edge of the casino was an enormous problem in Las Vegas and Atlantic City. It was rare in the big Strip casinos like the Miracolo, which made concerted efforts to prevent it. But it was extremely common downtown, where the low-rent casinos had neither the money nor the inclination to do much about it. Danny had probably passed a hundred kids like this on his way out of casinos downtown, but this was the first time he ever really noticed one.

Virgil tagged along behind Danny who was suddenly walking very purposefully. Danny looked over his shoulder and said, "Three-to-five her parents don't come back for another hour." They ducked into the gift shop and Danny picked up a *Supergirl* comic book and a box of Good & Plenty. As Danny was paying the clerk, Virgil said, "Interesting reading material."

"I never miss an issue."

"Have you ever pondered the parallels between the Superman myth and the story of Christianity?" asked Virgil.

"No, I haven't pondered that," said Danny, who was getting a little tired of all the Jesus talk.

"Think about it. A baby arrives from a distant planet. He's adopted by a rural couple. Early on it becomes apparent that this baby has supernatural powers. But these powers are largely kept under wraps until he's a full-grown man. At a certain age, he leaves Smallville and goes to Metropolis, a city rife with sin and danger. Rather like Jerusalem in biblical days. Superman becomes a kind of savior there, performing various miracles. Until it is discovered that kryptonite makes him human and vulnerable, just like the rest of us."

"Where does Super*girl* fit in?" asked Danny.

"That's what I was hoping you'd tell me," Virgil chuckled. "You bought the comic book. I thought you might know."

Danny went back to the little girl and handed her the comic book and the candy.

"This'll help you pass the time. Don't forget to share the Good & Plenty with your brother." He patted DeJesus on the head, and he felt his cold hand grow warm.

"Gee, thanks, mister!" said the girl. She beamed at Danny like he had given her a pony. Danny was at once surprised by how happy the girl was made by such a simple gift and how happy he himself was to give it.

"So shines a good deed in a weary world," said Virgil as they walked back toward the lion habitat.

"Shakespeare?"

"Gene Wilder. *Willy Wonka and the Chocolate Factory*," replied Virgil.

Danny felt the warmth in his hand spread to other parts of his body. It rose to his head where it began to feel a lot like anger. He walked up to a security guard posted near the lion cage. The guard was a fat black man. Danny got right in his face.

"What the fuck is your problem?"

The guard was somewhat non-plussed by this unusual greeting.

"Don't you see those kids over there?" Danny continued. "They've been sitting there for an hour waiting for their parents to come out of the casino. I thought you *cafones* were supposed to do something about that."

Danny gave the Italian word a Sicilian American pro-nunciation, even though he knew better, so it came out sounding like "guh-vones."

"What's a guh-vone?" said the security guard, blinking his eyes at the maniac in front of him.

"It's a fool, you asshole. Now what are you going to do about those kids?"

"Okay, okay, I'll take care of it. I didn't see them," said the security guard as he waddled off in the direction of the casino.

"Do you believe that freaking *melanzane?*" Danny turned to Virgil.

"What's a *melanzane?*"

"It's an eggplant, you asshole!" Danny pressed his hands together and wobbled them back and forth in the little praying gesture that Italians make when they're frustrated with someone.

"Oh, so you're a racist in addition to your many other fine qualities," said Virgil with a smile.

Danny laughed. He had been acting angry, which was very unusual for him, and he was enjoying it. For the first time in his life, Danny understood the phrase "righteous indignation." He'd been indignant before. Mildly indignant. Like when a waiter took too long to bring him his check. Or a maitre d' gave him a table by the bathroom. But he'd never been *righteously* indignant. It was an entirely new experience for him, and he was loving it.

Despite his apparent anger, in fact, he'd never felt better in his life than in the last five minutes. Buying that comic book for the little girl was the first act of selfless kindness that Danny had ever performed in his life.

Not that he was a bad man. Oh sure, he'd defrauded lots of people out of small sums of money over the years. But he wasn't really bad. Not violent. Not vicious. Not evil. Actually, he was a charming and likable person in a lot of ways. It's just that until this moment, he'd never done anything *good*. He'd never done anything for another human being with no expectation of getting anything in return. For the first time in his life, Danny felt an inner glow of happiness and peacefulness like he'd never felt before. He felt like he was in what the nuns in school used to call a "state of grace."

He was so overcome by this feeling that he did something he hadn't done since he was a little boy. He uttered God's name in something other than a curse.

"Thank you, God," he said, "for giving me another chance."

And he was rewarded for this little prayer by the sensation of a bullet striking his head.

WIN BY LOSING
SECTION THREE: SURRENDER

"You do not need to leave the room. Remain sitting at your table and listen. Do not even listen, simply wait, be quiet, still and solitary. The world will freely offer itself to you unmasked, it has no choice, it will roll in ecstasy at your feet."
—Franz Kafka

In every casino that is open twenty-four hours a day, seven days a week—which is to say, in nearly every casino—there is at least one craps table where the game never stops.

The next time you go into your favorite casino, see if you can find it. It's usually located in the center of all the other craps tables. It's the one that's open at four o'clock in the morning when all but the most degenerate gamblers have given up and gone to bed. It's the one that's open on Wednesday mornings, during the casino's slowest time of the week, when only a handful of hard-core players are standing around and a bored and desultory crew is going through the motions. It's the one that has to fill up with players before the pit boss will even think about opening a second one. In many casinos this table is identified with a little green sign on the side that says, "CP-1," or "Craps Table Number One."

Once a game of craps begins at CP-1, which happens on the first day the casino opens to the public, it never ends. It is the eternal craps game. Oh, they may have to clean the table from time to time. When that happens, they simply move the dice and the dealers to another table for an hour or so. But the game itself goes on. Hour after hour. Day after day. Year after year.

I want you to find this table in your favorite casino, and once you've found it, I want you to play at that table whenever you can. Get comfortable there. Find your favorite spot. Get to know the look of it, the feel of it, the smell of it. Get to know dealers and boxmen who work at this table, because the same crew will usually be assigned to this table day after day, shift after shift. It's Crew Number One at Craps Number One. I want you to get so thoroughly familiar with this table that you can picture it easily in your mind even when you're not at the casino. In other words, I want you to be able to enjoy the eternal craps game even when you're not physically present to play it.

I want you to be able to play at CP-1 in your mind when you're up in your hotel room. When you're at home in your easy chair. Even when you're in bed asleep. I want you to be able to play there in your dreams. Because the game is always going on. Whether your body is there or not, the game is going on and you are a part of it.

Once you have acquired the ability to play the game without being physically present at the table, you no longer have to gorge yourself on it when you are. When you're at the casino, you no longer have to behave like a starving man at a feast who doesn't know if he'll have a chance to eat again for another week or another year. You can take a break from the game without thinking that you might be missing something. And that break can last for one roll of the dice, or it can last for ten years. It makes not a bit of difference to the game itself how long you're gone. Because the game will go on without you. Even more importantly, the game will still be there waiting for you when you're ready to come back.

Only by admitting that the game is bigger than you are, stronger than you are, more permanent than you are, can you free yourself from its grip. Only then can you achieve the freedom that you need to play the game well. You must surrender to it before you can conquer it.

The forces at work in a craps game are much more powerful than anything you can muster in your own defense. The casino is more powerful than you. The "house edge" or "vigorish" on every bet is mathematically more powerful than any bet you can make or system you can devise. You may think of yourself as a lucky person and you can take the steps we've discussed in this booklet to make your own luck, but the whole concept of "luck" is much bigger than you are. Every day at the casino, some incredibly lucky things will happen and some incredibly unlucky things will happen. You have virtually no control over it. You only have control over yourself. Your job is to be standing at the craps table when the lucky things occur and seated at the bar when the unlucky things do.

That requires patience, of course. But it's a special kind of patience. It's not the kind of patience you exhibit by force of will when the bus you're waiting for is five minutes, ten minutes, twenty minutes late. That kind of strained patience will only get you in trouble. It will only serve to make you angry and frustrated. If you keep the steam bottled up inside your soul too long, it's only a matter of time before you blow your lid. You'll start pressing your bets and chasing your losses simply because you could wait no longer for the "luck" to show up.

No, you must be *in* the game, but not *of* the game. You must be willing to lose yourself, and lose your will, within the game in such a way that standing at the table with what appears to be saintly patience actually requires no patience at all. You must realize that the long stretches of time between lucky streaks are also an important part of the game, maybe the most important part—just as the golfer realizes that the long walks from shot to shot are an important part of golf.

But perhaps a better analogy to the game of craps is surfing. I've never even been near a surfboard and I have no plans to do so. But watching surfers ride those enormous Hawaiian waves on television has always struck me as the perfect metaphor for playing craps.

The surfer has no illusion that he is bigger than the wave, or stronger than the wave, or able, in any way, to bend the wave to his will. Instead, he *surrenders* to the wave. He yields to the wave. He lets his body be dominated and overcome by the wave in such a way that he *appears* to be in perfect control of it. Good surfers ride the wave, but excellent surfers actually become *part* of it. They haven't tamed the wave. It is much too big and powerful to tame. The only thing they have really tamed is their own fear.

And how do you tame your own fear in the face of something so mighty? First by surrendering yourself to its force. And secondly, by connecting yourself to a force that is even *more* mighty.

Do you think for one moment that Boris & Ivan, the magicians at the Miracolo, believe they have "tamed" their lions? They are much smarter than that! They know far better than you do that each of those lions is fully capable of biting off their heads at any moment. They *respect* their lions. They may even *fear* those lions. (What sane person wouldn't?) But they have tamed their fear. They have connected themselves to a force that is even stronger than the lions. They have connected themselves to the force of *hunger* in those lions. The desire for *survival* in those lions. They have even connected to the lions' *own* fear of human beings and their painful whips.

But the dice are much more difficult to tame than mere lions! They have no hunger. They feel no pain. They have no fear. They respond only to the unchanging laws of mathematics and physics. And there is only one force in the universe that is more powerful than the unchanging laws of mathematics and physics:

God.

Chapter 26

THE GALLERY OF SOLVED MYSTERIES

ANNY REACHED UP TO touch the wound in his head and when he brought his hand back down, it was covered with blood. But it didn't hurt at all. He knew from having once slipped in the shower that even a minor scalp wound could bleed like hell. So he assumed that the bullet had merely grazed his head.

In typical fashion, Peccati and Mortale had emptied the chambers of each of their handguns but only managed to hit two human beings in a hallway full of tourists. One bullet accounted for Danny's head wound and the other struck Virgil square in the chest. The force of the bullet threw Virgil flat against the wall, and he slithered down the wall and onto the floor in a heap as if someone had splattered the wall with a bucket of mud. When Danny glanced at him, he was clearly unconscious and, Danny concluded, probably dead.

Although Peccati and Mortale only hit two human beings, they did a great job of hitting the Plexiglas shield surrounding the lion habitat. Ten bullets altogether struck this wall, which shattered into a million pieces. There was panic among the tourists in the hallway, of course. But the three lions watched the scene very calmly. When it became apparent to them that they had been suddenly and miraculously freed from captivity, they did what any caged animals would do:

They walked out.

With the gunshots and the loose lions, nearly every tourist in the hallway made a mad dash for the exit doors to the side. There was a pileup of human beings screaming and clawing at these revolving doors trying to get out. Had the lions chosen to walk in that direction, they could've eaten their fill of human flesh. Instead, they decided to wander curiously and calmly in the other direction. Toward the casino.

In the casino, the ceaseless cacophony of slot machines had muffled the sounds of the gunshots, the shattered glass, and the screams of panicked tourists. No one in the casino knew that anything unusual was going on until the three lions came strolling in, looking from side to side and growling aimlessly. Nor did this strike many of the people in the casino as especially unusual. This was Las Vegas, after all. Most of the slot players didn't even look up from their machines long enough to notice the lions.

"Are those real or animatronic?" said one old lady to her friend seated at the adjoining slot machine, as she casually went through her purse looking for stray quarters.

"Those are animatronic," the other woman replied knowingly. "The ones in the cages are real."

Two of the lions continued walking out of the casino and onto the Strip, where they greeted the throngs of people on the sidewalk with the same mixture of cautious uncertainty and cynicism about Las Vegas publicity stunts. But the third cat had walked no further than the vestibule between the casino and the lion habitat when it became distracted by a child eating candy. A small crowd of people arranged themselves in a semi-circle around the peculiar scene.

"Isn't that adorable?" said a woman in the crowd.

Little DeJesus was sitting cross-legged with the lion curled up next to him like a tabby warming himself in front of the fire. He was feeding the lion Good & Plentys one at a time, and the cat seemed to be enjoying them.

As soon as the lions walked out of their habitat, Danny ran into it, figuring it was the safest place to be. He was hiding behind an artificial boulder in the front of the habitat, and from this vantage point, he could see everything that was happening around him. He could even see what was going on with the lions in the casino, which surprised him, because he didn't realize his vision was that good. He could also see Peccati and Mortale, their guns still drawn, trying to lose themselves in the crowd of tourists.

They gave up awfully easily, thought Danny. Maybe they were scared of the lions, he concluded.

Danny's eyes were drawn to Virgil, who had regained consciousness. He was sitting on the floor with his back to the wall, grimacing in pain and slapping the floor repeatedly with his open hand. It took a minute before Danny realized that Virgil wasn't in pain at all. He was laughing.

Virgil had removed the tiny Bible from the breast pocket of his denim jacket to discover that one of Peccati's bullets had struck it and been flattened into a disc the size of a silver dollar. Virgil was laughing hysterically at the irony, the coincidence, and the sheer cliché of it all. He waved the spent bullet at Danny and shouted, "From now on I'm going to keep this bullet in my pocket in case some crazy evangelist tries to throw a Bible at me!"

Even though he was hiding behind a rock and bleeding from the head, Danny couldn't help but laugh, too. Then he gave Virgil a little wave goodbye and started to plan his escape. Danny didn't want to go out through the casino; the two assassins might see he was still alive and decide to finish the job. He couldn't go out through the side exit, which was still jammed with tourists trying to escape, some of whom had been seriously trampled in the process. So Danny took the only other route available to him. He figured that there would be a conventional lion cage behind the habitat and, once back there, he could ask a zookeeper to let him out. Then he could go out an exit in the back and be far removed from Peccati and Mortale, who were running in the opposite direction.

The only obstacle Danny faced was a rather large moat that had been built for the lions to swim in and play. He looked for a way around the moat, but he didn't see one. So he slipped down one side and waded over to the other. It was about four feet deep. He scrambled up the other side and pulled himself out. He was soaking wet and strangely forgetful of all that had just happened. Why was he doing this anyway? He couldn't remember. He had a strong sense that he was no longer running away from something, but that now he was being pulled *toward* something. He crawled into one of the artificial caves in the habitat and, as he had suspected, found himself in a conventional iron-barred cage on the other side. A zookeeper was passing by at that exact moment and did what could only be described as a vaudevillian double-take.

"Could you let me out of here?" asked Danny politely.

"What the . . . ?"

"Could you let me out of here and tell me where the nearest exit is?"

"How did you get *in* there?"

"I can't remember."

"Where are the lions?" asked the zookeeper with growing alarm.

"I think they got out."

"*They got out?* Oh, my God!"

"Yeah, could you let me out of here, please?"

The zookeeper reached for the keys, which were hanging from a peg nearby, and unlocked the cage. He didn't know which was more amazing, that this soaking wet man was locked in the lion cage or that he appeared so serene about it.

"Could you tell me where the nearest exit is?" repeated Danny. "But not out front. I want a door that leads to the back of the building."

"Just keep walking down this hallway, through the set room and past the dance rehearsal room, and there's a fire door back there. It will set off an alarm, but I guess that's the least of your problems right now." The zookeeper answered Danny's question in a daze, as he wondered in mounting horror what kind of havoc the lions might be wreaking in the casino.

"Okay, thanks," said Danny, and he proceeded to walk calmly in the direction he'd been given, while the zookeeper cautiously stepped into the cage in search of his lions.

As Danny strolled through the set room on his way out, he saw many of the props and illusions from the Boris & Ivan show stashed in various places on the floor. He had seen the show several times before, even though he really didn't care for it much. In his opinion, it was nothing more than a blatant rip-off of Siegfried & Roy's show at the Mirage.

But Danny had to admit that the illusions in the show were fantastic. Unbelievable. Miraculous. Even better than Siegfried & Roy's. That's what kept him coming back. Every time, he'd tip the maitre d' more and more to get closer and closer to the stage—until the last time he'd seen the show, he was actually in the front row. But he *still* couldn't figure out how the illusions were done.

Now that he was only inches away from these boxes and props, however, he could easily see how they worked. The trap doors and mirrors were clearly visible.

"Oh, so that's how they did that," he muttered as he passed a cage where one lion had vanished into thin air.

"Oh, I see how it's done now," he said as he walked by a box where a woman had been sawed in half and then miraculously transformed into two lions.

"Why didn't I see that before?" he wondered. "I was close enough to see that trapdoor the last time I was here. Maybe it was the lighting."

An otherworldly calm surrounded Danny as he wandered aimlessly through this gallery of solved mysteries. He was vaguely aware that he was supposed to be frightened, supposed to be running away from something, but he couldn't remember what it was. He wanted to linger with these illusions even longer. But he still felt the insistent pull toward the rear exit.

As Danny approached the dance rehearsal room, he could hear the sound of voices and laughter. He peeked around the doorjamb and saw a male and female dancer rehearsing a scene from the show. He remembered the scene. They were supposed to be Adam and Eve in the Garden of Eden. It was meant to be titillating in the show, since they were wearing nothing but fig leaves and ballet slippers. The rehearsal room had floor-to-ceiling mirrors on all four sides and a dance *barre* that ran around the entire room. So it appeared to Danny, if he caught the view just right, that there were millions of Adams and Eves dancing in front of him.

He stood at the doorway and watched them rehearse for a while. It felt like a few minutes to him. Actually, it was closer to an hour. He didn't want to leave. He could've stayed there in the Garden of Eden for the rest of his life. But somewhere east of Eden, he heard the distant call of unresolved problems in his life. He remembered that someone was still trying to kill him. Somehow he knew that this was the same evil person who had killed Maria. He remembered that the FAA still wanted him for stealing an airplane, the U.S. Postal Service for committing mail fraud. He had money problems galore. There were lots of loose ends in his life. He had to tie them up before he could get to where he was going.

So Danny tore himself away from the dance rehearsal room and moved on toward the rear door, which he could now see looming in front of him with the word EXIT glowing in the semi-darkness. Standing underneath the light and eerily illuminated by it were the little Mexican girl and her baby brother from the casino. What are they doing back here? Danny wondered.

Approaching the children, he turned to the little girl and said, "Did your parents ever come back to get you, kid?"

"Don't worry about us," said the little girl. "It's time for you to go now. Thanks again for the comic book."

"It's time for you to go now," echoed her little brother. "Thanks for the Good & Plenty!" He directed Danny toward the door.

Danny pushed hard on the door handle and an alarm bell immediately rang. As he stepped outside, the desert sun was so bright it almost blinded him after spending so much time in the half-light of the backstage area. The sun was surprisingly high in the sky, and Danny wondered for a moment how long he'd been in the casino. He stumbled outside, blinking and shielding his eyes against the sunlight. With his hand touching his head, he could feel that the blood had finally dried. Disappeared, actually.

It was Christmas morning.

Book Three
PARADISO

In which our hero finds himself unjustly rewarded in heaven

Chapter 27

DA PIETRO

T WASN'T EASY FOR Danny to find Pentangeli. He had to make five telephone calls to various acquaintances in Atlantic City. Eventually, he learned that the top mob boss in A.C. was a man by the name of Frank Pentangeli, a big fat guy who always hung out in the back booth of the White House Submarine Shop on Arctic Avenue.

So he placed a call to the White House.

"You know the fat guy in the back booth?" Danny asked the person who answered the phone.

"Mr. Pentangeli?"

"Yeah, that's the one. Lemme speak to him."

"He's not here right now."

"Where is he?"

"How the hell should I know?"

Danny's heart sunk. But then the voice on the other line continued. "One of his men is here. You wanna speak with him?"

"Yeah," said Danny.

"Howya doin'?" said Benito Bazzoni, the flunky on the other end of the line. It was the way Benny always answered the phone. He'd heard it on a beer commercial.

"Where's Frankie?" asked Danny.

"Who wants to know?"

"Danny Pellegrino," said Danny with all the confidence he could muster.

The name didn't sound familiar to Benny, but he had just been promoted from tanning salon manager to bodyguard and he didn't know the names of all the key players yet. Rather than sound like an idiot by questioning the man any further, he decided to comply with the request.

"He's in Las Vegas."

"Where's he staying?"

But now the alarm bells went off in Benny's head. "Who the fuck is this again?"

Danny hung up. He cradled the phone in his lap and thought for a moment. Where would a wealthy Italian American stay in Las Vegas, he wondered. He dialed the number for the Bellagio, a number he knew by heart.

"Please connect me to the room of Mr. Frank Pentangeli," he said to the clerk.

"Mr. Pentangeli just checked in five minutes ago. I'm not sure he's in the room yet. But I'll ring it."

The phone was answered on the second ring.

"Howya doin'?" said Pentangeli, who'd seen the same commercial.

"This is Danny Pellegrino," said Danny, again with as much confidence as he could summon under the circumstances.

"Oh."

"I think we should meet."

"Man, you got more freakin' lives than a cat. Are Peccati and Mortale still alive?"

Danny figured Peccati and Mortale must be the hapless assassins.

"They were alive the last time I saw them."

"You mean they didn't accidentally shoot themselves in the mouth?"

"No."

"Too bad. It would've been an easier way for them to die. What can I do for you Mr. Pellegrino?"

"I think we should meet, Mr. Pentangeli. I want you to call off the dogs. The craps system is a piece of shit. It doesn't work."

"I've seen it work."

"Believe me, it's bullshit. Let me show you. We should meet."

Pentangeli figured that if this guy was dumb enough to walk down Dealy Plaza in front of the Texas School Book Depository with a red target painted on his back, who was he to talk him out of it? "Where do you want to meet?"

"You tell me," said Danny.

"Do you know Da Pietro's? It's a quiet place, good food, it's perfect for us. It's got one of those old-fashioned toilets in the men's room with a box and a . . . a chain on it."

Danny knew the place. But why in the world Pentangeli would identify it by describing the toilet in the men's room was a mystery. "Yeah, I know it. Shall we meet there? What time?"

"Where are you staying in Vegas?"

"I'm staying at the Stardust." The Stardust wasn't Danny's favorite hotel in town, but he had recently received a notice in the mail that he had three free nights waiting for him there anytime he wanted to claim them. So when he hailed a cab not far from the Miracolo, he told the driver to take him to the Stardust.

"Okay, I'll meet you in front of the Stardust after sundown. Around six thirty."

"You gotta call off the dogs, Mr. Pentangeli," Danny said again.

"We'll talk about it tonight," said Pentangeli and he hung up.

Danny stayed in his room at the Stardust all day. He was afraid to go out. He called room service for lunch and watched old movies on TV all day long. When six o'clock rolled around, he freshened up as best he could—considering he was still wearing the outfit he had on when he landed in the soybean field—and he took the elevator to the lobby. Pentangeli was waiting for him outside in a big black Cadillac sedan.

Pentangeli was in the back seat alone. Peccati and Mortale were in the front. When Danny got in the back seat next to Pentangeli, Peccati turned around from the driver's seat and said, "Where to, boss?"

"Down the road a bit."

Peccati had seen the movie *Casino* enough times to know that this meant he should drive to an isolated spot in the desert.

"Mr. Pellegrino," said Pentangeli as they got underway, "I need your help to perform a little experiment. When we get out into the desert, we're going to tie you up with a rope. Then I'm going to ask Mr. Peccati and Mr. Mortale to draw their handguns. Hopefully they won't hurt themselves. I'm going to ask Mr. Peccati to stick his gun in your left ear. And I'm going to ask Mr. Mortale to stick his gun in your right ear. Then I'm going to tell them to fire as many shots as they wish. And we're going to see if they hit or miss.

"If they miss, which is what I suspect they'll do based on past performance, I'm going to set you free. But if they hit you, which will be the result of some rotten luck on your part, I'm afraid you're going to die."

"What do you wanna kill me for?" asked Danny, with remarkable serenity.

"I think you know why."

"Look, I told you on the telephone. The craps system does not work. It's bullshit. I got sold a bill of goods by some jerk here in Las Vegas. I've lost more than $250,000 on it in the last two days alone. It's like any other gambling system in the world. It wins sometimes and it loses sometimes. Let me prove it to you. Stop here."

They were passing the last big casino on the road out to the desert, Mandalay Bay. Something about Danny's statement that gambling systems win sometimes and lose sometimes rang true in Pentangeli's ear. Against his better judgment, he tapped Peccati on the shoulder and said, "Pull into Mandalay Bay."

A doorman wearing a pith helmet opened the back door of the limo and Danny and Pentangeli stepped out.

"Mortale, you come with us. Peccati, you stay with the car. Don't move, this'll only take thirty minutes at the most."

Peccati waited in the car. It was a rented Cadillac, so he amused himself by fiddling with all the bells and whistles on the dashboard. He was just about to call some of his buddies in New Jersey with the hands-free satellite telephone system when Pentangeli and the others surprised him by returning less than twenty minutes after they'd left. Pentangeli looked mad. Danny looked relieved.

"Where to, boss?" repeated Peccati when everyone was back inside the car.

"Down the road a bit," said Pentangeli.

Danny had seen the movie *Casino,* too, and he knew what this meant.

"Wait! I proved to you it didn't work. You just lost twenty-five grand in there, and you were playing the system perfectly. What do I have to do to make you understand it doesn't work?"

Pentangeli was angry now. "Listen, asshole. Do you realize the trouble you've put me through this week? I killed three people because of you. One of them was my baby cousin. I killed a freakin' *woman* because of you."

Danny knew that he meant Maria, and he felt a stabbing pain of remorse in his chest. It was true, after all, that Maria had died because of his own greedy foolishness. But Danny didn't have time to wallow in remorse. Pentangeli was pitching a hissy fit.

"I killed one of my best bodyguards because of you. All because of you and your stupid craps system. So, yes, Mr. Pellegrino, I'm going to kill you. Someone has to pay for those deaths. Someone has to pay for all that unnecessary bloodshed. I don't like bloodshed, Mr. Pellegrino, it's bad for business."

Danny sat silently and stared out the window. For the second time today he was on the road to Calvary. It hadn't been a good day.

"Lord, help me," he said quietly. After forty years of not praying, it was his second prayer in twenty-four hours.

"Good thinking. He's the only one who can help you now."

"There's still a way to make money with this system," Danny said suddenly.

"The system is bullshit. You said so yourself. You proved it to me at the Mandalay. Now you're going to be target practice for Peccati and Mortale. God knows they need it."

"The system made a tremendous amount of money in the mail," said Danny softly.

"Craps by mail? Shut the fuck up. Craps on the Internet I've heard of, but nobody plays craps by mail."

"No, I was selling the system in the mail when I discovered that it really worked. Or that it looked like it really worked. But I was on my way to making a million bucks with it in the mail before I withdrew it."

"A million bucks?"

"At least. And that was just a test mailing. If we rolled it out, we'd be looking at five, ten million, who knows?"

"We?"

"Well, I need a partner. I'm out of money, Mr. Pentangeli. I need someone to bankroll another mailing. I'm talking about an investment of $300,000 or so that could yield a return of fifteen million." The figure was growing. "Then we could split the proceeds down the middle."

"Turn the car around," Pentangeli said to Peccati.

Peccati hit the brakes and turned the wheel so hard that the car literally spun around on a dime. Cars behind them and in front of them blared their horns and swerved out of the way.

"Nice work, Lou," said Pentangeli, patting Peccati on the back.

"I'm Peter, boss," said Peccati. He didn't want the credit for that fancy display of driving to go to anyone else.

"Where to, boss?" asked Peccati for the third time this evening.

"Da Pietro's," said Pentangeli, who turned to Danny like a kindly grandfather now and said, "That means Daddy Pietro's."

"Not really," said Danny cautiously. "It mean's 'at Pietro's house.' It's like *chez* in French. It basically means 'Peter's Place.'"

"Oh, really?" said Pentangeli pleasantly. "You live and you learn."

"Mr. Pentangeli! What a pleasant surprise!" said Peter Panetta, the roly-poly little proprietor of Da Pietro on Flamingo Road.

"Hey, Pete, how ya doin'? Table for two, please. My associates will sit at the bar. Give them whatever they want. But don't let them get drunk."

"Certainly, Mr. Pentangeli. I have your favorite table. Right this way." It was a table for six. But Pentangeli liked to spread out when he ate.

"Try the veal, it's the best in the city," said Pentangeli as they were seated and handed their menus.

Danny had eaten here before and he knew the veal was among the worst in the city. But, to be polite, he ordered veal picatta with lemon. They can't screw that up too bad, he thought.

Pentangeli ordered an antipasto of tomato and mozzarella *caprese,* a second course of *manicotti,* a veal chop *milanese* with *contorni* of spinach sautéed in garlic and olive oil, and a plate of string beans, also sautéed in oil and garlic. "I want to leave room for dessert," he said to Pietro by way of explanation for ordering such a light dinner.

"Che porco grasso," said Danny. What a fat pig.

Pietro's servile smile dropped like he'd just witnessed a traffic accident.

"What did you say?" asked Pentangeli.

"I said, 'How's the pork in this place?'" said Danny with a quick wink at Pietro.

"Oh, that's what I thought you said," said Pentangeli. "The pork is great. You wanna switch to the pork? Go ahead."

"No," Danny answered in Italian. *"Sto ceniando con un porco grasso, ma prendo il vitello comunque."* No, I'm dining with a fat pig, but I'll have the veal anyway, he said to Pietro.

Pietro quickly sized up the situation. He knew that Pentangeli was an important Mafia figure, but this guy must be *more* important. Maybe it's his boss. The horrified expression on his face brightened and he smiled knowingly at Danny.

"What did you say?" asked Pentangeli.

"I said, 'The pork sounds great, but I think I'll stick with the veal.'"

"That's what I thought you said. *Pronto, per favore, Pietro,"* Pentangeli added, eager to show both men that he could speak Italian, too.

"Da bere?" asked Pietro as he was leaving.

"No beer for me," said Pentangeli. "Just a glass of chianti."

"Nothing to drink for me," said Danny with another wink at the giggling proprietor.

It was interesting to note how slowly these ancient Italian dialects faded away. Both Pentangeli and Danny were third-generation Italian Americans born in New Jersey. But Pentangeli's family came from Sicily, so he pronounced *manicotti* like "manny-gut." Danny's family was Tuscan, so his pronunciation of *ceniando* sounded like "shay-nee-ando." Their grandparents would've been proud of them both.

Danny picked at his veal picatta, which was truly awful, while Pentangeli plowed through his five-course meal with relish. Danny began to think that anyone who couldn't speak Italian and who thought that this pedestrian Italian American food was good couldn't be very smart.

"Yeah, when all is said and done," said Danny as Pentangeli was finishing up his main course, "I figure we can clear twenty million from this mailing. We split it two ways, that's ten million for each of us. You could live on that, right?"

"I could get by," said Pentangeli with a smile, thinking that $20 million would be enough to get out of the tanning business once and for all. If this guy is stupid enough to think that we're actually going to split the money, he thought, let him go ahead and think so. "What exactly is involved in this mail-order business?"

"You come up with three-hundred large for the postage, the printing, the lettershop costs, and we'll split the proceeds."

"Three hundred large buys a lot of stamps."

"We'll have to mail a million letters to make it work."

Pentangeli did some calculations in his head.

"A million letters should come to $370,000 in postage," he said warily.

"We'll mail bulk rate," said Danny. "You see, that's why you need me, Mr. Pentangeli. You need my expertise."

"*Per il dolce?*" said Pietro, as he cleared off the plates.

"*La dolce vita!*" said Pentangeli. "You're exactly right, Pietro, it's a sweet life."

"He asked us what we wanted for dessert," said Danny.

"I knew that," said Pentangeli testily. "I'll have the cannoli. Try the cannoli, Pellegrino, it's the best in the city."

"I'll have an espresso," said Danny.

The espresso was undrinkable. Danny stirred it repeatedly and added pack after pack of sugar to it, as he'd seen people do in Italy many times, but no amount of sugar could make it palatable. So he sat there toying with the demitasse as Pentangeli polished off a pair of cannoli, then ordered another.

"Your espresso is no good?" asked Pentangeli.

"I'm not thirsty after all."

"You put too much sugar into it. You should drink it straight, like a real Italian."

"Let me go to work on this when we get back East," said Danny, letting the comment about the espresso pass, "and we'll meet again in Atlantic City next week. After the holidays."

"Fine," said Pentangeli with a mouthful of cannoli.

"Where should we meet?"

"At the White House Submarine Shop. I've got an office there. We'll split a sub."

"How do I know I'll get my half of the money?" Danny asked pointedly.

"You'll get it, you'll get it," said Pentangeli with a sly smile.

Danny smiled back beatifically.

Chapter 28

CONSPIRACY AT THE WHITE HOUSE

A FEW WEEKS LATER, Danny sat across from Pentangeli in his customary booth at the White House Submarine Shop handing him various papers to sign, work orders to approve, invoices to authorize, artwork and copy to proofread. Danny was essentially trying to make sure that Pentangeli got billed for every expense associated with the mailing and Pentangeli was blithely signing his name to everything Danny handed him with no intention of paying for anything. He figured he'd see if the mailing really produced the kind of profits Danny promised, then he'd worry about paying the vendors later.

"Now, I want to show you the copy, Frank, because I've made some improvements on what I wrote before and I'd like your approval."

"Show me a copy of what?"

"No, 'copy' is the word that we use in the advertising business for the text of our ads. Like when you read, 'See the USA in your Chevrolet,' that's called *copy*, and the person who wrote it is called a *copywriter*. That's what I do."

"Chevys suck."

"Now, on the outer envelope . . ."

"Corvettes aren't bad." Pentangeli's attention was wandering all over the map during this meeting. Danny had trouble keeping him focused. The truth of the matter was that Pentangeli wasn't particularly interested in the business side of this project, just the profit side.

"On the outer envelope, Frank, I had written the headline WIN BY LOSING! But in retrospect, I think that was a mistake. You see, one of the key things we try to do with a headline is to drive home the benefits of your product. People want to know, 'What's in it for me?' And your headline should answer that question. So that's why I've rewritten it to read, 'YOU CAN MAKE UP TO $1,000 A DAY PLAYING CRAPS—GUARANTEED'!'"

"Why so little?"

"So little what?"

"Why so little money? I made $50,000 with it over at Bally's and I wasn't even trying very hard. Ricky Three Pigeons, God rest his soul, made $30,000 with it at the Villagio in less than an hour. When I was looking at this system, I figured you could probably make $500,000 a day with it if you put a big enough bankroll behind it."

"Well, I don't know, Frank . . ."

"No, change this line," said Pentangeli, proving once again that everyone wanted to be a copywriter, even people who didn't know what a copywriter was. "It should read, 'YOU CAN MAKE $500,000 A DAY PLAYING CRAPS—GUARANTEED!'"

"Okay," said Danny reluctantly, "you're the boss. And I've made some other changes along the same lines in the letter copy. Here, take a look." He handed Frank a few sheets of paper.

Pentangeli studied them for a few minutes and said, "No, same deal. You're making the same stupid mistake here. You keep saying $1,000 a day when you should be saying $500,000 a day. Plus, you keep using all these faggotty words."

"Faggotty words?"

"Well, for example, you say 'You *might* win this' and 'You *could* win *as much as* that.' What are you, a freakin' lawyer? Come out and say what you want to say. Tell the people what they want to hear. Tell them that they're *going* to win five hundred large, not that they *might* win it. How long did you say you've been doing this?"

"Thirty years."

"Well, you suck, pal. I wouldn't hire you to write a newspaper ad for one of my tanning salons." Pentangeli always wrote those ads himself. He was a copywriter and he didn't even know it.

"All right, Frank," said Danny sheepishly, "maybe you're right. I'll make those revisions."

"Do it. But there's something more important we've got to discuss today. Where does the money come to?"

"What money?"

"The money that people send in for the crap system. Where does it come? Whose mailbox does it arrive in?"

"Well, I've got a rented mailbox in Montblanc that I use for that purpose."

"No, that's unacceptable."

"Unacceptable?"

"I want it to come to me."

"That won't work, Frank," Danny protested mildly. "I've got certain procedures and equipment in place for fulfilling orders. My office is set up to do that. It's easier if I pick up the mail, make the deposits, send out the booklets, and then split the revenue with you at the end of the month."

"No fucking way."

"Well, what do you suggest?"

"I suggest we use my fucking mailbox at my house in May's Landing. I make the fucking bank deposits. Then I'll send you a list of people to send the booklets to."

"You don't want it to go to your house, Frank. It's not professional."

"Well, then a post office box here in Atlantic City that *I* rent and that *I* have the only key to."

"Well, then how do I get *my* money?" asked Danny. This conversation was going even better than he had hoped.

"You'll get your freakin' money, for chrissakes. I'm good for it. I pay my debts. Everybody knows that." He turned to the proprietor of the White House Submarine Shop, who was walking by with a tray full of fresh submarine loaves. "Hey, Sal, have I ever walked out on a check here?"

"Of course not, Mr. Pentangeli."

"You see," said Frank, turning back to face Danny with a told-you-so look as if his clean record at the White House was all the proof anyone would ever need of his integrity. "You and I are both honest men. We don't need to make assurances to each other as if we were lawyers."

When Danny looked up at Sal the proprietor, he thought he caught a glimpse of someone he recognized sitting at the counter and eating a sub. From the back, it looked like David Invidia, the casino host at the Villagio, whom Danny had last left bleeding from the nose in a soybean field in Indiana. Sure enough, when the man paid his bill and stood up, Danny could see he was right. Danny stared down at his plate and hoped Invidia would walk out without noticing him. But he started walking directly toward their booth.

Before Invidia got within five feet of the booth, Danny looked up from his plate and began apologizing. "David, I'm sorry I punched you. I'm sorry I left you alone in the airplane. I'm sorry about what happened in the air. But I was desperate . . ."

"Don't apologize!" said Invidia with a hearty smile. "I should be *thanking* you. You saved my life. You saved it twice, actually. Believe me, Danny, there's nothing like a near-death experience to help a man get his priorities straight in life."

Danny breathed a sigh of relief. Then he noticed David was dressed very casually in the middle of the day, not his usual Armani suit. Had he lost his job? Was he still out on disability from the broken jaw?

"Are you still at the Villagio?" Danny asked.

"Naaah, I left there right after the holidays. No new job yet. But I'm in no hurry. I've been doing some charity work."

"Oh really?"

"Speaking of that, let me leave these with you fellas." He put two magazines on the table between Danny and Pentangeli. "If you get a chance sometime, take a look at them. No pressure."

"Okay," said Danny uncertainly.

"Well, I gotta run. But it's good to see you, Danny. And really, don't feel bad about what happened in the airplane. It's the best thing that ever happened to me in my life."

Invidia left and Danny picked up one of the magazines. It was a copy of *Watchtower*, the official publication of the Jehovah's Witnesses.

"You know that guy?" asked Pentangeli.

"Yeah, he was my casino host over at the Villagio. Yours, too?"

"No, but I've seen him around. I've seen him in the tanning salons."

"Handing out *Watchtowers?*"

"Yeah, that's right," Frank chuckled. "*Watchtowers* are real big in the salons. We put them in the reception rooms."

Danny wasn't sure whether he was kidding or not.

Chapter 29

JACKPOT!

"SONOFABITCH!" SAID RICHARD GOLDMAN.

Goldman was going through his decoy mail when he saw something that was so unusual, so peculiar, so bizarre that it made his eyes blink in disbelief.

I can't believe this, he thought to himself. Not only did the sonofabitch violate his cease-and-desist order, not only did he put this felonious promotion back in the mail, but now he's gone and broken every mail-fraud law in the book. Five hundred thousand dollars a *day? Guaranteed?* Has he lost his mind? He knows better than this. Lefkowitz knows better than this. Are they thumbing their noses at me? Are those bastards thumbing their noses at *me?* Well, I went to Harvard Law, too, you know. I'm going to send that prick up the river so long he won't be eligible for parole until the next ice age.

Goldman turned to his word processor with the intention of printing out another cease-and-desist letter, but then thought better of it. A cease-and-desist letter was far too friendly under the circumstances. What this situation called for was a nice threatening phone call. Man to man. He wanted to talk to Danny personally and put the fear of God into him. He wanted to hear that subtle change in the timbre of a man's voice that occurred when he first learned he was going to prison.

"Pellegrino Enterprises," said Danny in a pleasant tone as he answered the phone on the first ring.

"Richard Goldman. United States Postal Service. I think you remember me."

"Of course I remember you, Mr. Goldman. What an unexpected pleasure." He'd been expecting this pleasure for days. "How can I be of service to you, sir?"

"Mr. Pellegrino, I am in receipt of a letter here from your firm that troubles me greatly."

"From my firm? Which letter is that?"

"It's the *Win By Losing* promotion. Apparently, a revised one. It's got a new return address on it. And it has many other interesting changes. For example, it says, 'Win $500,000 a Day Playing Craps—Guaranteed!' on the outer envelope. Five hundred *thousand,* Mr. Pellegrino?"

"At least."

"It also makes various other misleading and deceptive statements throughout the letter. In fact, Mr. Pellegrino, if you look up the phrase 'mail fraud' in the dictionary, I believe you'll see a photograph of this letter there."

"I don't use a dictionary much anymore," said Danny. "I've got an automatic spell-checker on my computer."

"May I ask you how many of these letters were mailed?" asked Goldman tensely. He was holding a pencil so firmly in his fingers that it actually snapped in half.

"About a million, I believe."

"Do you realize that one million counts of mail fraud would leave you open to a potential sentence of five million years in jail and a $50 billion fine to the United States Government?"

Danny held his hand out in front of him and examined his fingernails, like a dowager deciding if it was time for a manicure. He sniffed deeply before answering.

"I'll bet you could buy a lot of aircraft carriers with that," he finally said.

"Yes, we could, Mr. Pellegrino. I'm glad you're taking this with such good humor. It seems like so many of the people I work with get frightened and defensive when I tell them they're going to jail."

"I'm going to jail?" asked Danny like a child who had been promised a trip to the beach.

"Lefkowitz can't get you out of this one, wise guy." Goldman growled this last sentence so closely into the phone that he could feel the little holes in the mouthpiece scrape against his whiskers.

"I don't see why *I* should go to jail. That wasn't my mailing."

"What do you mean it wasn't your mailing? It's a dead ringer for the mailing you sent out three months ago. The one we confiscated from your house. Except you've made it even worse."

"Naah. I gave the rights to that mailing to a friend of mine. I washed my hands of the whole thing. Look at that return address again. It's Atlantic City, New Jersey. Are you familiar with New Jersey, Dick? Do you realize how far Atlantic City is from Montblanc?"

"That doesn't mean squat. You could have a drop box in Atlantic City. They could be forwarding the mail to you from there. This is your letter. I still have a copy of this letter in my files. I've got you nailed to the wall, Pellegrino."

"Like I said, I was just helping a friend with that mailing."

"What friend?

"Guy by the name of Frank Pentangeli."

"Frank Pentangeli?" Goldman straightened in his chair.

"That's the one."

"*The* Frank Pentangeli? The Atlantic City mob boss? The Sultan of Suntans?"

"Who did you think I meant? The dead guy in *The Godfather*?"

"Are you telling me that you and Frank Pentangeli conspired to put out this fraudulent mailing?"

"Well, I don't know how much conspiring there was. I just gave him some advice and gave him permission to use some of my old copy. If you look into it, Ricky, I think you'll find that the return address is a mailbox in Atlantic City rented in the name of Frank Pentangeli. That Frank Pentangeli's signature is on most of the work orders, contracts, invoices, and so forth. Pentangeli even wrote a personal check to your employer, the United States Postal Service, for more than $200,000 in postage. Gee, I hope it didn't bounce."

"You and I need to meet."

"When?"

"ASAP. I can take the shuttle up to New York this afternoon," said Goldman. He was already reaching for his briefcase.

"Would you mind very much if my friend Sol Lefkowitz joins us?"

"I guess he should be there, yes."

"In fact, why don't we meet in Sol's office at four o'clock today. He's expecting us."

"You're not out of this yet, Danny boy. This is still your copy. You must have some involvement in this. And even if you don't, we can make it look like you did in court."

"Are you telling me that a representative of the United States Government would stretch the truth in court? I'm shocked! Well, we can discuss those issues with Lefkowitz. I have more stories to tell you about Pentangeli. Maybe we can work out one of those deals where you give me a pair of eyeglasses with a funny nose and a big house in Seattle."

Goldman hung up the telephone. He reached into his desk drawer where he had hidden a pack of cigarettes. He didn't want to leave them around the house where his wife would've found them. He put one in his mouth and lit it up. Cigarette smoking was *strictly* forbidden in federal office buildings. You would probably get in more trouble from smoking a cigarette in a government office than you would from running a prostitution ring. It wouldn't take longer than thirty seconds for someone in the hallway to start coughing obnoxiously. Probably only two minutes before someone else came into Richard's office and threatened to bring him up on charges. But he just leaned back in his chair, took a deep drag on the cigarette, and grinned at the prospect.

Let them come and get me, he thought. I'm untouchable. I've just nabbed a top mob boss on one million counts of mail fraud. I've hit the jackpot for government lawyers.

Chapter 30

"FREEZE, ASSHOLE!"

ENTANGELI VISITED HIS LITTLE rented mailbox at the Mailboxes Etc. on Baltic Avenue in Atlantic City every day for a week—despite the fact that Danny had told him that the earliest day they could possibly expect any returns would be on Good Friday.

Even then, Danny said, they'd probably just trickle in for a few days before they started to get a lot. "You'll probably get a few on Friday, a few on Saturday, and then a pretty good pile on the Monday after Easter. Then the following Monday will probably be our biggest day." But Pentangeli showed up at the mailbox every day anyway, just in case someone sent in their order by FedEx.

When Good Friday finally rolled around, Pentangeli showed up at ten o'clock, the precise moment when he knew the mail would be delivered and sorted into the mailboxes. He went to his mailbox and peered into the little window

There was nothing there.

"Oh, shit," he said. "Pellegrino told me we'd get some mail today. If that bastard lied to me, I'm going to kill him."

He opened the mailbox, figuring that there might be at least one letter stuck to the sides or stuck to the top. But no, there was nothing inside. Nothing except for a tiny slip of paper. On the paper there was a handwritten note. It said:

"Too much mail for box, see clerk at window."

At the window, the clerk handed Pentangeli two enormous mailbags filled to the brim with letters. He dragged the mailbags into a quiet corner of the shop, sat down on the floor, and opened one of them. He pulled out an envelope at random and ripped it open, almost tearing the contents in the process. There was a check inside for $40 made out to "Frank's Crap System." He ripped open another. There were two twenty dollar bills inside. He ripped open a third. There was a United States Postal Service money-order payable to "Frank's Crap System" in the amount of forty dollars. He reached deep into the bag with both hands, pulled out dozens of letters and tossed them into the air, letting them land on his head. He reached in again and pulled out another dozen envelopes. He rubbed them on his cheeks as if he were washing his face with them. He held several envelopes up to his nose and sniffed deeply. He could smell the money inside. He was so excited that he almost didn't hear it when a voice behind him said, "Freeze, asshole!"

"Freeze, asshole?" he thought. I know that line. That's from *Goodfellas*. The scene where they catch Henry Hill on the way to the airport with the girl in the floppy hat and all the cocaine.

He loved that line! He used to say it all the time. He used to love to sneak up on one of his flunkies from behind, stick a finger behind their ear, and say, "Freeze, asshole!" Bo Dietl was actually the guy who said the line in the movie.

Dietl was a former New York cop in real life who played himself in the movie. Frank liked Bo Dietl a lot. He heard him as a guest on the *Imus in the Morning* radio show all the time.

Frank Pentangeli turned around with a big smile on his face, fully expecting to see one of his buddies quoting his favorite line back to him.

Instead, he saw the barrel of a large handgun pointed at his nose. A United States Marshal was attached to the other end. Behind him, looking somewhat nervous about carrying his own handgun, but nevertheless sporting a satisfied grin on his face, was United States Postal Inspector Richard Goldman.

Chapter 31

ANOTHER SHITTY DAY IN PARADISE

DANNY PUT A NEW twist on the Witness Protection Program. He moved to Venice.

When he first floated the idea to Goldman and the other government lawyers in charge of his prosecution, they laughed in his face. Literally. So loud, so long, and so close, in fact, that Danny had to remove a handkerchief from his pocket and wipe his face like he'd been caught in a thunderstorm. But, in the end, he prevailed. He sold it to them as a cost-cutting move. And there's nothing the federal government likes better than giving the appearance of saving the taxpayer money.

"Look at it this way," he said. "If you keep me in the country, you'll have to give me plastic surgery and create a whole new identity for me. You'll have to train me how to do a different kind of job, then find a job for me to do. If you can't find one, you'll have to invent one. You'll have to buy me a big house in the suburbs, put furniture in it, and give me two cars. I'd stand out like a sore thumb if I only had one car.

"But if you send me to Venice," he continued, "all I'll need is a one-bedroom apartment and a new passport. Who needs a car in Venice? I won't need a job either. I can live off whatever I make from liquidating my assets here in America. I'll just be a retired American living in Italy and you guys can forget all about me."

Venice was not Danny's favorite city in Italy, although it was the favorite city of just about every Italian he'd ever met. Florence was Danny's favorite—in part because Florence was the ancestral home of his mother's family, the Alighieris.

But Danny had his reasons for choosing Venice. For one thing, there were casinos there. There were none in Florence. Secondly, the influence of the Italian Mafia was weaker in Venice than it was in Florence, and Danny figured he'd be a tad safer there. In Italy, the power of the Mafia was almost entirely a function of geography, gaining strength as you moved farther south. It was true to the extent that hardly anyone in Trieste was in the Mafia and nearly everyone in Calabria was.

But Danny wasn't overly concerned about the Mafia. He knew enough about it to know that the ties between the American and Italian mobs were almost non-existent nowadays. Even back in America, Danny knew it was highly unlikely anybody was looking for him. Pentangeli had been sent to jail for so long that his associates had written him off. In addition to all the mail-fraud charges, Danny's testimony also helped convict Pentangeli on the murders of Ricky Trepiccione, Maria Falcone, and Carlo Montagna. Pentangeli's subordinates were now battling each other for control of the tanning empire and some of Pentangeli's other businesses, including loan-sharking and conventional prostitution.

None of Pentangeli's former associates knew Danny anyway (except for Peccati and Mortale, who also went to prison for their connection with the three murders). Danny wasn't one of them, so he really couldn't be considered a traitor. He hadn't violated the oath of *omerta,* because he'd never taken it. Danny figured it was possible that his name appeared on a hit list somewhere, but it was so far down that list it would be like waiting for season tickets at Giants Stadium. Assassination, he eventually concluded, would not come to him in this lifetime.

He was so confident of that, in fact, that one day, just as a joke, he went to a custom T-shirt vendor near the Piazza San Marco and ordered a T-shirt that said, "WITNESS PROTECTION PROGRAM: Informer #N345J." He had the vendor put the name "ISCARIOT" on the back between the shoulders, like a football jersey. And he loved to wear the shirt around town, but hardly anyone got the joke.

Occasionally, an American tourist would point at him and laugh, but the Italians never seemed to get it. Italians, especially young Italians, were in the habit of wearing T-shirts with meaningless English words on them. Most of those words were just gibberish. Sometimes they made sense, but as far as the Italians were concerned, they were *still* gibberish.

Once, Danny saw an Italian teenager wearing a T-shirt that said, "Another Shitty Day in Paradise." Danny's Italian had gotten quite fluent by now, and in a friendly way, he decided to compliment the kid on his shirt.

As good as Danny's Italian was, however, it wasn't good enough to fool a Venetian. The people of Venice had an extraordinary gift for recognizing foreign accents. It was a part of their genetic heritage after more than a thousand years of living in one of the world's most popular tourist traps. A Venetian could tell when someone was born and raised three miles outside of Venice, and they considered those people as foreign as if they'd been born and raised in Peking.

"*La tua maglietta é buffa,*" Danny said. Your shirt is funny. Danny was sufficiently older than this kid to use the informal form of address. But it was a dicey thing. Children never objected to being addressed informally, but teenagers sometimes did.

"*Cos'é tanta buffa da quella?*" What's so funny about it, he snapped back in a tone that made Danny regret his informal approach.

"*Non sa cosa dice?*" You don't know what it says? asked Danny. He had switched back to the formal verb form.

"*No, non parlo l'inglese,*" said the kid disdainfully, as if only the goodie-goodies in school bothered to learn English.

"*Dice, 'Un Altro Giorno . . . er, Cattivo Nel Paradiso.'*" Danny gave a rather mild translation of the word "shitty."

"*Non posso vedere che cos'é tanto buffo da quello.*" I fail to see the humor in that, said the kid, and he walked away convinced that the man with the New Jersey accent had insulted his shirt.

So that's why no one ever commented on Danny's "Witness Protection Program" T-shirt. They simply failed to see the humor in it. As a result, Danny wore a sign on his back that clearly identified himself as a fugitive in the Witness Protection Program and he used it as a means of blending even more deeply into the daily life of Venetian society.

Danny began each day in Venice by visiting the cathedral of San Stefano and saying a few prayers in front of a side altar that contained a piece of St. Stephen's eyebrow.

Belief in God, Danny eventually came to realize, was like anything else in life. Like copywriting, or flying, or playing craps. You weren't born with it. Nor did it usually come to you in the form of a sudden revelation. It was something that you needed to learn, to study, and most importantly, to *practice.*

After his morning prayers he would go to the casino, which was located on a nearby island, easily accessible by one of the many water taxis that plied the canals of Venice. Most days Danny won money at the casino. Not a lot, but enough to supplement the modest income he got from his investments. Around one o'clock in the afternoon, he'd return to the central part of the city and enjoy a long lunch that could last anywhere from three to five hours, depending on how much wine he consumed and how many different courses the proprietor had to offer on any given day. He usually ordered fresh seafood, which was the mainstay of Venetian cuisine. A typical lunch might consist of a seafood antipasto, a seafood pasta, a meat course, a fish course, *contorni* of various fresh vegetables, and a dessert. Plus, an after-dinner drink. Some fruit and cheese. And an espresso at the end. More wine, too, of course.

Then, after lunch, Danny would do what the Italians called *fare passeggiata,* which literally meant "taking a stroll," but which actually meant "go girl-watching." (To the women, it meant "go guy-watching.") Dressing up and parading yourself in front of the opposite sex is the Italian national sport—not soccer, as is widely believed.

Occasionally, as a special treat, Danny would spring for a flying lesson, which was very expensive in Italy. He always told the instructor he wanted to work on stall recoveries, engine-out procedures, and recoveries from unusual attitudes. The instructor was always amazed at how good Danny was at these things. Most of his students hated doing them.

"*Bravissimo!*" he'd say with genuine enthusiasm.

"*Grazie,*" Danny would reply modestly.

Some might say that he led a lonely life in Venice, but Danny didn't think so. He was never all that much of a people person anyway. He got along well with people. He could make friends with people in a heartbeat. But he was happiest alone.

Or so he thought.

Everyone needs some companionship, however, so he bought himself a long-haired miniature dachshund and named him Satan after his old family dog. He took Satan with him on his evening *passeggiata* and this would often help him find a different kind of companionship. The Venetian girls were achingly beautiful—like Boticelli angels, only sexier—and they would flock to Satan and make a big fuss over him. "*Che carino, che carinino, che gassato,*" they'd say. He's so cute, just the cutest little thing, he even *knows* he's cute.

With his long, flowing red hair, Satan was such a peculiar-looking dog that people often stopped Danny to ask, "*Quale tipo del cane é?*" What kind of dog is it? He'd answer in a combination of English and Japanese, "It's a *bonsai* Irish Setter."

The puzzled expressions he'd get in response to this always made Danny laugh. But how are you going to translate a joke like that into Italian?

There was one particular Italian girl who seemed to fawn over Satan more than any of the others. She was the proprietor of a little shop in the touristy section near Piazza

San Marco that sold Carnevale masks and other little baubles made of Venetian glass. Danny thought she was a dead ringer for Maria Falcone. They even shared the same name—not that there was much coincidence in meeting a pretty Italian woman named Maria.

She liked the dog so much (and Danny, too, it seemed) that he made a point of stopping by her shop once a day, often more than once. She kept a jar of dog treats on her counter just for Satan. She was twenty years younger than Danny, but he was trying to work up the nerve to ask her for a date.

Then one day something happened in her store that gave Danny just the jolt he needed. After plying the dog with more than a dozen treats and fussing over him to no end, Maria reluctantly said goodbye as Danny headed toward the door.

"Ciao mio carinino! Ci vediamo domani! Non dimenti-carmi!" Goodbye my little cutie-pie. See you tomorrow. Don't forget me! She was crouched down on the floor to kiss the dog goodbye, but then she looked up at Danny and said, *"Ciao il mio capo di tutti capi!"*

Danny stood stock still and stared at her like he'd seen a ghost. Perhaps he had. He asked her for a date on the spot.

She sighed and said, *"Pensavo che non me lo avresti mai chiesto."* I thought you'd never ask.

Perhaps it was that unsettling encounter with Maria that put a peculiar idea in Danny's head when he was dining alone at Harry's Bar a few days later. Harry's Bar was a famous restaurant near the Piazza San Marco. It was very expensive, but the food was superb. It attracted rich and beautiful patrons from all over Italy and, in fact, all over the world.

On this late afternoon in May, the sun was beginning to set over the cathedral of San Marco looming behind him and it bathed the clouds and the Grand Canal in front of him in an exquisite half-light. The clouds were a salmon pink, and the canal was a deep sparkling blue. But those were just the dominant colors. There were millions of other subtle shades in both sea and sky that were brought out by the setting sun. The waning sunlight also caught the silverware and crystal wineglasses on the tables. It made the crisp white tablecloths look like French vanilla ice cream and gave the glasses of red wine so many rich and complex hues that you could sit there all night counting them if you were of a mind to do so.

Danny was alone, but he was surrounded by beautiful Italian women who were dining with their husbands, boyfriends, and probably "uncles," too, Danny surmised with a smile. They were all dressed to the nines, and the setting sun brought out the best of their clothing and jewelry, too. It sparkled off their diamond earrings and gold bracelets. It twinkled from their vivacious eyes. It gave depth and texture to their jet-black hair.

He was surrounded by so much beauty that his eyes didn't know where to look first. He would glance at the cathedral, then the canal, then the sunset, the women, the sky, the crystal catching the fading sunlight, the women again. The scene was a visual feast as rich as the culinary one he had just concluded. It was a beatific vision of unspeakable beauty.

Danny ordered an espresso and a sambucca from the waiter in what he proudly believed was perfectly pitched Italian. But the waiter walked away thinking, What is it with these Italian Americans from northern New Jersey?

Always with the espresso and sambucca. Don't they realize we have some of the finest cognacs in the world at this bar?

Danny lit a cigarette. *Everyone* in Italy smoked. In Italy, life was considered far too precious to waste time worrying about dying.

While waiting for his espresso, he continued to drink in all the beauty surrounding him. The effect was rather like drinking wine for hours on end, but never getting more than pleasantly buzzed. It was like the feeling you get in your mind somewhere between one glass of wine and three when all of your problems seem to melt away and all the truths of the universe suddenly seem clear. The problem is, you can never sustain that feeling for more than an instant. If you don't drink more wine, the feeling will gradually slip away. If you do drink more, you'll gradually get stupid, horny, and sick. Many unfortunate souls have become alcoholics trying to determine the exact amount of wine that can attain and sustain this sensation. For most people it is a futile and dangerous quest. But in Venice, Danny seemed to be able to do it every afternoon without any effort at all.

And it was in this state of *vino veritas* that it occurred to Danny that perhaps he had died and gone to heaven. Perhaps Virgil was right, after all. Heaven was not a place in the sky where angels sat on floating clouds and played the harp. It was a little piece of—what had Virgil called it?—"real estate" that just happened to make you happy. Virgil said that his heaven might look a lot like Caligula's, because that's where he was happiest. Danny was so sure at the time that he *wasn't* going to heaven, he didn't even bother to imagine what his own heaven might look like. But in retrospect, he realized that it might look a lot like what he was seeing at this very moment.

Danny recalled an Off-Broadway play that he'd seen in New York many years ago called *Sister Mary Ignatius Explains It All.* Nancy Marchand had played the title role, the same actress who later played the matriarch on *The Sopranos.* In the play, Sister Mary ascertains that one of her naughtiest students is in a state of grace immediately after going to confession. So she shoots the kid in the head with a handgun. Her reasoning? It was the most expeditious way to get him into heaven. She was doing him a favor.

Maybe that's what God did for him, Danny thought. Maybe He did Danny a favor. He found him in a state of grace, perhaps the first time he'd ever been in one, and He killed him before he had a chance to sin again.

Danny remembered how he felt when he bought that comic book for the little girl in the Miracolo. He remembered what a warm and deeply satisfying feeling was flowing through his body when he felt the bullet graze his head. But did the bullet graze his head, or did it *enter* his head? Either way, he would've felt no pain. There was no way to know for sure.

The truth, Danny eventually concluded, would be determined simply by how long he stays in Venice. If he gets sick and dies, he'll know that he wasn't in heaven after all. But if he simply continues to live, he'll know that he is.

So that's why Danny began every morning in Venice with a prayer asking God for grace and protection in the day ahead. And that's why he concluded each evening with a prayer of thanksgiving for the day behind.

And Virgil was wrong, by the way. I'm never too busy to answer prayers like those.

—THE END–

Author's Note

ERHAPS I SHOULD START out by apologizing to Dr. Juan M. R. Parrondo of the University of Madrid. (That's Madrid, *Spain.*) Yes, he's a real person and Parrondo's Paradox is a real scientific theory. But no, it cannot be applied to casino games. Or at least that's the official position of Dr. Parrondo, Derek Abbott, and Gregory Harmer—the three people who proved that you can indeed take two losing propositions and combine them into a single winning outcome.

The problem, as Virgil correctly points out in *Win By Losing,* is that the casino does not offer any wager that can provide the winning component of Game B. From keno to craps, every proposition in the casino is designed to have a slight (and sometimes not so slight) mathematical bias against the player. So keep that in mind before you take *Win By Losing* with you to Las Vegas. But of course, everything *else* Virgil has to say about winning at craps—from mastering your emotions to connecting with a higher power—is perfectly valid in the casino, as it is in life.

Virgil's theories about the origin of the universe also have some scientific validity. They are based, in part, on the work of a maverick MIT physicist named Edward Fredkin who believes (great simplification here) that the universe is a computer program. Professor Fredkin's ideas first came to wide public attention when he was profiled in *The Atlantic Monthly* in an article titled "Did the Universe Just Happen?," which was later expanded by its author, Robert Wright, into an excellent book called *Three Scientists and Their Gods.*

Fredkin steadfastly refuses to speculate on the religious implications of his theories, but that torch has been picked up by Ross Rhodes, who publishes a fascinating website called The Bottom Layer (www.bottomlayer.com). For the reader who wants to learn more about these ideas, Mr. Rhodes's website is an excellent place to start—not only for an overview of Fredkin's theories, but also for an attempt to place them in a religious and philosophical context.

Between the time I wrote this book in 2001 and when it was published in 2006, some of these ideas have gained popular currency. Recently, an independent film called *What the #$*! Do We Know!?* took an interesting look at the spiritual implications of quantum mechanics. Also, the continuing popularity of the Hollywood film *The Matrix* and its sequels is proof that seeing the universe as a computer program has some resonance in today's society. The first, and perhaps still the best, book to draw the connection between spirituality and quantum mechanics is Fritjof Capra's classic, *The Tao of Physics.*

The basic idea for *God Doesn't Shoot Craps* has been bouncing around in my head for many years. But it wasn't until I heard a remarkable lecture series on Dante's *Divine Comedy* by Dr. M. Craig Barnes, former pastor of the National Presbyterian Church in Washington, D.C., that the story began to crystallize into its current form.

Of course, I had a nodding familiarity with *The Divine Comedy* prior to that time and had read portions of it in college. But what was remarkable about Dr. Barnes's lectures was that they were the first time I'd heard Dante's masterpiece analyzed from the point of view of someone who actually believed in God. My agnostic college professors (like many Dante scholars) wanted to take religion out of the picture entirely and view *The Divine Comedy* as a political satire about medieval Florentine society—sort of a spaghetti-western version of *Gulliver's Travels.*

But in my view, that was not what Dante had in mind at all. His epic poem was exactly what it purported to be—a serious attempt to describe the nature of heaven, hell, and purgatory from the perspective of a middle-aged man who has strayed off the straight-and-narrow path into a "dark wood" and is wondering what the purpose and meaning of his life really is. For members of the baby boom generation like myself, *The Divine Comedy* may be the most relevant and timely work in the canon of classical literature. To write it off as political satire is to sell it woefully short. I urge you to take a fresh look at this masterpiece by purchasing Dr. Barnes's excellent book on the subject, *Searching for Home* (Brazos Press, 2003).

For the small portion of *Win By Losing* that deals with the issue of "mastery," I owe a debt of gratitude to George Leonard for his sublime little book on the same topic. Although Leonard's *Mastery* deals largely with the oriental martial art of aikido, it is must-reading for anyone who wishes to master any craft or skill— from playing craps to flying an airplane.

Some apologies and clarifications are in order:

The White House Submarine Shop is a real restaurant in Atlantic City, but it is not, to my knowledge, a hangout for the Mafia. It *is* a hangout for celebrities, the local *cognoscenti,* and anyone who loves a great submarine sandwich. Some of its fans have speculated that it's the spray of seawater in Atlantic City's air that gives the loaves at the White House a taste and texture found nowhere else in the world, not even in nearby Philadelphia where they also take great pride in their hoagies.

The restaurant where Danny and Pentangeli meet in Las Vegas, Da Pietro, is wholly fictional and bears no resemblance to any real restaurant in Las Vegas—certainly not to Pietro's, a fine Italian restaurant located in the Tropicana Hotel. The same goes for Caligula's, which is identified in the story as a topless bar on Paradise Road, but which, in fact, does not exist anywhere except in my fevered imagination. (Although you can't walk very far in Las Vegas nowadays without running into some joint just like it.)

Speaking of bars, I'm not sure whether Harry's Bar in Venice, which is a real and very famous restaurant, actually has an open-air terrace with a view of St. Mark's Cathedral. But if it doesn't, dammit, it *should* have, and I hope its many fans around the world will forgive me for taking poetic liberties with such an iconic landmark. (It was one of Ernest Hemingway's favorite watering holes.)

If you're a pilot and you have carefully crunched the numbers to determine that it's impossible for a V-tail Bonanza to get all the way from New Jersey to Indiana on a half-tank of avgas . . . thank you very much, but I'd rather not hear from you. I would only remind you that it is out of such impossibilities that miracles are made. (But let me say a quick thank you to my friend Massey Simpkins, retired captain for U.S. Airways, for cleaning up some of the more egregious aviation errors in the manuscript.)

And to my neighbors in Glover Park, if you're displeased with what I said about our community—and you have every right to be—I want you to know that I only portrayed it in such an unflattering light because I didn't want to let the word out about the friendliest, prettiest, and most charming neighborhood in Washington, D.C.

Some thank yous are in order, too.

First to my good friend, Bob Bly, himself the author of some fifty books, most of them on the subject of copywriting. Bob is in the habit of sending clippings of newspaper and magazine articles to his friends and clients on topics that he knows will interest them, along with a handwritten note that says, "FYI–Bly." I received one such "FYI–Bly" five years ago of an article in *Science News* about Parrondo's Paradox. That was the day *God Doesn't Shoot Craps* was born.

My agent Kim Goldstein of the Susan Golomb Agency in New York provided editorial advice and direction far beyond what any author has a right to expect from a literary agent. Her attention to detail, her understanding of the book, and most of all, her enthusiasm for it have been a source of great encouragement to me. I used to tease her that she'd never really succeed as an agent until she had a nickname like some of her better-known colleagues: e.g., Esther "Lobster" Newberg, Amanda "Binky" Urban, or Irving "Swifty" Lazar. After trying "Pilgrim," "Kiddo," "Kimmy-san," and many others in the hundreds of emails we have exchanged over the last two years, I have finally settled on one I like. She will forever after be known in my heart as Kim "Solid" Goldstein.

Deke Castleman has been the guardian angel of this book almost from the very beginning. Deke is the senior editor of Huntington Press and its flagship publication, *The Las Vegas Advisor.* I sent him an early draft of the manuscript, and he has taken it under his wing ever since, offering good advice on everything from casino grammar (he insists that "craps" is the noun and "crap" is the adjective), to literary agents, to the byzantine world of publishing. Deke is himself the author of several books on casino gambling and Las Vegas. The short essay on religion and gambling that comprises the epilogue of Deke's latest book, *Whale Hunt in the Desert,* is worth the entire cover price. And as a bonus, you'll get the best book ever written about David Invidia's real-life counterparts, casino hosts.

Let me send a "shout out," as they say these days, to my former editor at William Morrow, Jane Cavolina, who gave me tons of good advice about the publishing business and, even more importantly, a sympathetic ear for my constant whining and complaining. If you're as big a fan of *The Godfather* as I am, be advised that Jane and her sister wrote the best book ever written on the subject, *How to (Really) Watch* The Godfather. It's almost impossible to get your hands on a copy nowadays, but it's worth camping out behind used book stores to find it. Jane is also coauthor of the *New York Times* bestseller, *Growing Up Catholic,* and its many sequels.

Grazie milla to my dear Italian friend Cristina Bazzoni in Milan who helped double-check my tourist-level Italian—particularly the phrase used by Maria in Venice when she says to Danny, "I thought you'd never ask." It seems so simple in English, but in Italian it's a past imperfect conditional subjunctive—in other words, well above my grade level!

Who would've thought that my old college roommate, James F. Dean, would've grown up to become one of the world's finest website designers? Check out his work at www.goddoesntshootcraps.com, and if you'd like to hire him, you can reach him at justdean@pacbell.net.

Many thanks also to the superb publishing professionals at Sourcebooks for their excellent work on this project, especially my editor Peter Lynch, my copyeditor and production coordinator Michelle Schoob, and my publicist Tony Viardo. And a special thank you goes to Dominique Raccah, the *capo di tutti capi* at Sourcebooks, who "got it" from the beginning and fought for it to the end.

I'd love to hear your comments and questions about the issues raised in this book, and I will do my best to respond to each of them. The fastest and most efficient way to reach me is via email at richard@goddoesntshootcraps.com.

Finally, I'd like to thank the three women in my life whose love and support sustain me everyday: my sister Lydia, my mother Dorinne, and especially my wife of—can you believe it?—twenty-five years, Sharon.

Make that four women, my little dog Stardust, too.

Richard Armstrong
Washington, DC